DEMON OF THE DARK ONES

The War of Powers: Book Six

Here it is, folks. The final story, in every gut-wrenching detail. The blow-by-blow description of the ultimate, terrible confrontation between our trusty (and not so trusty) heroes and the forces of evil.

In order to save the human race from extinction at the hands of the alien *Zr'gsz*, and from the demon known as Istu, all-out war is declared. The only problem is that conventional weapons and spells will never win the war. The military strategy of Prince Rann, the ferocious fighting power of Fost Longstrider, the combined magics of the two princesses and the two genies are not enough.

As for the question: "How will they overcome such despicable adversaries?"—well, there is only one answer, and that answer is not a nice one.

THE WAR OF POWERS SERIES

DEMON OF THE
DARK ONES

ROBERT E. VARDEMAN
AND VICTOR MILÁN

**PLAYBOY
PAPERBACKS**

DEMON OF THE DARK ONES

Copyright © 1982 by Robert E. Vardeman and Victor W. Milán

Cover illustration copyright © 1982 by PEI Books, Inc.

Published simultaneously in the United States and Canada by Play-boy Paperbacks, New York, New York. Printed in the United States of America. Library of Congress Catalog Card Number: 81-83263. First edition.

Books are available at quantity discounts for promotional and indus-trial use. For further information, write to Premium Sales, Playboy Paperbacks, 1633 Broadway, New York, New York, 10019.

ISBN: 0-867-21012-5

First printing March 1982.

For cherry:
agent & sorceress
who made six out of one—
"it's better to burn out
'cause rust never sleeps."
love,
— vwm —

To all of you whose patience
exceeded my own—
Sharon & Cherry;
Geo. & Lana;
Mike & Marilyn;
Kathy & Melinda;
my parents & grandmother;
and, of course, always,
Kerry
— rev —

A Chronology
of the Sundered Realm

—20,000 The reptilian *Zr'gsz* settle the Southern Continent and begin construction of the City in the Sky.

—3,100 Istu sent by the Dark Ones to serve the *Zr'gsz* as a reward for their devotion.

—2,300 Human migration begins.

—2,100 Athalau founded by migrants from the Islands of the Sun.

—1,700 Explorers from the Northern Continent found High Medurim.

—1,000 Tension increases between the *Zr'gsz* and the human settlers.

—31 *Zr'gsz* begin active campaign to exterminate all humans.

—3 Martyrdom of the Five Holy Ones.

0 *The War of Powers*: Unable to wipe out the human invaders, the *Zr'gsz* begin to use the powers of Istu. Most of the Southern Continent is desolated. In Athalau, Felarod raises his Hundred and summons up the World-Spirit. Forces unleashed by the struggle sink continents, tip the world on its axis (bringing Athalau into the polar region),

7

cause a star to fall from the heavens to create the Great Crater. The *Zr'gsz* and Istu are defeated; Istu is cast into a magical sleep and imprisoned in the Sky City's foundations. Conflict costs the life of Felarod and ninety of his Hundred. Survivors exile themselves from Athalau in horror at the destruction they've brought about.

Human Era begins.

100   Trade between humans and *Zr'gsz* grows; increasing population of humans in the Sky City. Medurim begins its conquests.

979   Ensdak Aritku proclaimed first Emperor of High Medurim.

1171   Humans seize power in the Sky City. The *Zr'gsz* are expelled. Riomar shai-Gallri crowns herself queen.

2317   Series of wars between the Empire of Medurim and the City in the Sky.

2912–17   War between the Sky City and Athalau; Athalau victorious. Wars between the City and Athalau continue on and off over the next several centuries.

5143   Julanna Etuul wrests the Beryl Throne from Malva Kryn. She abolishes worship of the Dark Ones within the Sky City, concludes peace with the Empire.

5331   Invaders from the Northern Continent seize Medurim and the Sapphire Throne; barbarian accession signals fresh outbreak of civil wars.

5332   Newly-proclaimed Emperor Churdag declares war on the City in the Sky.

5340   Chafing under the oppression of the Bar-
        barian Empire, the southern half of the Em-
        pire revolts. Athalau and the Sky City form
        an alliance.

5358   Tolviroth Acerte, the City of Bankers, is
        founded by merchants who fled the disorder
        in High Medurim.

5676   Collapse of the Barbarian Dynasty. The
        Sky City officiates over continent-wide
        peace.

5700   The Golden Age of the City in the Sky
        begins.

6900   General decline overtakes Southern Conti-
        nent. The Sky City magic and influence
        wane. Agriculture breaks down in south and
        west. Glacier nears Athalau. Tolviroth
        Acerte rises through trade with Jorea.

7513   Battle of River Marchant, between Quin-
        cunx Federation and High Medurim, ends
        Imperial domination everywhere but in the
        northwest corner of the continent. The
        Southern Continent becomes the Sundered
        Realm.

8614   Erimenes the Ethical born. Population of
        Athalau in decline.

8722   Erimenes dies at 108.

8736   Birth of Ziore.

8823   Death of Ziore.

9940   Final abandonment of Athalau to encroach-
        ing glacier.

10,091 Prince Rann Etuul born to Ekrimsin the
        Ill-Favored, sister to Queen Derora V.

10,093   Synalon and Moriana born to Derora. As younger twin, Moriana becomes heir apparent.

10,095   Fost Longstrider born in The Teeming, slum district of High Medurim.

10,103   Teom the Decadent ascends the Sapphire Throne. Fost's parents killed in rioting over reduction in dole to cover Imperial festivities.

10,120   Jar containing the spirit of Erimenes the Ethical discovered in brothel in The Sjedd.

Mount Omizantrim, "Throat of the Dark Ones," from whose lava the *Zr'gsz* mined the skystone for the Sky City foundations, has its worst eruption in millennia.

10,121   Fost Longstrider, now a courier of Tolviroth Acerte, is commissioned to deliver a parcel to the mage Kest-i-Mond.

The Sundered Realm

To Northern Continent

North Cape

North Keep

GREAT NEVRYM FOREST

Kolinth.

Duth

City States

Nigh Medurim

LAKE LOLU

MYSTIC MTNS

Chendrun (KEEP OF THE FALLEN PEOPLE)

Harmis

THRUSHUR

SAMAZANT

Jar Nihen

BLACK MARSH

R. MARCHANT

LAVA FLOWS MT. OMIZANTRIM

PORT ZORN

Kubil

Witrix

WIR

HIGHGRASS

BROAD

Tolvirath Acerte CITY OF BONKERS

GREAT ROUTE OF THE

Quincunx (SKY CITY)

R. WIRIN

Deepwater

Thaisol

Bisinx

Kara-Est

ZHOU CHANNEL

THE SJEDD

BROKEN LANDS

SAMADUN

KEST-I-MON'S CASTLE

Brey

DYLA CANAL

WILDERLANDS OF DYLA

GOLDEN SEA

SOUTHERN STEPPE

GULF OF VELUZ

To JOREÁ

THE JOREÁL (OCEAN)

N

S

To Isles of the Sun

GREAT CRATER LAKE ETHEREALS

CAPE STORM

RAMPART MTNS

Athasar

Southern Waste

© 1979 VICTOR W. MILÁN

CHAPTER ONE

The man was a sadist, a killer, a eunuch. He was also a genius. But now Prince Rann Etuul gave little indication of those traits. He wore a plain robe that covered him from neck to ankles and made him appear to be little more than a hermit. The only outward signs that this man was different lay in the coldness of his tawny eyes and the network of fine scars glowing on his face where the light from the dying sun touched him.

He leaned forward, hands on a dilapidated table covered with maps, and stared out to the west. His mind worked methodically, savoring the sunset and the coolness and varied scents blowing in from the Gulf of Veluz. The songs of cinnamon birds and the evening lark mingled and vied for his attention over the cries of vendors in the city streets eastward and below his vantage point in the Hills of Cholon. He watched the western sky with little appreciation for the beauty of a vivid sunset. His mind was focused on a demon.

The Demon of the Dark Ones.

Rann tensed at the sight of a mote floating among clouds touched with the colors of gods. At first a spark less bright than the evening star, it grew and became cruciform. Growing still more, underwings burning with the reflected glory of the now hidden sun, it took on detail.

Thunder sounded. With a loud scrabbling of claws, the war eagle found a perch on the sill jutting from Rann's window. The window, like the others in the former Ducal Palace of Kara-Est, had been built in such a fashion that the opening was too small to admit the war bird, twice as tall as a man. Even the rider,

small and lithe like most Skyborn, had to duck to pass
through the opening before dropping to the stone floor.
The eagle's rider dismissed the mount, leaving it to find
supper and a roost in the aerie the fugitives of the City
in the Sky had constructed in a lesser tower of the
Palace.

The rider turned to face Rann. Her hair hung lank
about a face high of cheekbone and narrow of chin.
Under the grime and exhaustion masking her slightly
foxlike features, she might have been attractive. Her
hair was a lusterless tangled brown giving only hints of
its possible beauty when cleaned. She carried a bow and
quiver, and circling her left biceps was the gold brassard
of the elite Sky Guard.

"Sublieutenant Tanith," Rann greeted her. His voice
rang out like the pealing of a silver bell. When he desired, this tone increased the terror he inspired. He gestured toward a wrought-iron stand holding a large ceramic bottle and a goblet similar to the one he held.
"Drink, if you like."

"I'm on duty, sir," the Guardswoman said instinctively, her voice hoarse with dryness. Rann merely
looked at her. He was not above tricking the members
of the Guard into infractions of discipline. But in a
moment of reflection, the sublieutenant realized such
behavior belonged elsewhere, in the City in the Sky now
lost to the Demon. Too few of the Skyborn had survived the Demon's onslaught or the reptilian Hissers'
vengeance for Rann to further reduce their numbers
over petty crimes against corps discipline.

"Thank you, lord," she said, pouring the wine.

He permitted her to refill his cup. She drained hers
at a single swallow, then quickly filled her cup again.
Rann watched without comment. The mellow ale was
not that heady, and her farings would have given her a
great thirst.

"What have you learned?" he asked when she had
lubricated her throat sufficiently to speak in a natural
voice free of dry croakings.

"The City approaches, milord, even as you said it would."

"How far is it?"

"It should come into view sometime before dawn of the day after tomorrow. We could launch an eagle strike against it tomorrow." Her voice rose in hope that Rann would order such an attack. The Sky Guard had been shamed by the loss of their City. Tanith was like the other survivors who wanted nothing more than to redeem themselves and feel as if they were *doing* something to recoup their intolerable loss.

"And what did you see in the Sky City?" he asked, choosing to overlook her eager recommendation.

"The Hissers are at work, lord. They've completed the destruction they began the day . . . the day they cast us out. They build now. Defensive works, missile engines, and some construction that seems of no military purpose."

Gripping his left wrist with his right hand, Rann nodded above the rim of his goblet. He understood, or thought he did. No sooner had they turned on their human ally Moriana and the forces of her sister Synalon that earlier had been their common foe, than the *Zr'gsz* had set about erasing any hint of the nine-thousand-year occupancy of the humans who had supplanted them, the original builders of the City in the Sky. That done, it was obviously important to set their mark anew upon their recaptured prize to prepare to defend it.

Or to prepare to reassert their dominion over a continent. And eventually an entire world.

"The Demon," Rann almost hissed, leaning forward, his eyes gleaming in the last glow of twilight. "Did you see Istu?"

"My lord, I . . . I do not know." Tanith averted her eyes and bit her lower lip in consternation. For a heart-stopping instant, she thought he would reach across the table and seize her by the throat, shaking her the way a terrier killed a rat.

"What do you mean you don't know?" Rann's voice

was calm, level, deadly. Tanith now feared it more than if he had shouted.

"I saw Istu the day he was released, milord, as you did. A black shape towering in the sky like a doorway into darkness, his body like a man's but with horns set on either side of his skull. His eyes were slits of yellow fire." She shuddered at the memory. Better to face a hundred swordsmen than to even think about the Demon. "Like the Vicar of Istu, lord."

"That statue is his likeness. Now, I ask you again, did you *see* him?"

"Perhaps I did," she said, and met his polar stare. She managed to suppress another shudder. "But if so, he did not wear the same shape."

Breaking the bond of their locked gaze, Rann wheeled.

"Explain!" he snapped.

"I saw no such towering dark being as walked through the streets of the City on . . . that day. But the Skywell is filled with a blackness, lord, a rounded blackness that gleams like a giant black lens. I've not seen anything like it before. I thought this might be some manifestation of the Demon."

"The Black Lens." A look of stark pain flitted across Rann's ruined features. "One of the last tricks Istu concocted before Felarod bound him. And we must face it at the outset of this War of Powers."

He turned to her. Her eyes were wide above dark fatigue hollows. Rumors had flown among the ragged refugees streaming to Kara-Est and Bilsinx from the Sky City and the fury of its returned builders that a second War of Powers lay at hand. She had tended to dismiss such sayings as idle gossip.

The scarred lips of Prince Rann confirmed those rumors as truth.

"And skyrafts, Sublieutenant. Did you see any?"

"Few, lord. Ten or a dozen flew around or beside the City, but no more than that. We were observed, I think, but none pursued us." Her teeth showed bright in the twilight dimness of the room. "They've learned that lesson, at least!"

Rann waved his hand. The dearth of skyrafts mystified him, but it was only a minor mystery. The reptiles holding the City might have dispatched their fleets elsewhere for some arcane mission. A few sharp skirmishes since the day the City was conquered had demonstrated that, without magical aid, the skystone craft the Hissers rode couldn't survive long in the sky against the eagles of the bird riders. It was a trivial fact. The real enemy was the Demon of the Dark Ones. Against him the might and speed of the war eagles were little more than a sparrow smashing senselessly into a stone wall.

Rann chose not to tell the officer of the insignificance of the superiority to which she had alluded with such feral delight. He did not play his torment games with his own soldiers. Not now, not when so few remained. As spurious as it was, he would let her revel in the superiority of eagle over skyraft. All humans needed what comfort they could find now.

He sipped the ale. His cheek muscles contracted to give him a slight squint.

"The others remain to shadow the City?" he asked.

"Yes, lord. Four of us alternate resting on the ground and following the City. We've had luck in the form of clouds to hide in." She drank again from her own cup. "But still, I think they know they're being watched."

Rann nodded. That was one of the disadvantages of aerial observation. As a general rule, if you can see your foe, he could also see you. But this, too, meant little. Such was the strength of the reptilian Vridzish that they didn't care if they were spied upon or not. They now held the City—and had freed it from its once-set course over the center of the Sundered Realm. Using this immense aerial rock raft as their base, they could now travel at will and lay siege to even the most heavily defended cities.

"Well done, Sublieutenant Tanith. Go below and get some food and rest. You've earned them."

She paused beneath the doorway arch and asked, "Do we strike them tomorrow, lord? Or wait till they come to us?" In the dusk, her eyes shone with their own inner light.

"I shall take your suggestions under advisement, Sub-lieutenant. I assure you I'll undertake no weighty strategic decision without first consulting you." Feeling the lash of his irony, the officer turned and fled.

He listened to her heels tackhammering down the stairs. He had been harsh with her. That struck him as an ill omen. He usually controlled himself with far more precision. His skill in inflicting hurt led naturally to his knowing how not to inflict it, and when not to. This had been one of those occasions.

He shook his head and poured more ale. He was losing his grip in obvious ways. It was a new problem for him, more alien than the ways of the reptilian *Zr'gsz*. Though he knew how to manipulate that problem to maximize the despair and suffering of others, he didn't know how to cope when it came to haunt him.

Prince Rann knew fear. Great fear, overwhelming fear, for the first time in his life.

Her fear almost as tangible as the perfume of the two burly youths standing behind her, Governor Parel Tonsho fumbled at the door of her apartments, the brass key clicking against the lockplate as her fingers jumped and jittered. To cover fear and clumsiness alike, she cursed the smoky yellow glare of the oil lamps set in alcoves along the hall. If either of the youths realized that her difficulty had any cause but the dimness of the corridor, neither spoke the thought aloud. One did not maintain a much sought after position in the Governor's harem by being quick to find fault.

The key finally slid home with a thin screeching. Tumblers clicked and the door opened. She cast a quick look up and down the hallway before pushing into the darkened chamber beyond. Her pretty-boys were skilled with swords, but if the doom she'd feared so long had decided to overtake her now on the eve of battle, neither these two nor an army like them would help her in the least.

Then she was in the foyer, her heart hammering, as though she'd escaped a stalking, half-seen menace. A lamp flared in the room. With an odd relief she saw the small, neat figure sitting at ease in a fur-draped chair, hand raised to turn up the lamp even more. The long-awaited doom had come and, in coming, removed all fear of the waiting.

The door closed softly behind her. She sensed that neither of her kept youths had entered.

"I suppose," she said bitterly, "it would do me little good to call for help."

Prince Rann smiled the lazy smile of a cat that has awakened to find a mouse creeping across an expanse of open floor.

"Does it surprise you that your playmates are in my employ?"

"No." Her lumpy body sagged against a cool, plastered wall. Her pitbull eyes closed to weary slits. "Not really."

"Come in and sit down, milady Governor. Join me in a glass of this excellent Jorean Chablis. I find it vastly more palatable than that turpentine you Estil squeeze for yourselves." He gestured at a square bottle cut from blue glass bearing the wax seal of a renowned Jorean vintner.

Knowing the hopelessness of her situation, she saw nothing else to do but comply. The soul of graciousness, Rann poured full the crystal cup he had set out on the stand at his elbow, rose, handed her the glass, then eased back into the chair.

The thick furs strewn across the floor clutched at her feet as she walked to the divan opposite Rann. Cushions sighed protest as she dropped listlessly, spilling drops of white wine down the front of her purple silk tunic.

Reflexively, she took the glass in both hands and gulped the wine, needing the warmth and reassurance of its alcohol more than the sweetish taste.

"You've done well for yourself under the aegis of the City in the Sky, Governor." Rann's eyes, cat-yellow in the light, appraised her over the sparkling arc of his glass. "You've already accumulated a Tolvirot banker's ransom worth of new furs and silken cushions to replace those spoiled during the late, uh, unpleasantness. And by the diligent scrubbings of your servants and application of incense, you've almost managed to eliminate the smell of the blood that was spattered so liberally throughout these quarters."

At his words she twisted at her necklace of tiny seashells so violently that the strong silk thread snapped. The shells clattered to the floor in a pink and yellow rain.

"We have even provided you with a new seraglio to replace the one Colonel Enn found necessary to have shot down in this very room. And you still possess one of the finest cellars in all the Sundered Realm." He hoisted his glass in salute, drained it, swirled the wine across his palate for a long moment before swallowing. "No, all in all, the yoke of the City has lain lightly on your shoulders, Governor Tonsho. This you must admit. And in my turn, I admit that none other could have done as splendid a job administering the recovery of your city. You have amply earned both the rewards we your conquerors have lavished on you, and—" He leaned forward, eyes hardening, brightening. "—and the confidence we put in you."

Knowing the hopelessness of her position, she dashed her glass into fragments on the marble floor at his feet.

"Enough of this fencing. You know what I've done, damn you. Isn't that why you're here?" Her puffy face twisted in a sneer. "Since we're both admitting so much tonight, let's get it all out into plain sight."

He laughed.

"Ah, my good Governor. Of course I knew who employed those assassins in Bilsinx. Trying to assassinate me before we attacked Kara-Est was a clever move. Had I been in your position, I'd have done much the same myself." He sipped wine. "By the way, you'll be pleased to know that the young mage who saved me recovered not only from the trauma he suffered when the magical communications geode to which he was tuned shattered over the killer's head, but that he also escaped the massacre in the City."

As he spoke, a spark appeared in Tonsho's almost colorless eyes. She ran her hand repeatedly through her frizzy, graying hair. Rann smiled. She was allowing herself to hope.

"Or do you refer to the team of assassins you sent off for to Tolviroth Acerte, when you'd learned I'd be coming to Kara-Est after we were forced from the City? I'm afraid they won't be carrying out their mission. We intercepted them at the dock." He dropped a hand to his sword belt and toyed with something thrust between leather and tunic. "You were better advised to go with Medurimin fighting masters, as you did the first time. The Brethren of Assassins are much overrated, I fear."

Parel Tonsho hadn't risen to Chief of the Chamber of Deputies and de facto ruler of the richest seaport in the Realm by being slow witted. But it still took several seconds for the portent of Rann's statement to penetrate her numbed mind. She uttered a strangled sob and covered her face with chubby hands. He had learned all.

He sat quietly drinking as she wept. Soon, the ragged rhythm of her sobs faltered, broke. She raised a tear-wet face to his, jaw quivering with the effort it took to defy him.

"Did you bring that for me?" she asked, gesturing at the object he toyed with. "Do you plan to tranquilize me, to make it easier to carry me to your torture chambers? Or does the tip carry some terrible poison that will give me a lingering, painful death?"

He raised an eyebrow.

"This?" He took his hand away from the object. Briefly, Tonsho wondered that she hadn't remarked on it before. It was a hand dart used by the savage tribes-folk of the Thail Mountains, a bit over a handspan in length, carved from yellow wood, fletched at one end with yellow bird feathers. The tip was weighted with a ring of stone strapped to the shaft by strips of cured human skin. From the tip jutted a stiff black spine. It was incongruous for Rann to carry such an artifact; one similar had been used on him by the Thailint savages to drug and capture him. Before a band of his bird riders could rescue him, the prince's genitals had been burned away by the tribal leman.

"No," said Rann softly, shaking his head. "It's not for you. It's for an experiment."

She forced her upper lip to curl into a sneer.

"Whatever you'll do to me, you'd best start now. You'll need most of tonight to make final preparations to oppose the new inhabitants of the Sky City."

"You surprise me, Tonsho, you really do. I know how you dread the very thought of pain. And for that very reason I have come to personify all you fear most. It was, I grant, a factor in choosing you as Governor of Kara-Est. I judged that your fear would keep you in line. Yet you dared hire assassins a second time, knowing they would fail." He touched the glass to his lips. "That took spirit, Tonsho. I always judged you had great moral strength, but I didn't judge it could over-come your physical cowardice."

"I had to do something." She almost spat the words. "You hold my people in bondage."

"And you, as well," he said quietly. She shrank back, seeking shelter among the velvet cushions. Her flesh crawled as she considered the way she had just spoken to Rann, whose pleasure was the pain of others, whose face was her most familiar nightmare, whose elegant hand held her fate like a palmful of sand. He had her in a horror as excruciating as any physical torment; and he took no notice.

"As for preparing for the city's defense," he went on in a soft voice, "there is to be none."

She stared blankly.

"That's what I came to tell you. Get out. There won't be a Sky Citizen inside the walls of Kara-Est by the time the sun rises over Dyla. Kara-Est is doomed. For us to defend your city against Istu is to lose precious men. We can ill afford more losses."

"But Synalon! She's a mighty sorceress! I've not forgotten how she summoned the greatest air elemental seen to smash our ships and how, against all nature, she brought forth a salamander and forced it to cast itself into the waterspout. Can't she use those magics against the City and the Demon?"

Rann threw back his head and laughed. To one who knew him better than Tonsho—who knew him only as a nightmare figure—it was a strident, rare sound. She merely winced. To her, Rann's laughter was a thing to fear.

"Synalon *is* a mighty sorceress," he said when he had recovered himself, "but her sister defeated her in a duel of magics. And that same day Istu cast Moriana from the City like a man puts out a tomcat at night."

Her eyes narrowed until only wet yellow gleams of reflected lamplight showed between the lids.

"Why do you tell me this?"

He leaned forward. Had this been anyone but the devil Rann, Tonsho would have said he had a look of . . . desperation.

"You are able. You took a crushed, conquered city and made it a functioning seaport again in a matter of weeks. You've a rare gift. In the days to come, humanity will need all such gifts it can muster, if we're to have the slightest chance of survival."

To her amazement, she laughed in his face.

"What do you care for humankind?"

"More than you might think, milady Governor." His smile thinned. "More than for the damned *Zr'gsz,* at any rate."

"No, no, I can't believe this," she moaned, grasping her temples with both hands and rocking back and forth. "It's a trick." She raised her pallid face, fear and uncertainty etched in the flesh. "That's it! You trick me into abandoning my post so you'll have an excuse to put me to death."

"If I wished to put you to death, do you think I'd need an excuse?" He was becoming exasperated. Only rarely did he argue. "Or if I desired you removed from office, that I'd go to such lengths to manufacture one? Tonsho, all I'd need to do is spread the word that you had been negotiating with the Wildermen of Dyla to deliver your city to them. You'd soon be writhing at the post out in the Plaza, with the sorry collection of marionettes we've set to playing Deputies standing by bobbing their heads and applauding my wisdom and justice."

He saw that he fought futilely against her adamantine fears. Such sorry stuff as reason would not dispel her image of him any more than Synalon's magic could turn the wrath of Istu away from Kara-Est. He stood, smoothing wrinkles in his midnight blue trousers.

"Good evening, Governor Tonsho," he said.

"Highness." He stopped. "Now that you've failed to work your trickery on me, where do you go?" She all but giggled the words, giddy at her escape from pain and her imagined triumph over the wily prince.

"I've an appointment with Her Majesty to discuss tomorrow's events. I plan to tell her exactly what I told you. Perhaps she'll find it less amusing." He bowed. "I do hope your wit serves you equally well with Istu. Goodbye."

"Do you jest, Rann?" Synalon spun from the window and faced him squarely. "Evacuate?" She laughed, the sound evilly clinging to the very stone of the walls.

Standing by the door, Rann absently eyed the ala-

baster curve of her throat. Tonight the princess had
arranged her hair in two raven wings standing upward
and out from the sides of her head. On a woman with
less beauty or presence—or less power held in dubious
check—it would have looked ridiculous. On Synalon it
stirred both lust and dread. Her slender body was
wrapped in a gown of some gauzy stuff, more diapha-
nous than translucent, that showed the pink points of
her nipples and the trim dark thatch between her thighs.
Rann's tawny eyes, drifting downward now and again
against his will, could almost pick out the fine tracery of
blue veins on the flawless, milky skin, of breasts, belly,
well-shaped legs. He knew she had dressed in this
manner solely for him. Such was the game they played.

The black-haired enchantress stopped laughing and
gave him a cool, appraising look.

"Come, Prince. Tell me what you really intend. How
shall we face this menace?"

He grimaced, as if she had made to strike him.

"I wasn't joking, Your Majesty." On arriving in Kara-
Est after the flight across the Quincunx lands, Synalon
had reassumed the title of queen, though of what she
had failed to specify. From his unique position, Rann
generally disdained to give her that title and addressed
her as Highness. But now much rode on her good favor.
If he could get it by feeding her vanity, he would do so.

"We are prepared for defense," she said tolerantly.
"We have walls against ground attack, and our eagles
fighting beside the Estil gasbags and rooftop engines
will make short work of the skyrafts used by the stinking
Hissers."

"Very well. The Vridzish we may defeat. But not
Istu."

"No?" A frown clouded her fine features. "I have
meditated much since we were driven from my City. I
have some new tricks, half-man."

Ignoring the jibe, he shook his head and replied,
"Moriana defeated you, and she couldn't best Istu.
Moreover, Istu had just awakened when she faced him.

He had yet to come to his full power." He slapped his gloves across the palm of his left hand. "No, Your Majesty. If your sister could not defeat Istu, neither can you. We have no chance of defeating the Fallen Ones."

"But my own powers . . ."

"How much of the powers you've come by of late have been through the dispensation of the Dark Ones? I doubt they will allow you to muster strengths which they have lent you against their sole begotten son."

She folded her arms. Mad blue sparks danced in her eyes and crackled in the roots of her dark hair.

"Would you have us skulk away in the night then, cousin? Come, I thought you were a man in spirit, if not in flesh."

The scars at eyes and mouth turned white with strain.

"We would only throw our lives away."

"What of it?" she demanded, head held high. Blue flames raced along the wings of her hair. "If it's our lot to go down to defeat before these inhuman scum, then we shall die fighting, as befits the Skyborn! Let the groundlings flee, if they wish."

"While we live there's always a chance of finding some way to win," Rann said doggedly. "Felarod did, after all."

"Damn Felarod!" she spat. "That creature!" As a devotee of the Dark, Synalon had always despised the man who had undone the Lords of Infinite Night before.

"His enemies are now our own, cousin," Rann pointed out. "But if you hold him in such contempt, why not seek a way to do him one better?"

She smiled and turned away, the gown swirling like mist around her long, sleek legs. Below her spread the glimmers of the seaport city, red torches, yellow lamps, green lanterns bobbing at the corners of ships out in the harbor. Somewhere in the distance a dog barked. The wind had veered to come up from the fens with the thick, moist breath of corruption riding on it. She drew it in like a fine perfume.

"Maybe I will. Moriana was a weakling at heart. She let me live when I lay naked and powerless against her. I am steel at the center, not mush. If Istu would pit his will against my own, it may be the Demon who is surprised." Her words glowed with hatred. The Demon's progenitors had used her for their devious ends and cast her aside. Her pride still smarted over the injustice. Had a human injured her pride, death would have been painful and long. So fierce was her rage that she would forge from it a weapon fit to wound even the Lords of the Void.

Rann sighed. Like Tonsho, Synalon was a genius in her own way. He had to grant both women that. But he had long ago learned the sad lesson that not all of genius were stable.

"Is that your answer?" he asked, his voice as soft as wind among swamp reeds.

"Yes." She spoke without turning. "We fight."

The corners of his mouth drew up in an expression that wasn't a smile. His left hand dropped to his left boot-top, withdrew the yellow dart which Tonsho thought he'd brought for her. His hand whipped up.

The dart blurred across the room. Wary as a unicorn stag stalking a hunter, Synalon had half spun when the missile thunked home in soft, white flesh between her ribs. Red blossomed like an insane flower against her skin's pallor.

Both Rann and the Thailint poison were quick acting, but neither was fast enough. Rann's face twisted in agony as blue-white lightning lashed from Synalon's fingers and bathed his right side in flame. They fell together.

The doors burst open. Young Cerestan of the Guard stood there, eyes wild and hair awry, curved blade in his hand. He saw the royal cousins sprawled on the floor a few paces apart and gasped. The Guards crowding in at his back stopped and looked on in horror.

But both forms refused to remain still. Synalon lay on

her back, arms outflung, closed eyes turned to the vaulted ceiling, her entire body spasming. Rann, his jacket and tunic smouldering, painfully hoisted himself from the limestone floor.

"It is done." The words fell from Rann's lips in jagged fragments. "Cerestan, see that the evacuation continues. We must be away from here before . . ."

Strength left him. He fell face-down on the cold stone.

CHAPTER TWO

"I know little of practical magic but have read much of the theory in books," the small, round man said. "But from what I do know, yes, it could have been an illusion and nothing more."

Fost Longstrider leaned back in his chair, fingering his chin thoughtfully. The appearance of the goddess Jirre at such an opportune time at the Battle of the Black March troubled him. Moriana Etuul was a great sorceress, yes, but she had been physically and emotionally drained by the Zr'gsz magic and was hardly able to fling a small lightning bolt, much less maintain a greater than life-sized illusion. The battle had been ill-conceived due to the bickering between the various factions comprising the army, and Fost was still more than a little surprised at the victory against the superior army of reptiles. His eyes narrowed. He didn't have to ask Oracle the question. The being—the projected image—read it from his mind.

"It seems to me," the image of the little man went on, "that an illusion properly cast, especially by one who'd never performed such a spell—and the Princess Moriana had not—might befuddle the caster as well as its intended objects. So, assuming that the apparition of the goddess Jirre was no more than it seemed, it still might have served to uncover untapped reserves of power within Moriana. Focusing that power might account for the destruction of the Zr'gsz skyrafts when the apparition struck its lyre. The way the Hissers died when she swept through them can be attributed to suggestion. But as you pointed out, it stretches credibility beyond the breaking point to speculate that the rafts themselves possessed some consciousness for the illusion to play upon. I," said Oracle firmly, "therefore conjecture Moriana has unsuspected powers that caused the craft to disintegrate."

Oracle possessed much of the knowledge stored in the great Library of High Medurim and shared it willingly with Fost. The real body of the entity called Oracle lay in the next room. It was nothing more than a gleaming blue-white mound of fungus the size of a peasant's hut. The nutrient vat in which it rested bubbled and reeked like garlic, but this didn't stop the legion of savants whose droning penetrated the wall in a beehive buzz as they read aloud from ancient volumes. The more they read, the more Oracle absorbed into its consciousness, and the more information it could integrate, evaluate and pass along to Fost.

The living, thinking, reasoning fungus was a triumph of genetic magics commissioned by the Emperor Teom.

In spite of Oracle's logic, something nudged at the former Realm-road courier's mind. Oracle had learned much in its short existence. Perhaps too much from Emperor Teom and his sister-wife Temalla when it came to subterfuge and intrigue. Fost felt that Oracle held something back, but the illusion of a pudgy, self-content man sitting cross-legged beside him was unreadable.

"You're being less than candid," Fost accused. "That body of yours is no more than an illusion, yet you are able to cast it all the way to the Black March to view the battle. I'd say that shows more than theoretical acquaintance with magic."

The pale eyes slid from his gray ones.

"There's magic and magic, my young friend, and—"

"Young?" Fost snorted. "With all due respect, I'm not as young as you, who were first cultured in the vat a scant three years ago. And as for magic, *I'm* one who truly knows little of it, but I do know the kinds. There's extrinsic magic, the ability to manipulate powers like

elementals and lesser demons, which was passed to the
Etuul bloodline by the Hissers back in the days before
the reptiles were driven from the Sky City. And there's
intrinsic magic—Athalar art—springing from the powers of the magician's own mind. Moriana's hardships on
the slopes of Mt. Omizantrim honed her intrinsic powers
to the point where she was able to best Synalon's largely
extrinsic magic. Befuddling minds so only illusion is
perceived is clearly intrinsic magic—and happens to be
exactly what you're doing to me, you charlatan."

Oracle spread his hands and smiled.

"No evading the question," Fost pressed. "Was the
apparition of the goddess Jirre simply illusion—or
something more?"

The cheerful mask dropped from Oracle's face. He
hesitated, and his eyes seemed to probe Fost's very soul.

"Are you sure you want the answer to that, my
friend?" he asked in a soft voice.

"Uh, no, maybe I don't." Fost licked dry lips. He
had thought he needed the answer. Now he wasn't so
sure of himself. Moriana had learned much during her
stay in the Hissers' city of Thendrun. Some of her newfound knowledge struck him as truly alien, a thing
better suited to the reptilian than the human. And if she
had somehow accomplished the impossible feat of actually summoning a goddess to do her bidding, she ranked
as the most powerful mage in all of history.

"You fear the gods, don't you?" Oracle asked after a
long silence.

"I fear the fact of their existence. No, not even that.
I dread living in a world that's a battleground for forces
beyond it. If the Dark Ones exist, and the Three and
Twenty Wise Ones of Agift, too, fine. That's no concern of mine. But if they choose to settle their differences on this little mudball wrapped in a blanket of air
where I live. . . ." He shuddered at the magnitude of it
all. Sometimes it was difficult enough dealing with
human royalty. This transcended petty, bickering hu-

manity and opened the Universe to unknowable dealings. "I don't know if I can bear the thought of being
no more than a pawn in a cosmic chess game."

Oracle's face mirrored the pain Fost felt.

"You must bear it, my friend," he said quietly. "Istu
is loose again, and a Second War of Powers is already
being fought. Whether you like it or not, you are one of
the principals."

In moody silence, Fost sat and remembered. The
Battle of the Black March had been swung from defeat
to victory for humanity by the startling, unexpected
apparition hundreds of feet tall that may or may not
have been the goddess Jirre herself. After Fost had
talked himself into believing it only an illusion, the
image of Zak'zar, the Speaker of the People, had appeared at the victory feast in Emperor Teom's pavilion.

The *Zr'gsz* leader had destroyed the triumphant mood
with twin revelations. Humankind had won a feeble
victory; the Sky City carrying the Demon of the Dark
Ones easily conquered the great city of Kara-Est. Even
more unsettling for Fost was the shattering indictment
of his lover, Moriana Etuul. Zak'zar revealed that
Moriana had lain with one of the Hissers to seal her
alliance with the People, and that she, and all of the
Etuul bloodline, were descended from another human-
reptile union nine thousand years earlier.

Fost's walls of self-assurance had slumped into ruin.
He had endured so much, and now he was forced to
withstand even more. It wasn't enough that Moriana
had once killed him, driving her dagger deep into his
back. Athalau, the city buried in the glacier beyond the
Rampart Mountains, held many objects of magical lore;
one of them, the Amulet of Living Flame, had restored
his life. And Fost had followed Moriana, not for revenge
but for love. Her act had been one of patriotism and
idealism directed toward saving her precious Sky City
from Synalon's demented rule. Fost could even admire
Moriana for her devotion to her subjects, though his
hand unconsciously went to the spot where the dagger

had been driven into his body. He had endured all that and more until this moment.

Now he hardly knew what to believe.

With a sardonic bow, Zak'zar's image had winked out, leaving Moriana alone in a sea of silence. Fost had wanted to go to her, to comfort her, yet found himself stunned and immobile. She had left the tent and gone into the night. Fost had been sure he would never see her again. But the next day just after dawn, Moriana had returned to the encampment of the Imperial armies, obviously distraught but forcing herself into composure. She bore up well under the hostile gazes and proved herself truly regal by her demeanor.

Seeing her again had washed away some of the misgivings Fost had. He loved her; what matter that she was not altogether human. As Erimenes the Ethical, an Athalau ghost bottled for fourteen hundred years, had pointed out, the *Zr'gsz* blood was diluted by several hundred generations. The philosopher's spirit, usually acerbic and argumentative, had mellowed considerably since Fost had first come upon him. No longer did Erimenes seek out the vicarious thrill of bloodshed and voyeuristic sex. His contact with another Athalar spirit, the nun Ziore, had caused Erimenes to temper his behavior greatly. For that Fost was thankful. Dealing with the emotion-twisting knowledge of Moriana's heritage was problem enough for him at the moment.

About her liaison with the Hisser to complete their military aid pact, Fost discovered it meant little to him. He knew she had had other lovers when they were apart. He himself had stayed far from celibate while tracking her across the continent; what was one more lover between them? If one of Moriana's lovers wasn't human, he was more nearly so than the hornbulls Moriana's sister had imported for her own wayward pleasures, on the advice of the ever-helpful Erimenes.

"Tell me of the gods, Oracle," Fost asked abruptly.

The small man smiled.

"You wish a discourse on theology?"

"No, but I think I'd better have one just the same."

Oracle sat for a moment, rocking back and forth. Outside, the afternoon sun had sent the residents of High Medurim scurrying to shelter to escape the glare and heat. Here in the marble precincts of the Palace it was cool, and a stick of incense smouldered in a corner of the cubicle taking the sting from the smell of Oracle's nutrient pool next door. Fost's eyelids turned heavy in spite of the coolness. He and Moriana had arrived only the day before, a long and dusty ride on the heels of arduous battle. Emperor Teom had reckoned the menace on the frontier serious enough for his personal attention, but with that settled and the *Zr'gsz* massacred, he had felt the precarious civil unrest in his capital called for a prompt return. This resulted in little time for rest for any of them.

The humming of the savants next door had a soporific effect, too. Fost found himself trying to follow their sing-song reading, their education of Oracle.

"To theology," said Oracle. "Best begin with the Dark Ones, since everything does begin with them. No, don't shudder." He shut his eyes and spoke in a low, rhythmic voice like an incantation. "In the beginning was the Dark, single and undivided, holy. And the Masters dwelt within darkness and nothingness and all was at peace, for all was One, and this was the blessed rule of Law.

"Then Perfect Dark was disturbed by Light, and the Oneness became Two. And the Masters of the Void set to destroy this defilement. But a mistake occurred, even then indicating Perfection had been lost. The Light was not destroyed; it was dispersed. Bits of Light were scattered across the face of the Dark. And some cooled and became Matter, and some of these specks of filth began to quiver with Life, the ultimate perversion. And so was Chaos born.

"And it came to pass that Gods rose up in opposition to the Dark, Gods favoring Light and Matter. First one, then two, then many; and so the efforts of the Masters to return all things to Unity were thwarted by the accursed, the Lords of Light and Chaos. Many were their numbers, and their names were legion.

"But the Masters of the Void, who do not suffer their names or numbers to be known, gave their only begotten son to the Universe, that it might one day be returned to the rule of Law and Darkness, and the great struggle was commenced."

Oracle paused, took a deep breath he hardly required, then opened his eyes.

"This was taken from the preamble to *Gospels of Darkness*. The Library has translations going back to the First Migration. It is one of the most ancient of texts. I take it you've not seen or heard this before?"

Despite the coolness, drops of sweat stood out on Fost's forehead.

"No, I've never come across that."

"It's peculiar, given your lust for knowledge, that you've shied away from the subject of religion," said Oracle. "Also revealing." Fost's youth in Medurim had been split between petty thievery in the streets and evenings filled with study in the massive Library. He had originally entered the Library hoping to find easy prey; the master had enticed him with stories ranging far beyond his humble imaginings. The wealth he had removed had been knowledge, a commodity far greater than mere gold klenors.

"I suppose. What about the Three and Twenty?"

The little man rubbed his chin. It gave Fost an eerie feeling since it was among many gestures Oracle had copied from him in trying to perfect the humanity of his simulacrum. It was like shaving in a mirror and seeing a hand hold a razor to a stranger's face.

"The first thing to understand," said Oracle, "is that the Twenty-three are ladies and lords of Chaos, and few generalities can be made about them. It is written in old, old tomes that once humanity's gods each had a single attribute: war, birth, lust, fire, water. Worship in such a fashion is rare today, although you find traces of it among the Thailint and Dyla savages, and the more de-based cultures of the Northern Continent. On the other hand, each of the Three and Twenty represents several principles and has several attributes. With a few exceptions, of course, since these are first and foremost Chaotic deities. This disparity between old religion and new tends, I believe, to support a thesis I formulated before you came to High Medurim." Oracle cocked his head to one side to see if Fost still listened.

He did and asked, "And what's this theory of yours, Oracle?"

"I do not believe humanity is native to our world."

Fost's eyebrows rose. Though Oracle smiled indulgently at his attempted interruptions, he held relentlessly to his subject of the confusing and confused array of gods and goddesses.

"I'll discuss my theories of how humankind came to this world with you later. But bear with me for a short while longer.

"Chief of the Three and Twenty is generally held to be Jirre. Jirre's the goddess of both Creation and Destruction, a typically Chaotic contradiction. But this contradiction may be only apparent. Her devotees argue that Creation and Destruction are two sides of the same coin, hence only one goddess is required. Another way of viewing it is the Dualist philosophy, which holds that Twoness, not Oneness, is the natural order of things. That accounts for the creation of Light in the first place. Of course, that doctrine raises unanswered questions of its own since Light and Dark are but two faces of the same coin.

"But I see your eyelids drooping. I fear I bore you like that discursive old fart, Erimenes." Oracle spoke faster to hold Fost's attention. "You're already familiar with Ust, the Red Bear; Gormanka of wind and wayfarers, your patron of couriers; Somdag Squid-face. There are others, of course, less commonly known."

"Wait, wait, wait." Fost held up both his hands in despair. "This is going too fast for me. I'm not sure I can work through the contradictions in all you're telling me."

"I told you that these are lords and ladies of Chaos. In a nutshell, Justice, alone of the attributes of Chaos, is immutable but takes many forms. Law always takes a similar form but its nature changes according to what best serves the ends of the Elder Dark. I admit it doesn't make much sense, even to me. But it is often said that expedience is an attribute of Law and Darkness, and Justice cannot be expedient."

Fost stretched, yawned.

"You're the one doing the talking, but my throat's as dry as dust," he said. "Thanks for the lesson."

Oracle arched a pale eyebrow.

"The lesson's far from complete," he said, "but I perceive the chamberlain, the one you always think of as 'the slug,' approaches along the corridor. He doubtless means to drag you to another rehearsal or lesson in protocol. As always, it was a pleasure speaking with you. I look forward to our next session together."

"I'd look forward to it more," said Fost, rising, "if we could talk about something less unnerving and more coherent." But the image of the little, fat man was gone, leaving Fost alone with the smell of incense, the sound of mumbling savants, and the petulant pit-pat of the chamberlain's sandals coming down the hall.

CHAPTER THREE

The thick stone walls of the temple muffled the bustling sounds from without as they muffled the oppressive heat. Fost and his companions wandered along the cool flagstone-paved aisles, glimpsing here and there priests robed in the color of the deity they served, or worshippers laden with small offerings to plead their petty cases, seeking the mending of hearts or the winning of good luck for themselves and bad luck for their enemies.

"What I want to know," said Erimenes the Ethical, laying a long, vaporous blue finger beside his beaky nose, "is why the Temple of All Gods, by rights the fairest in all the Sundered Realm, should be so prodigiously ugly."

Fost laughed, winning him a dirty look from a pinch-faced priest in a white and yellow robe. The pillared hall swallowed the sound without a trace, however, so that only those nearby heard. It might have been that among the deities whose likenesses were housed here were those who did not disapprove of voices raised in laughter.

"You can thank the Northblood Barbarians for that," he said. Ziore tilted her head, partly in respect for the sundry deities and mostly to hear his words, which were spoken now with decorously lowered voice. He saw Moriana looking on with apparent interest, and his heart lifted. There were times since the battle when she seemed to be drifting into another world, a world divorced from this one. Anything that captured her interest and took her away from her own problems merited his approval. That Ziore likewise appeared interested also heartened him. The nun's ghost and

Moriana had become closely linked in a way that he could not truly fathom. Their emotions merged into something beyond telepathy. If Ziore smiled, that communicated directly to Moriana's mind.

He nodded polite acknowledgement to a statue of Ust the Red Bear as they passed. The god was one of Fost's patrons, entrusted with guarding the Realm Roads, and he felt an obligation to pay slight obeisance since he had called upon Ust so many times in the past. In spite of his reflexive invocations of the bear god, he wondered if it did any good. He had no proof one way or the other, yet the hetwoman of the Ust-alayakits, Jennas, believed in the god. The time he had spent with Jennas getting through the Rampart Mountains and crossing the length of the Sundered Realm had instilled in him a healthy respect for—if not belief in—Ust. Jennas had predicted this War of Powers long before he had seen the signs forming. Whether her knowledge came from shrewd insight into the ways of man or true revelation by Ust, Fost couldn't say. Either way, Jennas was a superior woman of rare courage and even rarer abilities.

"The barbarians knew only a few of the Wise Ones when they invaded nearly five thousand years ago. Like most barbarians who pride themselves on virile vigor and their superiority to effete civilized folk, the first thing they did on conquering Medurim was to settle down to emulating the Medurimin citizen in earnest. They somehow decided that gods prefer ostentation. So, they rebuilt the Temple of All Gods according to their own ideas of splendor fitting for a house of deities." Fost waved a scarred hand. "These are the results of that wild, misguided fit of building."

They looked about. Some of the statues stood free on pedestals, while others were sheltered in alcoves, the gods' and goddesses' preferences determined by their devotees. But the statues mostly predated the barbarian dynasty and were not what captured the eye.

In his youth, the unschooled and half-wild street

urchin named Fost thought that the Temple was ugly.
From the outside, its hewn granite blocks were set in
massy tiers appearing to form crude steps in the ultimate
shape of a pyramid. Now that Fost was grown and had
seen other architectures offered by cities in the Realm,
he *knew* the place was an eyesore.

Inside was no better. High up, where the tiers jutted
together, crossed and criss-crossed a spiderweb of struts
and supports of wood and iron. The Temple's original
plan called for the stepping-in to continue until the ranks
of stone met. Planning exceeded expertise in construction. The huge blocks were poorly balanced and would
fall if the building had continued upward as intended.
The Emperor Gotrag II had ordered his artificers to
roof over the partially finished upper structure. The
lofty courses were dangerously unstable, as a result, and
the latticework of joists and struts grew more complex
with every passing year. Should one single succeeding
Emperor fail to add bracing, the Temple roof would
certainly collapse.

"But whoever heard of square columns?" demanded
Erimenes on a rising note of outrage. The genie whirled
about in a tight vortex of blue mist as he pointed out
the offending supports. Ziore wavered nearby, her substance lightly mingling with his and giving the philosopher silent approbation. "And who saw fit," he continued, "to build them of alternate blocks of rose granite
and whatever that ghastly chartreuse stone is?"

"It's a type of limestone," explained Fost. "And in
answer to both the other questions—the Northern
Barbarians."

Ziore looked puzzled and slightly pained.

"Forgive my asking, Fost, but I thought the Northern
Barbarians founded High Medurim, and that the residents were descended from them." She bit at her non-
existent lip, fearful of giving offense.

Fost laughed.

"They did; I'm descended from them, just as you
and Erimenes and Moriana are mostly descended from

the Golden Barbarians. The Golden Barbarians have achieved a static society while the Northern ones have locked themselves into a cycle of renaissance and regression; every few centuries they work themselves up to the level of barbarism, then they fall to fighting and knock themselves back to savagery. They call it progress."

They stopped in front of an alcove containing still another of the seemingly endless statues of a goddess. It was a conventional enough rendering of a lovely, slender woman bearing sword and lyre. Fost was struck by the resemblance between the chiselled stone features and those of the illusion Moriana had brought forth in the Black March. The exiled Sky City princess had duplicated well, never having set foot in this Temple before.

If she had duplicated, Fost found himself thinking.

Wordlessly, Moriana slipped the strap of the satchel containing Ziore's jug from her shoulder and handed it to Fost. She stepped forward and fell to her knees in front of the statue, placed a sprig of blue wildflowers at the statue's feet and bent her head in prayer. Fost held his breath, half-expecting and half-dreading some sign. But the statue remained stone.

Moriana finally uttered a small sigh and rose.

"The goddess thanks you, milady," came a voice behind Fost.

Fost turned to see a stout, short man dressed in green and gold, with a fringe of gray hair hanging lank from the base of his bald head. Around his neck rode a gold chain supporting a medallion struck with the signs of sword and lyre. His eyes shone surprisingly green and youthful from a leathery, seamed face.

"It's I who have come to thank her," Moriana said.

The priest's brow knit, then his face underwent a remarkable migration of lines and wrinkles that eventually sorted out into a broad beam of joy.

"But you, Princess Moriana, are the one who called her down to succor our folk at the Black March!" He dropped to his knees and reached an arthritic hand out to catch the hem of her gown and raise it to his lips. He fumbled a moment, uncertain when he found no skirt, then took the hem of her suede tunic and kissed it instead.

"This is the happiest day of my life! All my devotions are rewarded. I come at last into the presence of one truly touched by blessed Jirre!" Great tears of happiness rolled down his round cheeks. Even Fost, skeptical of priests and politicians, was moved by the intensity of the emotion displayed.

Tears gleamed at the corners of Moriana's eyes as she reached down and helped the little priest to his feet.

"You need not kneel to me," she said. Fost thought she was going to tell him it hadn't been Jirre at all but rather an illusion she had summoned to confound the Zr'gsz. But her eyes caught Fost's, a corner of her mouth quirked upward, and she said nothing.

"They cried at the portal that you were within," the priest babbled in rapture. "But I did not dare hope. Joy, joy!"

"Wait a minute," Fost said. "Who was crying at the portal that Moriana was within?"

"The mob."

Fost swallowed. He exchanged bleak looks with Moriana. There was no need to ask which mob it was. News of the way Moriana had brought the battle to a conclusion had preceded the returning army by a full day. Coming between that news and the first tired riders had been the tidings borne by Zak'zar of Kara-Est's destruction and Moriana's lineage. When Moriana had entered High Medurim, she had been beset by two masses of people, one throwing flower petals and naming her holy and the other naming her witch and traitor to her kind. It was even rumored old Sir Tharvus wandered the streets dressed in a mendicant's rags and egged on the violent faction. He had lost brothers in battle and blamed Moriana. If a mob truly gathered at the Temple door crying Moriana's name, she and her companions were in danger.

As the priest hopped from one foot to the other pleading to be told what troubled the holy lady, Fost corralled a worried-looking woman in white and red. He found that, as he had dreaded, half those thronging the Temple screamed for Moriana and the other half screamed for Moriana's blood.

"But won't the ones who call you saviour protect you from the others?" asked Ziore.

"More likely the two factions will pull her apart in a tug of war," Fost answered grimly. "It's happened before." He had lost his own parents to a riot many years ago when the mob rose up in rage at learning the dole was to be cut to cover the expenses of celebrating Teom's ascension to the Sapphire Throne.

"If I must face them, then I shall," she said, tossing back her hair. "Where's my sword?" Moriana walked toward the front of the hall.

Fost seized her arm. Her eyes blazed as she spun on him, but she neither broke his grip nor fried him with a lightning bolt.

"You won't defeat the Dark Ones by getting yourself torn to pieces on the Temple steps," he pointed out.

"What would you do? Do you want me to cower among the statues until the mob rushes the gates and drags me out? If I must die, I'll do it on my own two feet, with my head held high."

Fost knew it wasn't bravado speaking. She had gone to what seemed certain doom in the Sky City and the Circle of the Skywell to face the Demon Istu himself. She had succeeded in slowing the Demon's pace long enough for many of her subjects in the City to escape; not once had she wavered in front of that black, soul-sucking being.

"No need," he said. "Where are the Wardens of the Temple?"

Grasping the peril of the situation, the portly priest

gathered up his skirts and hustled off in search of one
of the brown-robed custodians of the Temple. Two
figures soon returned, both tall, both with brown hoods
drawn well up and closed to cover their faces. They
carried faded leather satchels containing ceramic jars
slung over their shoulders. They paused for a moment
listening to the battle raging on the other side of the vast
structure, and then hurried off through the puddles and
refuse that desecrated the interior of the Temple. They
slipped through a side door and made their way through
the city's alleys.

They dined as they generally had since coming to
High Medurim, alone in their apartments except for the
two genies. After they had finished, the chamberlain
arrived all atwitter to go over the protocols they would
be called on to observe on the morrow when Teom
invested them both as nobles of the Empire. When the
man left at last, pale hands fluttering like a mother bird
drawing attention away from her nest, they both felt as
tired as if they'd been forced to run around the entire
city of Medurim—twice. A sultry, sticky sea breeze
blew in through the windows, laden with the smell of
dead fish.

Moriana had a stack of scrolls and books piled in the
corner, grimoires that a servant had brought over from
the Library. But she claimed to be too tired to make
sense of them. For his part, Fost toyed with the notion
of paying a visit to Oracle.

He just as quickly discarded the idea. Since the night
of the orgy celebrating their initial arrival to the city,
Empress Temalla had taken to popping out at him as
he walked the corridors, particularly at night. He knew
all too well what would happen if he angered her, and
he was running out of tactful refusals to her sexual
overtures. The last time had been the most embar-
rassing. He had admitted—lied—that he had contracted
an uncomfortable fungus infection from riding so long
in a wet saddle. At that, the Empress had laughed up-

roariously and told him she was too old to believe in a child's fable and that he must have gotten the blight by becoming more familiar with his war dog than was conventional, even by High Medurim's permissive standards. He had been blushing quite authentically when they parted.

Fost and Moriana finally retired for the night, to separate pallets. Though she had not rejected his company since the battle, she hadn't encouraged intimacy, either. He had considered asking for separate quarters, yet hoped that their nearness would again spark the feelings for one another they'd lost. He undressed quickly and lay down, turning his face to the wall and trying to ignore the rustlings and shiftings Moriana made as she disrobed.

The two Athalar spirits had been cooing and making calf-eyes at one another constantly while the humans ate. Before going to her own bed, Moriana poured them together in a bronze vessel Teom had provided for just that purpose. There were many times Fost wished Erimenes and Ziore had remained as hostile to one another as when they'd first met. He had thought their incessant squabbling wearisome, but it was nothing compared to this. Thanks to Ch'rri, the Wirix-magic spawned cat woman and a healthy dose of aphrodisiac vapors, the two genies had discovered the art of incorporeal lovemaking. They may not have had bodies but they carried on like pigs in rut. In spite of the squeals, moans and titters, sleep soon found Fost.

Walls of light, flowing curtains of blue and scarlet and white shifting relentlessly, colors blending seamlessly one into another circled Fost. He reached out an arm turned curiously insubstantial. Warmth met his fingertips. He pushed into the colored fog and the wall vanished, revealing a long corridor.

Unafraid, Fost walked forward. His feet met only softness, as if he marched on the very stuff of which clouds were made. The particolored walls remained just beyond his reach as he walked and walked and walked, for what seemed an eternity. Suddenly, he realized he had acquired a companion.

"Erimenes!" he cried out in surprise. "You have feet!"

"Of course I do, dear boy. Did you suspect tentacles —or perhaps another head?" The spirit appeared as tenuous as ever, but now Fost joined him in this ghostly state.

Ziore reached out and caressed Fost's cheek. Surprised, yet curiously calm at all happening to him, he caught up her wrist. His fingers momentarily felt substance, then his fingers flowed through her forearm. He couldn't tell if it were she or himself lacking real dimension.

"Ahead," came Moriana's voice. "How lovely it is!"

Fost felt ineffable calm. His friends had joined him in this dream world, this dream. He looked in the direction Moriana pointed. Unbidden, the name "Agift" came to mind. This was the home of the gods and goddesses. His mind flitted around the idea this was more than simple dream, then hastily moved from such conjecture. He was too caught up in the swirling nothingness at the end of the corridor. Even as Fost watched, the mists solidified into a subtly hued chamber filled with light that cast no shadow.

He blinked, then noticed a table at the far end of the room, the figures grouped around it strangely familiar to him.

Radiant in her gown of green and gold, Jirre rose as the four approached.

"Daughter," the goddess said to Moriana. "It is good to see you again. I had not planned on it. You may thank Majyra for this meeting." She nodded to a young woman at the head of the table, stately in a lavender gown that left milkwhite shoulders bare. Deep red hair was piled atop her head. Her eyes shone out as black as night.

"Sit and be welcome. You can stay only a short

while." As she spoke, her gown's color changed to icy blue.

Fost hadn't noticed the four chairs before. He and the others took seats and faced the Three and Twenty Wise Ones, their gods and goddesses.

"We are not all here," said an older woman to Majyra's left. "Tothyr and Avalys won't come because they find Majyra too frivolous, and several of the others are missing for whatever reason. Who can say with us?" She drew deeply on a leaf-rolled cigarette, then blew the smoke out. The smoke danced and formed fleeting caricatures of those missing from the table. Fost blushed when he recognized the acts being performed by those smoky figures.

"I thank you for your hospitality, Lady Majyra," said Moriana, gathering her wits more rapidly than Fost. Of them all she took this with the most aplomb. Even Erimenes remained uncharacteristically silent in the presence of the deities.

"And to you, Jirre," continued Moriana, "I offer my thanks and eternal devotion for the aid rendered at the Black March."

"You are welcome," said Jirre, a smile curling her lips. "I truly wish I could do more. But as I told you, I cannot."

"What of the others? My world is your domain. The Dark Ones threaten it. Can't you take an active part in defending it?"

Several of the deities stirred impatiently. Fost felt the shape of the chamber altering, as if the emotions rising somehow changed the very physical dimensions of the room. He sensed that few of the Three and Twenty assembled were favorably disposed toward him—or Moriana.

"Let me explain," Jirre said, looking down the table and silencing the grumbles. "We summoned you here to tell you that we cannot aid you. Or if aid might be possible, then it must be given indirectly."

"But why?" asked Ziore.

"The ways of gods are not the ways of men," pontificated Erimenes. The spirit fell silent when Jirre scowled in his direction.

"We have grown apart from your world. Even brief visits to it are tiring for us. There is also the fact that we tried our might against the Demon of the Dark Ones before. We failed. And we were stronger then." Jirre spread her hands in a gesture of helplessness. "There are other reasons, but those are the primary ones."

"Well, we're grateful for the help you've given us this far," said Fost, wondering at himself for speaking so familiarly to the Wise Ones. "Lord Ust," he said turning to a huge bear sitting a few feet away down the table, "you especially have my thanks for aiding me."

Ust frowned and rubbed his cheek with a claw.

"You've been a dutiful son," he rumbled, "though like all of them you think of me most often when in distress. But I cannot recall intervening on your behalf. You seem well enough equipped to sort out your own problems."

"But," Fost sputtered, confused, "but that time the Ust-alayakits rescued me from Rann and his killers and spared my life because I called on you . . . and those other times when Jennas told me you had aided me. You didn't?" He felt hot tears of frustration stinging his eyes. He had come to have faith in Jennas and her forecasts. He felt cheated she'd failed him in this way.

"Jennas is my chosen," the bear god said in his rolling bass. "Her I do watch over, for she leads my people. But you—if someone's been helping you, it hasn't been me." He scowled, his eyes turning red. "An impostor, is it? Just let me find out who—"

"Ust, control yourself," chided Jirre. "Your muzzle is growing."

"I won't sit next to a *bear,*" declared Majyra. "They smell!"

Reddish hair retreated from the bear god's face, and his face and brow took on a more human appearance.

But he huddled himself down and growled as if hating the shape change.

"Best I return you to your bodies," said Jirre. "I am truly sorry. Our hopes and best thoughts go with you, for what they're worth."

Fost felt the chair dissolving under him. He stood rather than be dropped to the floor. Beside him were Moriana, Erimenes and Ziore. They bowed. There was nothing to say, although Fost's mind churned with unanswered questions. Jirre had dismissed them. When a goddess bids a mere mortal leave, it was best to depart.

As they walked back the way they had come along the auroral hall, the shifting hues of the walls faded from view and were replaced by swirling fog. Gradually the others drew ahead of Fost. Though he picked his own way through the foggy terrain as quickly as he could, they moved inexorably away, hardly seeming aware that they did so. Fost felt panic grip his throat when they vanished into the misty distance.

"Be calm," a voice said beside him. "I wanted a word with you in private."

Fost turned and saw one of the Wise Ones. The goddess seemed tantalizingly familiar, yet he could place no name to her. She had remained silent in the hall while Jirre spoke.

As if reading his mind, she reached out and plucked a tiny rose from behind his ear, saying, "Now do you know me, Fost? I am Perryn." A dulcet laugh filled his ears, yet had a peculiarly flat quality to it. "Perryn Prankster, some call me."

The goddess of laughter and anarchy handed him the miniature rose.

"I will tell you something, my friend," Perryn said, laughing at Fost's discomfort. "It might be that the Wise Ones, aligned together, could defeat the Dark Ones and cast Istu back into spaces between the stars. It just might be," she said, grinning savagely. "And it might be that you should thank me for helping prevent it."

"Thank you?" cried Fost. "But you've thrown us to the Dark Ones, left us defenseless!"

"Not defenseless. Felarod defeated Istu before without our aid."

"But the World Spirit . . ."

"Is a thing apart, closer to you than to us. It is not of Agift but rather of a more basic origin. In many ways, it and Istu are so similar." She shook her head. "Because you're ignorant in matters of the gods, I will state the obvious and not think less of you for it. We are us and you are you."

Fost looked blank.

"Our interests are not yours," said Perryn, eyes boring into Fost's gray ones. "If we fight for your world and conquer it, it will be ours. No longer yours, except by our sufferance."

"This is all . . . hard to accept." Fost licked dry lips.

"It'd be harder for one raised a pious believer. We are good allies but poor masters."

She clapped Fost on the shoulder and said, "You'd best get along now. Remember not to count on assistance from us." Perryn smiled wickedly, adding, "Well, perhaps a little. I do like you, mortal. You're cute." The goddess laughed and this time the waves of mirth smashed into Fost's brain like ocean waves against a beach. His head rang as he felt himself spinning away.

He cried out, "Perryn! Who was it who helped me before, if not my patron Ust?"

Ghostly laughter brought Fost awake. He sat upright, drenched in a cold sweat, his heart triphammering wildly in his breast. He took several deep draughts of the fish-smell laden air and calmed down.

"What a dream," he said to himself, reaching up to brush away the perspiration on his forehead. A single tiny rose was clutched in his right hand.

CHAPTER FOUR

"Wasn't that the most lovely aurora last night?" chirped Zunhilix the chamberlain as he flitted about the apartment. "I'm sure it was a most auspicious sign for your investiture."

Fost and Moriana looked at each other.

"We didn't see it," the princess said.

"Oh, but I'm sure you had better things to do than watch the sky, didn't you?" He tittered, hiding his petal-shaped mouth behind a delicate white hand.

Fost felt exasperation and a tightening of the muscles in his belly. It had been some time since he and Moriana had lain together, and the strain he experienced now was as much emotional as physical. But paramount in his mind was the question of what had happened the night before. Aurora? His eyes darted to where one of the servants made up his bed. Nothing but a withered stalk of the miniature rose remained on the bedside table. Yet he had clutched that delicate, living flower in his very own hand the night before. A sense of being little more than a leaf caught in a millrace seized him.

"Most certainly my companions had something better to do than watch the sky," Erimenes piped up. "But unfortunately, all they did was sleep. I'm beginning to despair of those two, chamberlain."

As two plump stewards, painted even more gaudily than their master, laced Fost into a molded gilt breast-plate, the courier rolled eyes up in his head in mock horror at the genie's words. It seemed nothing kept Erimenes's libido at bay.

"Now, Erimenes," chided Ziore. "I thought I kept

you too busy to care what *they* did." The nun's spirit produced a throaty and quite unvirginal chuckle.

"Of course you did, my love. I simply find myself grieving that our young mortal friends are so profligate of the little time they have in life as to waste the nocturnal hours on a pastime as unrewarding as sleep. They actually went to bed to sleep! Great Ultimate, what a waste! It is solely concern for their well-being that motivates my interest in this matter, nothing more."

Ziore made a skeptical noise. She may have been besotted with the lecherous old ghost but she wasn't *that* besotted.

Ignoring this byplay, Zunhilix busied himself attending to Moriana's coiffure. It was her one concession to Medurimin mores. She would wear a sculpted breastplate and back, a kilt of gold-plated strips of hornbull leather and glittery gold greaves, just like Fost. Zunhilix had pleaded with her to wear one of the stunning selection of ceremonial women's ensembles he had at his disposal, from weblike concoctions of Golden Isle shimmereen that left breasts and pubes bare to a chaste, long-trained robe of green lacebird silk. Sternly she had shaken her head. She was not eager to be invested as a noble of the Empire, no more than Fost, but both had deemed it impolitic to refuse the great honor Teom had offered them. Not only did they need the help of the Empire in battling the Fallen Ones and the lizard folk's Demon ally, the situation in city and Palace was such that they needed his goodwill to continue living. The mobs demanding Moriana's head grew increasingly bold. But if Moriana had to add some insignificant Imperial title to that which was her birthright as lawful heir to the Sky City's Beryl Throne, she was going to do it as a warrior, not as one of the simpering damsels of the North.

To mollify Zunhilix, who had fallen to weeping and tugging at his pointed beard on learning how adamant Moriana was, the princess had agreed to allow the chamberlain and his staff to do as they liked with her hair. The warrior's investiture garb included a helmet of dubious value in real battle due to its impractical design. To their mutual relief the helmets needed only to be carried beneath one arm during the ceremony. This gave Zunhilix free rein with her hair.

Eyeing her sidelong now as the stewards laced up his cuirass at the sides, Fost had to admit the chamberlain and his elfin crew had performed admirably. Moriana's hair had been washed in aromatic herbs, then brushed by giggling stewards until it shone like spun gold. Then it was swirled atop her head and held in place with golden pins, then hung about with fine gold chains bedecked with glittering emeralds that set off her seagreen eyes.

In her gleaming breastplate, with long, slim legs carelessly sprawled beside the stool on which she sat, her finely-coiffed head held high with great hoops of gold wire dangling from either ear, the princess made a fantastic spectacle, splendid and exotic and enticing. Fost felt himself hardening futilely against the steel cup of his codpiece. He squirmed on his own seat, eliciting further laughter from his own attendants who immediately noticed his predicament.

A cool breeze gusted through their suite, tinted with subtle fragrances of the Imperial garden and tainted with tar and rotting fish from the harbor. The Imperial Palace, unlike the Temple of All Gods, was no product of barbarians obsessed with mass and size. Justly famous Imperial architects at the height of their craft had wrought their superb best in the design. Everywhere were cool white marble and clean lines. And meticulous care had been paid to the circulation of air so that even the northern wing of the Palace where guests resided remained comfortable throughout the sultry summer days.

Fost rose and examined himself in a full-length mirror.

"Not bad," he said, more to himself than to the others. He was a tall, powerfully built man, raven-haired, with startling pale gray eyes looking forth from a tanned and considerably battered face. The Medurimin ceremonial armor was silly, but the frivolity of the outfit somehow made the man within seem more rugged. Secretly, Fost was delighted. He had been uncomfortable being dressed by others. However, he had to concede that the half hour perched on the stool trying not to fidget or growl when a steward squeezed him under the pretext of sizing him had proven worthwhile.

"Magnificent," applauded Erimenes. "I have never before truly appreciated how well-matched a couple you are. Tall, lithe. Moriana as radiant as the sun, Fost dark and brooding. In that gear even your habitual expression of surliness is not unbecoming, friend Fost."

Fost winced.

"Oh, Erimenes," said Ziore. "I think they both look marvelous."

"Yes, yes." Zunhilix bobbed his head, basking in the reflected glory of his creations.

Cradling his sharp chin in one palm, Erimenes studied first Fost and then Moriana, and nodded judiciously.

"The design of those kilts is quite propitious," he said, "in that merely by elevating a few of those strips fore and aft the two of you can easily clear for action. The good ship Fost can ram Moriana in the stern, or perhaps seat himself on a chair and ready his pike to accept boarders!" He smirked with delight at his own risqué metaphors.

"Erimenes," Fost said sharply. Moriana turned away, color burning high on her cheeks. Ziore reached with an insubstantial pink hand and tweaked one of the philosopher's ears.

"Ouch!" he exclaimed. "How could you do that, woman?"

She leered.

"The same way I can do this," she replied, and reached for the front of his loincloth.

"You don't have to go," Moriana said quietly.

"Huh?" was Fost's confused reply. His mind churned, as he tried to figure out what she meant.

Her shoulders rose and fell in a sigh.

"You don't have to come with me. I'm the one who loosed the Fallen Ones on the world. I must deal with them or fail in the attempt. That's my destiny. This is no fight of yours."

Fost turned a foreboding thunderhead of a look upon Zunhilix. A query died in the chamberlain's throat and he hurriedly gathered up the skirts of his robe and his covey of underlings and fled. When the doors had shut behind them, Fost turned to Moriana.

"It's my fight, too," he said, low-voiced.

She shook her head, and her eyes were jewel-bright with unshed tears.

"I've lost too much already by letting those I care for follow me into peril."

His heart thrummed like a bowstring, and though he knew he should not, he blurted, "Is that why you've been so cold to me? Because you're afraid of drawing me into danger?"

She nodded and turned away.

"First I feared you would reject me because of my . . . my heritage. Then it came to me that I was a bane to all I've loved, or who have loved me. Darl died on my behalf, along with so many fine men and women. Brightlaugher the Nevrym boy, and poor old Sir Rinalvus, and before that Ayoka my faithful war bird, and Kralfi and Catannia whom Rann tortured to death to torment me . . . and you, whom I loved most of all!"

"And me," Fost said, nodding. "Alone of all those, I died by your hand, and for my death alone you bear responsibility. And yet here I am." He raised his brawny arms to shoulder height and made a deep, courtly bow. His eyes remained fixed on Moriana's slender frame. He saw a delicate shiver of dread pass through her and the silent word "why?" form on her lips.

He straightened and laughed softly at his own tangled, often confused motives. A question Erimenes asked beside a campfire in the days before Chanobit and the treacherous battle there—a question he had since asked himself a hundred times in a hundred different ways with no better answer than the one he had given the sage.

"I could be romantic and say that I would rather die at your side than live without your love. And—" With a surprised twitch at the corner of his mouth, he finished, "—and that would be true, oddly enough." He looked quickly away. Such words embarrassed him. "But let's be practical. If you fail, neither I nor any other human of the Realm will long survive you, save for ones like Fairspeaker and others who play traitor for the Dark. And even they wouldn't last for long, not if they depended on the sufferance of the Dark Ones. Let me put it this way. I'd rather be with you than away from you, and I'd be in no more danger at your side than anywhere else." He smiled, regaining some of his composure. "And perhaps I can even be of service to you, milady."

She stretched out a hand to him.

"Never call me that. To you I am Moriana—or, if you will, love." She smiled through tears running down her cheeks and spoiling Zunhilix's carefully applied makeup. "And you have done much to help me already."

He went to her, mouth pressing to hers, tongue questing. He felt her cool fingers moving urgently against his thigh. He drew his face back from hers.

"Much as I hate to gratify Erimenes by following his advice . . ."

Her mouth muffled his words.

With a brave shout and a clash of spears on bronze round shields, the Twenty-third Light Imperial Infantry marched in review past the wooden bleachers that had been erected in Piety Plaza. Squinting against the glare of the afternoon sun, Fost was able to conceal his reflexive grimace of distaste. They made a brave show with their brightly feathered round helms and their shield devices of a fist gripping a barbed spear, and their hobnailed boots rang in perfect unison on the broad blocks of blue-veined marble. But at the Battle of Black March they had bolted like frightened lizards, tails high and elbows pumping. They were typical Imperials: parade ground beauties.

The four-story structure vibrated in sympathy to the measured tread of the regiment. Instinctively, Fost clutched at the bench beneath him.

"I hope this damn thing doesn't collapse," he said sidelong to Moriana. She cocked a brow at him. "It's happened before," he said defensively.

She shrugged slightly and turned her attention back to the parade, but not before giving him a smile that caused a comfortable warmth to grow in his groin. When they had permitted Zunhilix and his attendants back into their apartments, the chamberlain's emaciated features had crawled with horror and his hands fluttered like agitated white birds when he saw the dishevelled condition his charges were in. He had only a half hour before the investiture ceremony to patch up the damage. Nonetheless, he had rapped out brisk orders to his underlings, and by the time the brightly-plumed officers of the Life Guards had arrived to escort them to the Plaza, they both looked as good as new. Zunhilix might have been effeminate and prone to twitter, Fost reflected, but he got things done. All things considered, he might do a better job commanding the Imperial armies than the officers now in charge.

Fost glanced to his left, where Teom and Temalla sat side by side, a particolored parasol shading the stinging sun from their pasty white skins. The Emperor and his sister-wife smiled and waved at the marching troops from the midst of a flock of courtiers and dignitaries, all as brightly hued as so many tropical birds, and chattering as loudly. Temalla noticed Fost and favored him with a lewd wink, at the same time dipping one pale shoulder slightly so that her milky gown exposed an ample, burgundy-tipped breast to his view. He swallowed and looked across the square, over the heads of the marching troops.

A detachment of the Watch tramped by beneath. These were special riot troops, as well-trained as the regulars and vastly more experienced, given the Medurimins' penchant for rioting. They sported burnished blue plate armor, short swords at their hips, small spiked target shields on left forearms and over each right shoulder lay a halberd with an eight-foot ironshod haft.

"Weren't these the men who killed your parents, dear Fost?" came Ziore's tentative, curious, soft words.

He glanced at the satchel resting on the bench by Moriana's hip. All had agreed, Erimenes with the worst possible humor, that it would be best for the genies to remain out of sight today. The city was feverish with talk of magic; to have a ghost hovering in the bleachers would do nothing to calm the dangerous passions of the anti-Moriana faction and might even incite to violence those favorably disposed toward her.

Fost shrugged.

"I don't really know," he said in a voice equally soft, but laden with emotion. "I was only eight when it happened. I never got a clear account of how they died. It was during festivities like this, only grander. Teom was being crowned. The mob caught the rumor that their dole would be reduced to pay for the celebration and rioted. But who killed my parents? The guard, the mob, what difference?"

Lacking telepathic skills, Fost was unable to read any unstated response on Ziore's part, and she made no attempt to broadcast it. He guessed the cloistered genie was shocked at his apparent callousness. But the death of his parents had been history for twenty years, and he had cried all the tears he had for them long since.

"One thing the death of my father and mother taught me," he replied to the still silent nun, "later, when I had the chance and maturity to think it over. The fact that a group is oppressed doesn't mean it's any better at core than its oppressors. If the rioters killed my parents, they did so no less heedlessly than the guardsmen would have done." He flicked sweat from his forehead where it threatened to bead and roll into his eyes. "This transition from guttersnipe to noble of the Empire makes little impression on me."

He looked around at the panoply of fabulous costumes, a profusion of gilt so extreme it transcended bad taste and achieved silliness. He thought of melting down any five hangers-on and getting enough gold to keep the entire Imperial Navy afloat for a whole year. He smiled mirthlessly. He knew how things were done in High Medurim. The state of their army showed that all too clearly. All things considered, the gold was probably better off where it was. At least, it wasn't going to finance further bloodthirsty follies on the Northern Continent.

Off to the south, slate-blue clouds hung over the foothills of Harmis. Flashes of yellow heat lightning played among them with a dull rumble. Fost thought he caught the scent of ozone mixed with the aromas of the day. Nearby vendors fried sausage and sold it wrapped in paper with hot mustard and sweet seaweed. The men and women around him were drenched in the rarest perfumes, some sweet, some tart, only a few exotic and elusive, wordless. Intermixed with these heady odors came the rank smell of war dog droppings, the heavy smell of farmed land south of the city, the pressing, intrusive odor of unwashed bodies. They kept Fost's memory turning ever backward to his childhood, for smell is the most reminiscent sense of all.

A heavy gonging rattle like giant coins shaken in a sack drew him back. Sensing a shift in the crowd noise, a note of subdued hostility like the warning hum of a beehive when an intruder nears, he looked down at the street. A strange, outlandish sight greeted his eyes. A full troop of Highgrass Broad dog riders rode by at a trot, colored streamers flying from the spires of their helms, their scale armor ringing to the tempo of their war dogs' gait.

"I've heard of these," Fost murmured to Moriana, seeing her puzzled frown at the presence of the High-grass mercenaries. "They just got back from serving out a contract in the Sword Kingdoms, battling the southern Northern Barbarians." The Sword Kingdoms lay above the equator, in the northern half of the Northern Continent. "Teom heard about them when their ship landed here in Medurim and hired them for the city's defense. Wise move, too."

Moriana looked skeptical.

"They do have an impressive collection of trophies," Erimenes said. Fost's companion had been unable to stay in his jug like Ziore, but in the babble of the crowd no one was likely to notice either words or a partially exposed blue head peering from the satchel.

The genie was correct. Every other dog rider held lance couched in a stirrup with one hand and a captured banner or insignia proudly aloft in the other. There were bicolored, slender pennons of rival Highgrass units, flags worked with the devices of a score of small cities and minor nobles, and the beaten-brass plaques the Northern Barbarians used in place of banners.

"There," gasped Moriana, pointing. "See that white, spiralled staff hung with human skulls? It's the tusk of a thunderfish. That was the sacred war totem of the Golden Barbarian horde we fought in the savannas west of Thailot six years ago." She shifted her hand, now pointing to other units. "Red and black streamers —that would be Captain Mayft's troop."

"The Gryphons," Fost added. "It's easy to see why they call themselves that." It was indeed. Like their riders, the big, thick-legged Grassland war dogs were all encased in scale armor. Each beast's head was covered with a steel mask worked in the shape of a beaked, sharp-eared face which gave the animals the appearance of wingless gryphons. Most of the riders had mask visors as well, but rode with them raised to reveal the typical broad, sun- and wind-tanned Grasslander features.

"They're a free company, aren't they?" asked Moriana, with a trace of distaste. At Fost's affirmative, she shook her head. "I don't see how one can hope for discipline from such as those."

There were dozens of bands of Grasslander mercenaries, from small squads up to regimental size. They were formed to a dizzying array of models. Some were based on clan affiliations, others on village of birth, still others on religious creed. Some were wholly communal, sharing rations and booty and bodies, as well, in great orgies. Others were stern and abstemious. Captain Mayft's Gryphons were one of the least interesting varieties, a purely volunteer company raised at its commander's own expense.

"Obviously one can," Fost replied dryly, "since here they are, still together six years after you first encountered them. And they've done pretty well for themselves. I doubt they paid klenors for those trophies."

"Bought with blood and life," cackled Erimenes from his satchel. "Obviously. Oh, what battles they must have fought!"

Moriana turned away. The dog riders clattered on past, lance heads winking in the sun, heavy unstrung bows riding in dogskin cases beneath the skirt of each saddle, to take their place in ordered ranks among the other troops assembled at the far end of the broad avenue. The native soldiers drew away from them; the foreign mercenaries were little loved by their ostensible comrades in arms.

Fost smiled grimly. With the exception of a few truly tempered units such as the Imperial Life Guards, the Grasslanders were unquestionably the finest troops on hand. For precisely that reason they were hated. He would not have ridden in Captain Mayft's saddle for anything, and not only because he was a poor dog rider.

Diplomacy had failed, so Fost had finally come out and flatly refused Teom's offer to become Grand Marshal of the Imperial Armies. Moriana would have made a better commander; she was trained to war and well seasoned in battle strategies both physical and magical.

In High Medurim, women fighting masters were accepted out of necessity, since many masters of the first quality hailed from locales in which women were not raised as docilely as they were within the Empire. For that small concession, the City States reckoned Medurim decadent. Certainly, they would accept no woman as general over them.

As for Fost, he had no desire to commit suicide. He had been resented enough when Teom had named him mere marshal, and that was a position without power or influence. The lords of Imperial arms would sooner have a foreign barbarian from the North or a hairy, uncouth wild man from the Isles of the Sun placed over them than a commoner bred in the gutters of their own city.

Finally, the parade was over. The great gates—gilded, of course—of the temple across the Plaza swung open. Out marched the bull-necked, heavily bearded Patriarch, Spiritual Protector of the Empire, clad in vestments of cloth of gold. On his head he wore the tiara, a three foot, gem-encrusted golden cylinder, surrounded by flying buttresses and less functional protrusions of silver. After him in bright array came the lesser prelates. Last of all came the Sexton, more profoundly bearded than the Patriarch, his whiskers as white as sea foam and stuffed into his girdle to keep him from stumbling over them.

He was a full one hundred thirty-eight years old, emaciated, and somewhat befuddled by all the hoopla around him this day. He had an uncanonical pushbroom propped over one skinny shoulder, not knowing what all these people were doing tracking up his pristine Plaza but sure that a broom would be needed before the ceremony was over. An alert acolyte relieved him of the implement after only a brief scuffle, and the ceremony resumed.

Ignoring the byplay, the Patriarch launched into his benediction in a voice remarkably shrill and thin for one so stoutly built. His voice reminded Fost of a mosquito's whining as he went through the liturgy. Fost was thankful for the annoying voice; it was all that kept him from falling asleep. A half-dozen spearmen had collapsed in ranks from heat and ennui before the Patriarch, with a final flourish of his golden staff, announced his blessings on High Medurim and the proceedings.

Temalla's sharp elbow nudged Teom awake. He blinked and shook his head, confused as to his surroundings, causing Fost to reflect that truly rank hath its privileges. The Emperor stood, cleared his throat, then fumbled for his notes stashed away in the front of his immaculate gold-trimmed robe.

"Thank you, Holy One." He clapped his hands. At once, a stream of nearly naked dancing boys and girls poured into the streets from beneath the bleachers, strewing flowers and marring the mood of chaste piety, though by the way the Patriarch's black eyes glittered beneath beetling black brows it was clear he didn't take the interruption amiss.

Teom paced down the tiers of bleachers with a servant trotting at his heels keeping the parasol between sun and Emperor. Though the Imperial party sat at the midpoint of the bleachers, Teom didn't have to fight his way through a horde of notables. A broad, clear swath ran down the center of the stands, with the nobles seated on either wing. He had made it down only one flight of steps when it became apparent to all that the Emperor had been taking counsel with a bottle, and the Imperial tread, while grand, was none too steady.

In the center of the wide wheel of the Plaza, a small kiosk had been assembled hurriedly after the troops passed in review. An avenue crossed the Plaza left to right, running between high, stately, marble edifices. The troops were drawn up in armed array to either side. The hewn granite walks flanking the street were thronged with thousands of Medurimins, jostling, shouting, haggling with vendors. Young boys and girls dressed in identical white robes circulated throughout the mob, their skirts hiked high to reveal plump, rouged buttocks. As Teom wove down through the bleachers, a cry rose from the crowd. The Emperor acknowledged it with a fond nod and a wave of his pale hand. But something in the sound caused Fost to tense.

"My word, this is tedious," grumbled Erimenes. "When do we get to the good part?"

Teom mounted the dais where he was being embraced and kissed on both cheeks by the bristly bearded Patriarch.

"This is as good as it gets, I'm afraid," Ziore answered peevishly.

"Perhaps there'll be a riot," Erimenes said hopefully. "Medurim is famous for the fine quality of its riots, I understand. Sometimes they rage for weeks, with considerable looting, burning and raping. Now *that* would be a sight to see, especially after this."

Fost shivered despite the heat that sent rivulets of sweat steaming down the back of his armored shell.

"Don't say that," he muttered.

Preliminaries over, Teom began to announce the names of those who should step forth to be recognized. Though this ceremony had been decreed expressly to honor those who had distinguished themselves in battle, Fost didn't know most of the names called out by the red-faced herald at the Emperor's side. Not even their faces were familiar. He did recognize Foedan, a tall, knobby man with high-domed forehead and deeply sunken brown eyes. And Ch'rri, the mutant cat woman, who at the call of her name shook out her broad wings with a thundercrack and glided down to stand before the dais, her long hair streaming behind. A rumble rose from the crowd. Whether in approval for her voluptuous nudity or out of superstitious dread of her strangeness, Fost couldn't tell.

Fost ran a finger around the inside of his linen collar beneath the cuirass. The armor sweltered fearsomely.

"I know more of those who aren't here," he said in an aside to Moriana, who nodded, busily mopping her own brow with a cloth from a bowl of scented water brought by a page.

Harek was absent, the small argumentative Assembly-man from Duth; he had fallen under the blades of the *Zr'gsz*. The immense bulk of Magister Banshau of the Wirix Institute of Magic was conspicuously absent, fortunate in the light of the bleachers' continuing threat to collapse. He still lay recovering from wounds received during the abortive coup. Nor was the Dwarven Jorean Ortil Onsulomulo on hand. The half-breed captain was on board his ship making preparations to sail with a cargo of Medurimin patricians who were less than optimistic about the outcome of the new War of Powers and thought this a propitious time to relocate to Jorea or the Sword Kingdoms.

Also missing was the gaunt old knight, Sir Tharvus, last of the three Brother Knights of the Black March. He had disappeared after the victory in his home country. Dark, dire rumors were whispered about his current doings.

The first to the platform were duly honored. Ch'rri accepted the rank of marquessa by seizing Teom's head with both hands and kissing him deeply, so that he flushed red from lack of air. Lascivious hoots rose from the crowd. This being High Medurim, such doings were not wholly alien even to the elaborate Imperial punctilio, so proceedings were not delayed, though it looked as if Teom wished they could be to pursue Ch'rri's further gratitude.

The herald cleared his throat. His eyes darted over the bleachers and signalled to Fost an instant before the call went out.

"Fost, called the Long-Treader, Marshal of High Medurim, arise and come forward," he intoned in a voice several sizes too large for him. Fost managed to grimace only slightly at the mangling of his name, got to his feet, crossed his arms and waited.

The herald blinked myopically. This was irregular, but Fost was not going to walk down in front of all those people alone. It had been arranged in advance that he and Moriana should go forward together. Obviously, arrangements had been mislaid.

The waiting game stretched on for long seconds. Fost began to regret the whole thing, particularly since he roasted inside his armor. At last, the herald blinked, cleared his throat again, and boomed, "The Princess Moriana, Pretender to the Throne of the City in the Sky, step forward and be recognized."

Moriana rose and the two went down hand-in-hand, she tight-lipped at being called second. They were halfway down when Fost became aware of the weight bumping at his right hip.

"Damn," he swore.

Moriana squeezed his hand.

"It's all right. I forgot to leave Ziore behind, too."

"Just as well we brought them, I suppose. Erimenes would probably heckle me from the stands."

"Very perceptive, friend Fost," the genie tittered.

"Quiet!"

They approached the kiosk and, after a slight hesitation, fell to one knee before it.

"Fost Long-Treader," the herald said again.

"Long*strider,* you dunce!" hissed Erimenes.

Paling at being corrected out of thin air, the herald cleared his throat again.

"Fost Longstrider, rise and approach the Presence."

His hand itching to clout the spirit's jug, Fost rose, stepped forward the requisite three paces and went to one knee again, thanking Zunhilix silently for providing padded greaves.

"For Honors Won and Services Rendered on the Field of Battle," the herald began, his words ringing with pomposity, "it pleases his Sublime and Imperial Majesty, Lord of All Creation, Conqueror of the Barbarians, Caster-down of the presumptuous Fallen Ones—" Erimenes snickered. Fost squeezed his eyes shut and prayed to be struck by lightning. "—to invest you Archduke and Knight of the Empire."

Fost started up but the herald droned on relentlessly.

"As such you are elevated to the highest ranks of Imperial patrician. Know that from this day forth you shall receive all perquisites appurtenant to your exalted rank: the right to stand between Sub-Archdukes and Grand Archdukes in the bedchamber of Their Imperial Majesties—"

"Is that good?" whispered Erimenes.

"It means I outrank the boy who empties the chamberpots."

"I thought the Palace had waterclosets?"

"The Guilds won't let them abolish the job. Now shut up!" Fost felt a million eyes on him. He was sure that the herald heard the byplay but the man plowed ahead with his recitation.

"—and of *droit de seigneur*—"

"*That's* promising," said Erimenes, this time not even bothering to whisper.

"Hush!"

"—and to administer the High Justice, and the Low Justice—"

"What's that?"

"It means," said Fost, exasperated, "I can hang thieves and collect taxes. Or maybe hang tax collectors. Same thing."

"—and to be immune to seizure of person and all real property without direct order of His Celestial Majesty, wherever the Writ Imperial shall run."

"Ought to be safe as long as you don't wander off the Palace grounds," Erimenes said. Fost shook the satchel. Erimenes's words were cut off by his sputtering attempts to avoid the buffeting.

The herald's words droned to an end. Fost felt the heavy jeweled scepter Teom held thump him on first the left shoulder, and then the right. The clanging seemed to fill the entire Plaza as his armor quivered under the onslaught.

"Arise, Sir Fost, O well-beloved subject and servant of the Sapphire Throne."

None too thrilled at having attained the exalted rank of servant, Fost pushed himself upright. His left knee emitted a splitting crack. He wobbled to be caught and kissed full on the mouth by the Emperor. Released, Fost staggered backwards to Moriana's side. The Emperor's aphrodisiac perfume made him unsteady and decidedly aroused, even though this was hardly the time or the place for such things. Backing up a half pace, he stumbled again. Moriana's strong arm circled his waist and held him upright until he cleared the cloying perfumed vapors from his head and regained his balance.

"Well done, Your Grace," Erimenes told him sarcastically.

"Moriana Etuul," the herald roared, pointedly ignoring the extra voice chirping in from time to time, "Princess and Pretender to the Beryl Throne, Mistress of the Clouds, beloved cousin of our Emperor Teom the Magnificent, arise and approach the Presence."

Moriana did as she was bid, but before she could step forward, a loud rumble like an avalanche in progress rolled from left to right across the Plaza.

"Thunder?" asked Fost.

"We should be so lucky," shot back Erimenes. "Look to your left."

His heart nearly jumped free of his chest.

"Death!" shouted the mob as it crashed like surf against a line of blue-plated Watchmen, who stood their ground with halberds levelled. *"Death to the foreign sorceress!"*

A sergeant rapped an order. The gleaming blue line of Watchmen took a step back and prepared for the crowd.

Across the cordon of armored Watchmen a figure arthritically mounted the steps of the Ministry of Sanitation. A tall figure, thin almost to the point of emaciation, clad in torn and faded tunic and trousers that had once been as red as freshly shed blood threw up his frail matchstick arms and emitted a wordless screech of pure hatred. The crowd surged, rallying to him.

"Seize the witch, the traitress!" shrieked Sir Tharvus of Black March, flinging out an accusing arm and pointing straight at Moriana. "Slay her, slay the betrayers of humankind who shelter her in their bosoms! They are traitors and deserve to die with her!"

Roaring like a rabid animal, the crowd surged forward.

CHAPTER FIVE

The halberds flailed, blades rising to flash white-hot in the sunlight, rising again to the company of screams to gleam the dull red of blood. The mob faltered. It momentarily lacked a leader, someone to urge them forward into the face of death. The faint-hearted in the crowd began to edge away from the soldiers. But the crowd didn't disperse. In the back rallied tight knots of angry citizens. Parties of stout men in dusty aprons finally pushed forward, hauling great chunks of pale-veined white stone. The others in the mob heartened and began to chant cadence as their newfound heroes cast the hundredweight blocks. Unwieldy in their cara-paces, a half-dozen Watchmen went down beneath the crushing chunks of marble.

It was enough. The crowd rushed forward again while Sir Tharvus's voice whipped it, crying out for blood. The remaining Watchmen fought, then vanished from sight as if they were sailors drowning in the vast Joreal Ocean. Teom stared, his eyes wide with terror at what befell his troops. Fost gripped the hilt of cere-monial sword and swore. Moriana had her own straight blade, but Fost's broadsword had been judged too un-orthodox for the investiture. That left him armed with a weapon hardly fit for swatting flies.

The soldiers assembled down the avenue held ranks, though whether by design or confusion of their officers there was no knowing. Across the hundred yards of cleared space in the Plaza raced the crowd, waving sticks and bats and other makeshift weapons. Above their shrill cries came the shriller chants of Sir Tharvus. Mad-ness had seized him and lent his frail frame power

70

beyond reckoning. And that power transmitted to the crowd and fed their pentup hostilities. There was carnage.

"You hoped things would get better," Fost told Erimenes, pulling the satchel flap back from over the jug inside. If he and Moriana were about to be murdered by the mob, Erimenes might as well get an unobstructed view.

"Stop!" The voice tolled like a great bell, drowning even the strident cries of Sir Tharvus.

Quiet descended over the crowd scattered across the marble flagstones of the Plaza. Down from the bleachers strode Foedan, tall and unafraid, holding his arms wide as if smoothing the jagged emotions of the crowd. The crowd faltered, lost impetus. He walked toward the bloodstained leaders. Fost and Moriana clearly heard the padding of his soft suede boots on the marble.

"Cease this display," he said. The mob stared at him, weapons hanging limp in a hundred hands. "This woman has saved you from destruction. You should fall on your knees with gratitude, not attack her like so many jackals."

"But . . . but she's a witch!" a voice faltered from the middle ranks of the crowd.

"She is a sorceress. Were she not, the Fallen Ones would have arrived in these streets by now, bringing with them flame and thirsty blades. You and all your families would be dead, the death meted out by the damned reptiles!"

"Don't listen to him!" Tharvus shrieked. "Slay her! She sold out humanity to regain her throne. Slay her!"

Still the mob remained poised on the knife edge of indecision.

"No," Foedan said, not loudly but distinctly.

"He'll never hold them," said Ziore. "Moriana, do something."

Fost's stomach twisted to a sudden premonition.

"No!" he shouted. But it was too late.

Moriana raised a hand, swept fingers in an intricate

gesture. A globe of pure white light appeared over Foedan's head, competing with the sun in intensity. A moan of fear and awe swept through the crowd. The knight gazed at the mob, not seeming to notice the luminous display above his head.

"See? He's sold out, too!" Tharvus cried. His eyes blazed with a mad light as bright as the mystic sphere hanging over Foedan. "Behold, the witch has set her mark upon him!"

The crowd gave throat to an animal cry of rage. They fell upon the lone, unarmed knight with club and cleaver and bare fists. He stood unmoving until the seething bodies hid him from view.

Teom yelped like a scalded cat and raced to the steps of the Temple crying, "Sanctuary! Give me sanctuary!"

The platoon of Life Guards that had attended him on the bleachers went clattering by the kiosk and up the wide steps after their master. They ran as much to protect him as to save their own hides. No amount of training prepared their officers to face sure suicide by standing and fighting off this mob.

"What ho!" Erimenes sang out. "A battle!"

"I'm glad the prospect pleases you." Fost drew his blade and held it in front of him without conviction.

One of the members of the masons guild who had helped strike down the Watchmen raced at Moriana, swinging a long pry-bar he had used to lever up chunks of the paving marble. She snapped out of her fog of horror at what her attempt at help had won Sir Foedan and backed with a ringing clang of steel on iron. She fought to retain her grip on the sword as the stonemason attacked again and again. A laborer swung a hammer at Fost, and he had no time to worry about Moriana.

Fost's blade crossed the haft of the hammer with an odd sound. The workman reeled back, mewling like a lost soul.

"Shrewdly struck," congratulated Erimenes.

Fost stared. The man's right hand hung from a rag of skin, yet Fost's parry hadn't come anywhere near it.

Then Fost saw that his sword had bent itself into an L shape around the hardwood shaft nearly severing his assailant's hand at the wrist.

"Come on!" he shouted to Moriana. She thrust into the twisted face of an attacker and spun, following him back to the bleachers with the mob hot after them. The flimsy wooden structure thundered and vibrated beneath frantic feet as the assembled notables fled the wrath of the populace. The mob was pouring into the Plaza from both directions now. As hazardous as the bleachers were, they offered the only ground on which to make a stand. As Fost and Moriana went booming up the stands, a hairy-armed man made a grab at Erimenes's wavering form.

"Unhand me, you rogue!" shrilled the genie.

"Oh, my darling, are you hurt?" cried Ziore. Fost moaned. The man snatched again and seized one of the straps flapping wildly on Fost's kilt. His sword useless, Fost swung Erimenes's satchel and caught the man squarely on the side of the head. The man fell backward and went cartwheeling down the tiers of benches. One of the benches at the bottom gave way under the added weight with a loud snapping noise. The man's back was obviously broken.

They made the top of the bleachers and turned, momentarily ahead of the pursuit. Here the angry crowd could only come at them with difficulty, and some of the most vocal members of the mob sheered off short of the steps, wary of the bleachers' penchant for falling. The would-be killers came in ones and twos. Moriana was able to send them reeling down again, gashed and bloody, while Fost propped his sword tip against the bench and tried to kick it straight again.

He slipped, slashing his right calf, cursed, looked accidentally over the edge. The hard marble of the Plaza was a good forty feet below. There was no escape that way.

"Where the hell are the soldiers?" he shouted, swinging his almost-straight sword against a long-haired man hacking at him with a billhook. The blade struck edge-on and didn't bend. Fost put a sandaled foot in the man's belly and sent him staggering into the sweat-streaming faces of a dozen fellows.

"Don't expect help from them," Moriana panted through a lull in the attacks. She pointed her chin up the street.

"It appears your elevation is resented more than any-one anticipated," Erimenes said dryly. "Or perhaps the Twenty-third is paying off some long-standing grudges against the City Watch."

The lightly armed but more numerous infantrymen had thrown themselves against the massively armored Watch, preventing them from coming to the aid of the Imperial party. In the other direction, Imperial troops fought each other, too. Fost shook his head and spat blood. A blow had caught him in the mouth, and he hadn't noticed it until now.

"Their commanders won't even stand trial for this," he said bitterly. "Look. Teom's out of it."

Moriana glanced across the sea of bobbing heads that flooded the Plaza. Teom and the innumerable clerics had disappeared. The great gilt valves of the Temple were shut and guarded by a line of Life Guards with raised shields and lowered spears. A fresh wave of attackers flowed against Fost and Moriana leaving no time for talk.

An apprentice stonemason dressed in a leather jerkin thrust at Fost with a shortsword taken from a dead Watchman. Fost disengaged and ran the man through. Screaming, the apprentice toppled off the verge of the bleachers, but not before the courier had wrenched the sword from his grasp.

Fost turned back and found a big man almost on top of him, swinging a makeshift club at his head. He caught the thick wrist in his free hand and aimed a disembowelling stroke at the giant belly squashed against his hips.

"Ellu!" he gasped into a face he knew well from the streets of his childhood. He faltered.

He recalled in a flash the foundling kitten they'd found and nursed together with scraps of food purloined to ease the complaining of their own bellies. No such memories stayed Ellu's now-fat hand.

"Traitor!" he snarled through spit and a cloud of reeking breath. He twisted his burly arm free of Fost's grip and cracked him across the face with his cudgel. Fost saw blackness and dancing sparks, fought to keep his balance with heels dangling over emptiness.

Ellu raised the club to finish him off. His arm stopped in midstroke, as if caught and held by an invisible hand. A look of consternation gripped the man's florid features. Then Moriana seized his shoulder, spun him from her lover and struck him down, crying her thanks to Ziore for staying the man's hand with her emotion-confusing powers.

Dizzy and nauseated, Fost dropped to his knees.

"It's lost," he croaked. "We can't stand them all off. The War of Powers is lost here and now." A blackness beyond physical oblivion clutched at him.

He felt Moriana's hand on his shoulder, looked up through red mists of agony. He heard barks, snarls, screams, saw the crowd streaming away to the right, eastward toward The Teeming in which he'd been born. No one had reckoned with Captain Mayft and the outland cavalry. Now they came with lances couched and war dogs snapping left and right and made reckoning of their own with the mob.

Slow and lazy the stained wooden deck rocked beneath Fost's bare feet. He smoothed wet hair from his face, drank in the salt air rich with the tar and cordage smells of the big ship and felt more relaxed than he had in days.

He stood near an opening in the rail. A rope ladder had been let down from the gap to hang just above the dancing green surface of the sea. As he watched, a slim hand reached out of the waves, catching the bottom rung. In a few seconds, Moriana was lithely scaling the side of the ship, shimmering with wetness.

Like him, she wore a minimum of clothing. To a simple loincloth like the one knotted around his waist she had added a brief halter bound about her chest.

"I must say the princess makes an impressive sea sprite," remarked Erimenes. His jug had been lashed to the railing so that he could watch Fost and Moriana swim without fear of being tossed into the sea by the sway of the ship.

"A good thing this is a Tolvirot craft with a mixed crew," said Fost. "If Moriana appeared dressed like that on deck of an Imperial vessel with an all male crew. . . ." He shook his head.

For all that, he found himself appreciating the suppleness of her body and her great beauty. He approved, heartily.

"Have fun with the sharks?" he asked as Moriana stepped on deck.

She nodded, doing a brief dance as her feet accustomed themselves to the heated deck. Fost glanced over the side to where lean, silver shapes knifed through the water. A wedge of fin broke water hard beside the ship. A blunt snout thrust above the surface and a dead-gray eye regarded the deck with inhuman detachment. Fost shivered, but Moriana called out to the creature and waved. It slipped soundlessly into green water and vanished, all thirty feet of it.

"You shouldn't have left the water when they arrived, Fost," chided Moriana, wringing out her long hair. "They're very friendly. It's fantastic to ride on one. They're so fast, they move so cleanly, with such strength —it's like being on the back of an eagle, almost." Her voice dropped and her eyes were troubled. He slipped an arm around her shoulder and hugged her reassuringly, savoring the feel and smell of her tanned flesh.

"Friendly?" He shook his head, grinning. "I could

swim down the throat of that monster without getting scraped on his teeth along the way. And I'm not even sure he would consider me as more than an appetizer served before the main course. I prefer not to take my chances with a beast like that."

"Perhaps we need such powerful friends." Her tone was not wholly joking.

"I wonder if it's true what Oracle said," asked Ziore, hovering at Erimenes's side with her fingers vaporously mingled in his. "That in the old days the world belonged to the *Zr'gsz* and the giant lizards and the great furred beasts, the hornbulls and mammoths, that humanity came here from somewhere else and brought certain animals with them, dogs and pigs and sharks and those darling little animals Teom showed us just before we left, the new ones imported from the Far Archipelago. What did he call them? Horses?"

Erimenes sneered.

"That's right," answered Fost, ignoring him. Teom had taken them into the menagerie he kept outside the north wall of the Palace, on the very bluff overlooking the harbor. The Emperor had chattered volubly as if a second attempt on his life and throne had not been crushed in a bloody street battle only two days before. The new acquisitions to his enormous zoo filled him with delight, for they were rare beasts with intriguing legends surrounding them. Indeed, Fost thought they were rather cute. Tiny elfin things, the largest male no more than eighteen inches high at the shoulder. They were built like hornless deer, but their small hooves were continuous, not cloven. They had long silky brush tails and similar manes of hair growing down their necks. Their dished faces held eyes liquid brown and large.

In their last interview with Oracle a little later, Fost had mentioned the beasts. Oracle's eyes lit up.

"I have heard of such," he said eagerly. "Do you know the most intriguing legend of all concerning them?" The four had shaken their heads, Erimenes with a crabbed look. He hated being lectured to by someone more knowledgeable.

"It is written in old, old documents that once these creatures called horses grew larger than the biggest war dog, as large as Nevrym unicorn stags, and that they were tamed as dogs are now, to be ridden in travel, the hunt, war."

"But they're so tiny," objected Ziore.

"The ones surviving today are. They were a special breed, nurtured by the scholar-priests of the Far Archipelago as objects of amusement and wonder. What happened to the others?" He shrugged imaginary white shoulders. "What happened to the cattle of olden days, short-coated like riding dogs, with horns set on either side of their heads? The only beast in the world today who wears his horns like that is Istu himself—oh! Your pardon, Princess," he said to Moriana, who had suddenly colored and dropped her eyes. The mention of the Demon had triggered a train of memories in her that were anything but pleasant.

"I suppose you think all this supports your ridiculous theory that humanity came to the world from another plane of existence," said Erimenes, elevating his nose to a contemptuous angle.

"I do, in fact. The legends aren't conclusive, but they point strongly to the possibility that we—or you, I suppose—originated elsewhere."

"It also points strongly to the certainty that our kind is given to flights of imagination," Fost pointed out, loath to rank himself with Erimenes in debate with Oracle. "The Archipelagan Reduction states as a matter of principle that the simplest theory to account for a phenomenon is the most likely to be true."

Erimenes turned his sneer on him.

"I'm ashamed to learn you've been taken in by the naive and simpleminded doctrine of Reductionism. We sages of Athalau had more wisdom than that."

"Did the Athalar sages ever disprove the Reductionist axiom?" Oracle asked with interest.

"Ah, no, not exactly. But there are contentions too patently absurd to require that wise men waste their precious time deigning to disprove them."

The discussion had gotten tangled in sticky strands of epistemology. Only Moriana remained aloof, lacking the others' interest in abstract knowledge for its own sake. The question of humanity's origin on this world or elsewhere was never solved, unsurprisingly.

Moriana took her place at the ship's rail by Fost's side, pressing her hip against his. He smiled lopsidedly. He didn't dare turn from the rail now, not without revealing the state of his scanty loincloth and displaying to the entire crew of the ship Endeavor the extent of his interest in the nearly naked woman. She sensed his discomfiture—or maybe read it from the surface of his mind. Since recovering Ziore's jug from the glacier-swallowed city of Athalau, Moriana's mental abilities had been increasing. She began to rub her hip slowly back and forth against his, teasing him until he felt as if he would explode.

"You shouldn't start something you don't mean to finish," he said.

"Why not finish it? You seem to have a good start. A very good one, from what I can see from this angle." She leaned forward and peered down meaningfully.

His mind tumbled and roiled like a storm-wracked ocean. For no reason, he remembered the conclusion of the final talk with Oracle. The others had gone ahead after offering their farewells. The projection of the "man" had requested Fost to stay behind.

"Will you win?" Oracle had asked.

"I'd hoped you could tell me," Fost answered.

"I have insufficient knowledge."

"I don't know," Fost said, sighing deeply. "Moriana is as powerful a sorceress as lives, perhaps the strongest in centuries. But is she Felarod?"

"Even Felarod needed Athalau and the aid of the World Spirit."

"Athalau lies buried in a living glacier, an intelligent

being named Guardian. He—it—was created by the first War of Powers and is entrusted with . . . guarding Athalau from intruders."

"Yet you penetrated it once before."

Fost ran fingers through his hair.

"We've had this out, Moriana and I. I think she knows we'll have to return to Athalau to seek the means to overthrow Istu—if it can be done again. But now she's concerned mainly with getting to the City of Bankers with this draft Teom has given us so she can raise troops and supplies to try to check the Hissers in the Quincunx." He shook his head. "I have to admit the menace of Istu and the Dark Ones is great enough that it's easy to forget the purely physical peril the Fallen Ones pose. If their armies defeat us in battle, the relative strengths of the Powers is moot. But I think Moriana fears—or maybe resists—the idea of confronting the Powers with which Felarod trafficked so long ago."

"But it must be done. I know enough to tell you that."

They sat in silence for a time, flesh and blood man and a figment of an alien mentality.

"If you win," Oracle finally said, "will you come back here? You are my friend. And you look upon me as a friend rather than a challenging project in scientific sorcery or a surrogate offspring of a man who fears both he and his era will be without issue."

"I'm touched," Fost said truthfully. "I'll come back." He mentally added, If I can, if I live, if there's anything to come back to.

"I can tell you one thing, friend Fost," Oracle said diffidently. "Though I don't know if I should."

"Go ahead."

"You have been troubled by the profound question of why you continue with the mad adventure. At first you thought it was because you were in love. Erimenes claimed you continued because you feared being alone. Now you have the added motive of wishing to do all possible to preserve humanity and throw back the ultimate orderliness offered by the Dark. There's truth in all these, I think. But I perceive a further, even more fundamental truth."

"What's that?" He tapped fingers tensely on one thigh.

"Why," said Oracle, a broad grin splitting his moon face, "you go along because you want to see what happens next. You have a great curiosity." The grin widened even more. "And that's as good a motive as any."

A seabird's cry passed Fost on its way downwind, breaking his reverie. He let his fingers trail down Moriana's back until he found the wet, warm curve of her rump. She jumped when he pinched her and jammed an elbow into his ribs. Laughing, they came into one another's arms for a long kiss. Breaking apart, they headed below to the portside cabin they shared. Though most of his thoughts were for happy lechery and enjoying Erimenes's pitiful, futile pleas to be brought along to watch, he still had time to tell himself Oracle was right.

His curiosity about what would happen next drove him onward.

Considering the difficulties they'd encountered on their way from North Keep, the twice-longer journey around the northeast shoulder of the Realm passed with almost ridiculous ease. A huge Imperial Navy ship had escorted them to the delta of the River Lo marking the easternmost extent of the Imperial dominion. Teom's parting gestures to them were of a truly Imperial magnitude, as well they should be. Not only did he owe his continued life and throne to them, specifically to Moriana, the king actually felt a certain kinship with her and her companions. Alone of all those surrounding him, these stalwarts were objects of Teom's real affection. Getting them out of the Empire safely was the most gracious thing he could do. Two serious attempts to overthrow him in a matter of weeks, interspersed with a desperate battle with the reptilian invaders, constituted an ominous record even by High Medurim standards. The intervention of mercenary Captain Mayft and her heavy dog riders on the day of the investiture had broken up the mob and foiled the plot hatched by the commanders of several Imperial Army regiments in concert with the mad Sir Tharvus to overthrow Teom and Temalla and murder Fost and Moriana. It had also caused such a violent reaction on the part of the populace that the mercenaries had to be released from their contract and sent trotting home with a huge bonus. Tharvus was still on the loose crying for Teom's downfall and Moriana's death, and it seemed that more Medurimin citizens heeded his call each day. So Teom was only too glad to see the last of his controversial guests and did all in his power to speed them on their way.

One last bit of ill-tidings had arrived before they could quit the Imperial city, however. The day before the Endeavor was to sail there was a great commotion at the gates of the Palace ground. After hurried consultation with Teom's surviving advisors, the gates were opened to admit a ragged, desperate, footsore band of refugees.

Grimpeace, King in Nevrym, and a scarred and battered retinue sought asylum.

"That damned Fairspeaker came back," Grimpeace told Fost after they had gripped forearms in greeting. "With fifty skyrafts laden with Hissers. They dropped down on Paramount just as dawn turned its upper branches gold. They drove us—drove me—out of the Palace like ferrets starting rabbits from their hole."

Fost and Moriana had nodded with grim understanding. Someone, Fairspeaker or the canny Zak'zar of the People, had a shrewd grasp of tactics. Had they attacked the Lord of Trees from the base, as many others had tried and failed at, they would have found themselves battling upward level by level against a foe who couldn't run but must fight and sell themselves as dearly as possible. Attempts had been made to force Paramount before; none had succeeded.

But with skyrafts dropping in from above, the startled defenders would be driven downward, level by level along a path to safety their foes had thoughtfully left open. A quick strike by the Hissers and their turncoat allies and the defenders found themselves in the foyer of their own keep, with the enemy holding the rest against them. A simple plan, and a deadly one.

Moreover, an assault borne on skyrafts avoided the problems of passage among the eldritch trees of Nevrym. Fairspeaker and his ilk were foresters and could never be seduced from the trail by the sleights of the trees. But as intruders had often found in the past, those who walked the ways of Nevrym unbidden met with a multitude of fates, none pleasant. The Hissers had flown above; the trees were impotent to stop them.

"What are you doing here?" Fost asked his friend in puzzlement. Nevrym had seceded from the Empire during the Barbarian Interregnum and had kept its king and sovereignty when the rightful native dynasty was restored. There was little love between High Medurim and the Tree. Lifestyles and modes of government were too different.

Grimpeace's brown eyes had slipped from Fost's, and the courier knew the answer before the man spoke it.

"I've come to make submission to the Emperor and beg his help," the exile said softly.

Fost's first impulse was to shout, "You can't!" but he schooled himself against it. Grimpeace bore a heavy burden of responsibility, weightier than Fost could readily imagine. Also, Fost himself had bent his knee to Teom just a few days past with no good result. He pointed that out to Grimpeace.

"Teom can barely cling to the Sapphire Throne with both hands and all his toes," he said. "If you must sell the free birthright of the forest, can't you at least get a better deal?"

Grimpeace shook his great head, bone-weary and bitter at all that had happened.

"Where else can I go?"

"Back to the forest. Fight a guerrilla war against the intruders. Make a treaty with the trees and unicorns. They can't desire Hisser masters."

Still the king shook his head.

"Too many of my people chose to go in with Fairspeaker. The Hissers control too much."

"They can't be everywhere," pointed out Moriana.

"No, Princess, not everywhere. Not yet. You have stymied them at the Marchant—for now. And the Watchers of Omizantrim have all but closed the skystone mines."

"See!" cried Fost, eagerness seizing him. "It *can* be done. You can do it, too! Go back and fight them on your own ground, where all the advantages are yours."

"The advantages are those of Fairspeaker and the other traitors," Grimpeace said bitterly. He sat heavily in a creaking chair. "Besides, the heart's not in me for such a war. I must face reality. Mayhap all I'll find here is my own death fighting to defend these stinking crowded streets from the Fallen Ones. But better that than to skulk like a thief through Nevrym-wood, *my* wood, while the monsters at Thendrun sit like kings within the Tree."

There'd been little more to say. Grimpeace parted from Fost with a few uncomfortable words, bowed courteously to Moriana, and was gone. The encounter had left Fost deep in black depression. It wasn't just the misfortune of his friend that possessed him or the triumph of the evil Fairspeaker. The tradition of almost fifty centuries, the tradition of Nevrymin freedom, lay in ruins at the clawed feet of the Vridzish. Kara-Est was a raw wound in the soil at the head of the Gulf of Veluz; Wirix had not been heard from, even via magical means, for weeks. The Empire was tearing itself apart from within, while the Hissers squatted in their fortifications across the Marchant and watched with chalcedony eyes, waiting until the stone thunderhead of the Sky City darkened the sky above the homeland of their enemies.

He had the awful sense that the People were victorious everywhere, that such pinpricks as the defeat in the Black March and the interruption of the Omizantrim mining operations were sad, silly, futile against the might and cleverness of the lizard folk and their patrons. Istu had scarcely shown his strength and yet the dominion of humanity fractured like rotten stone.

Fost was impotent with Moriana that night. Not even Erimenes found voice to complain. And Moriana hardly seemed to notice, her thoughts distant and her body tense. They clung to each other, unsleeping, unspeaking, needing the reassurance of closeness rather than the release of desire.

Oared galleys had warped Endeavor out of the harbor the next day, accompanied by her escort. No cheering crowds lined the waterfront to see them go. Teom's advisors had insisted on keeping the time and manner of the departure secret. Teom and Temalla took leave of them at the Palace with tears and presents and lingering kisses, but did not go with them to the dock. Only painted Zunhilix, his normal ebullience subdued, and a detachment of Guards had accompanied them to the docks.

They did not leave unnoticed, however. The tugs pulled Endeavor within a hundred yards of Onsulomulo's ship the Wyvern, already riding low in the scummy water with her hold swollen with the goods of refugee patricians. And there was Ortil Onsulomulo clad only in Jorean kilt and dawn light, golden on the rail of his vessel, dancing and playing a mournful hornpipe. He was a strange one, this half-breed, but he had in his way been a friend and they were sad to see the last of him. Somehow, though, Fost couldn't find it in him to worry about Onsulomulo. The half-breed claimed the gods and goddesses watched over him, and the evidence bore this out.

The wind came from the port quarter, fair for passage west to the turning of the land, fairer still for Tolviroth. They made good time to the place where the outflow of the Lo stained green seawater brown. Their escort made a slow turn, dipped flag in salute and began to pull back for High Medurim, a proud and lonely remnant of lost Imperial might and grandeur.

Despite Fost's apprehensions, there was not real trouble. A flotilla of galleys with drab sails set had come out of North Cape Harbor when the Endeavor passed in sight of Northernmost Peak to try to claim this rich prize for the Dwarves' revolutionary government and its new allies, the *Zr'gsz*. Big as she was, Endeavor was a smart sailer with a good Tolvirot hull, and she put them easily in her frothy wake.

Down came the sails, out went the oars, and the Dwarven ships began a waterstrider crawl in pursuit. Endeavor's master, a native Tolvirot only a few years Fost's senior, medium built with the broad shoulders and dancing tread of a fencing master, casually ordered an onager unwrapped from its oiled cloth coverings. The Endeavor had been laid for deepwater and open sea storms. She was much more strongly built than any oared war craft, and could carry heavy engines, true shipkillers, whose workings would damage the lighter hull of a war ship. Captain Arindin stood with one hand in the voluminous pocket of the embroidered green coat he was never without, calmly munching a fruit held in the other, while his crew unshipped the onager and set it bucking, hurling great rocks against the pursuing galleys. The fourth shot sent a hundred-weight stone smashing through the bottom of the leading vessel, breaking her back and foundering her in the rollers heaving in from the line of squalls hanging far to the north. Abruptly less avid for the chase, her companion ships crowded around to assist in rescue operations. One was so intent on breaking off the chase and aiding the damaged ship that the would-be rescuer rammed another just aft of the bow and holed her. The last sight the Endeavor had before twilight drew a dark curtain over the scene was a confusion of uncontrolled ships and angry heads bobbing in the swells.

"If the wind'd died we might have had hot work," was Captain Arindin's only comment.

An eeriness, a foreboding, attended the rest of the voyage, or so it seemed to Fost. Dark clouds hung like a line of distant cliffs in an unbroken wall across the northern horizon, sometimes sending down dark mutterings of thunder, flaring by night with maroon lightnings like no other Fost had seen. Sometimes it seemed that huge shapes stalked among the clouds, and sometimes there were splashings and tumults in the sea, too far for Endeavor's lanterns to reach even with their cunning lenses of Tolvirot manufacture. The loudness became all the more unsettling for that. Alarum was cried shortly after midnight and Fost and Moriana came tumbling onto deck, she in a cloak, he naked except for his woebegotten mail vest.

No attacker threatened.

A huge wheel of light, eight-spoked and hundreds of feet across, rose from the depths to make the surface bubble and glow a yellow-green a thousand yards ahead of the Endeavor. As the astonished passengers and crew watched, the monstrous colored wheel sank a score of feet, then, still clearly visible, moved toward them, spinning faster and faster as it came. It cleared the keel of Endeavor and passed beneath them without sound or heat, though the heavy ship rocked at its passage. It crawled along under the long wake of the ship and was soon gone from sight. Arindin ordered wine broken out and, fortified with drink, the vessel's folk went back to duty or bed.

Erimenes and Ziore chattered brightly about what the apparition might have been and where it might have come from. The Tolvirot mariners, hardheaded as they were, seemed disconcerted and exchanged muttered speculations of their own as they clambered into the rigging to dress the furled sails. Fost and Moriana said nothing about it between themselves. Privately Fost thought the wheel was a sign, a proof, that the reality he had grown up to accept was unraveling all around him.

The Powers intruded more and more into his daily life.

No further disturbance occurred until Endeavor rounded the coast, headed south for the Karhon Channel and Tolviroth. Fost was on deck drinking wine, enjoying the double moons, the stars, the velvet sky, the warm rich smells of the land breeze and the comfortable speculation as to what awaited him when he joined Moriana in their cabin in a few minutes. His reverie was broken by a footfall behind him. He turned to see Moriana, her face strained and pale. At first he thought the cunning light playing down on them from the twin moons caused the effect. Then he knew it was no illusion. Tears glowed brightly in the corners of her eyes.

"Come," she said urgently, gripping his sleeve.

"What's wrong?"

"Come on!" she hissed at him. He went.

A lantern shed mellow light in their cozy cabin. Fost looked around, saw nothing unusual, said so.

"On the bed," Moriana said tonelessly.

For the first time, he noticed the flower lying across the pillow they shared.

"A gift from the crew? Is that what's bothering you?" He laughed reassuringly and slipped his arm around her waist. "It seems more thoughtful to me than anything else. Besides, I thought your emblem was a rose."

"Look at the color."

He frowned, took his arm away and went to the bed, bending down to more closely examine the flower.

"Don't touch it," she said. He shrugged. To humor her, he didn't reach out for the flower.

He went cold all over. The flower was black. Not just the bloom itself, but the stem and long, long thorns, as well. He recoiled, fear clutching at his stomach.

"What . . . ?"

"It means the Dark Ones wish us to know they've not forgotten us," she said.

CHAPTER SIX

Wholly at ease and hoarding the sensation like a marooned man hoards crumbs of a rapidly dwindling food supply, Fost ate small, tart berries from an iced bowl and admired the scuff marks his boot heels made on the marble table in front of him. The bankers of Tolviroth Acerte had given the city its name. But the other residents of Tolviroth did not have to *like* the bankers, and his birthplace notwithstanding, Fost had come over the years to consider himself as much a Tolvirot as anything. So he ignored the scandalized looks from the reed-thin clerk behind the reception desk and propped his feet on the marble table while he relaxed in a soft chair and plied himself with iced fruit.

"Do you have to do that?" Moriana demanded, striding to and fro nervously. "We've come here to ask for money."

"We've come here to demand money, against the Emperor's note," Fost corrected. He popped another grayish berry into his mouth, sucked cool juice down his throat, chewed the skin and swallowed. "Besides, you're doing more damage to the place than I am. You're wearing a hole in the carpet."

The clerk, sexless in a long brown toga, gave Fost another venomous look and went back to scratching entries in a leather-bound ledger spread across the desktop.

"You mustn't worry, Moriana," said Ziore. "Certainly there will be no trouble with the bank honoring Teom's draft."

Fost looked thoughtful but said nothing.

"Remember the good fortune I had the last time I dealt with the bankers of Tolviroth?" Moriana said, her words edged in irony.

"But you didn't visit this particular institution on your last trip."

"That's why I chose it this time. I'm leery of dealing with people who turned me down once before."

A squarely built woman of medium height appeared in the painted stucco archway. Her eyes roved over the room, hardly stopping on any of the people there, as if she considered all beneath her notice. She turned, as if to leave, then hesitated. Her gaze stopped on Moriana. No hint of emotion tainted her calm face.

"Princess Moriana?" she inquired in a courteous but cool voice.

"Yes," said Moriana. "Freewoman Pergann?" Fost smiled in approval at her remembering Tolvirot protocol by choosing the proper form of address. The bankers were touchy about such matters. Protocol meant as much to them as did the proper pomp and ceremony to the chamberlains tending the patricians in High Medurim.

The woman showed even teeth and her manner chilled even more, if possible.

"*A* Freewoman Pergann. I'm one of the Daughters of Pergann." She swept the small group again with a gaze that revealed nothing. Fost vowed never to get into a game of cards with her. He had the feeling Pergann knew everything about him after a single glance while he could never begin to fathom her depths. "If you would be so kind as to step into my office."

Fost lifted his feet from the table, trying not to call attention to himself. The woman wore a severely cut ice-blue tunic with balloon trousers tucked into the tops of low, soft boots. This wasn't the garb he'd come to expect from bankers, nor was her attitude. She lacked the usual supercilious manner of other Tolvirot bankers and even approached glacial coldness toward them.

Since he had not been excluded from the invitation, he picked up Erimenes's jug and followed the woman and Moriana, who had scooped Ziore's jar into her arms.

Freewoman Pergann seemed no more nonplussed to have the odd assembly of mortals and ghosts facing her across her own desk than she had been to discover them in her anteroom. The desk itself was plain, dark anhak wood, of more modest dimensions than the androgyne secretary's in the waiting room. With his usual tact, Erimenes pointed this out before anyone else had a chance to speak.

"Ostentation," answered Pergann, with a thin smile, "is fine out front to impress the customers, or so Mother believes. The company is still hers. I work here and see no need for extravagant display." She pinned Fost with her cool eyes. He felt like a bug being placed in an exhibit, but without the passion normally the domain of avid collectors. "Usually folk are somewhat impressed by the lavishness of the waiting room's decor, if not its attention to dictates of taste. But then, most of our clientele falls between the extremes of those too wealthy and those too barbaric to possess taste."

Fost flushed at the implied insult and studied the wooden carvings on the wall that were the cubicle's sole decoration. They were Jorean, portraying the equinoctial devotions to the goddess Jirre. They were old, stained by time and Tolviroth's humid climate. Fost glanced down at Erimenes's jug, hoping the genie hadn't noticed the subject matter of those carvings. For a staid banking office, they were quite risqué. But the spirit gave no attention to mere bric-a-brac.

"About the Emperor's draft, Freewoman," urged Moriana.

The woman's mouth set into a thin line. At first glimpse, Fost took it for intransigence, but soon realized that the woman was reluctant to say what was on her mind.

"I can see no profit in being circumspect in this matter, Your Highness," she said finally, "though it gives me no great pleasure to tell you this. The cheque is worthless. There's no money in the Imperial account to cover it."

"None?" Moriana blinked rapidly. "But that's impossible!"

"With all due respect, Your Highness, it does not speak well of your knowledge of Imperial fiscal policy that you find the penury of Emperor Teom's account so startling. A nation that will cast clay slugs, fire them in a kiln, cover them with pewter wash and call that _coinage_ is capable of anything from a financial viewpoint, anything save responsibility." She spoke of the Imperial Treasury's latest seigniorage scheme in the same tone one might use to speak of someone who enjoyed eating dog excrement for breakfast.

Realizing she might have been harsher on Moriana than intended, she softened her tone and said, "Let me explain about money. Economics has few laws. One is that devalued money will soon replace more valuable coin. No one continues to use a one klenor piece of silver when the Imperial pewter klenor buys the same amount of goods." Pergann leaned back and said, smiling, "It does speak well of your own fiscal attitudes that you find the Empire's doings so hard to grasp."

"I . . . I still find it hard to believe there's no money in the Imperial accounts. You're sure? There's nothing?"

Pergann's eyes and face hardened slightly.

"I would not be a responsible banker if I made inaccurate reports to my clients," she said primly. "Your friend there with the big boots is smiling. You're from Medurim, sir? Or know about it?"

"I was born there," admitted Fost.

"I might have guessed."

He wasn't sure how to take that. He reached out and gripped Moriana's hand firmly in his.

"Don't be upset," he told her. "We're not penniless— at least you're not. You're Queen of the Sky City. That withered old goat Omsgib will have to open the Sky

City accounts to you." Realizing the unflattering description of one of Pergann's fellow bankers, he added, "Uh, sorry, Freewoman."

"No pardon needed," she said gravely. "I see that for all your roughness of manner and need to elevate your feet, you are an astute judge of character."

Moriana rose, saying, "We won't take up any more of your time, Freewoman. Thank you for seeing us."

"You're quite welcome. I hope we can have dealings in the future, dealings of a more mutually productive nature."

Fost stood, too, paused uncertainly, stuck out his hand to the banker. She shook it with strong, dry fingers. Then she came around the desk to hold open the door for him and Moriana.

"Great Ultimate!" Erimenes yelped as Fost passed through. "Have you seen what they're doing on that hanging?"

Ostentation at the House of Omsgib-Bir went more than skin deep. Tulmen Omsgib faced his motley visitors across several acres of desk, nodded judiciously, and popped a jellied sweet into his mouth. His thin beard, long face, high-bridged nose and big, sad eyes made him look like a goat, an effect accentuated by the unconscious nodding of his head up and down as he chewed.

"It is a pleasure to see you again so soon, Your Highness," he said in a voice so oily it might have been poured from a bottle.

"Let's not mince words, Omsgib," snapped Moriana. "You never expected to see me again when you sent me penniless from your door. You were so smugly sure my sister would win. And did you think she might reward you for failing to release the City's funds to me, the rightful ruler?" She laughed, a harsh, strident sound. "I'm sure Synalon would have rewarded you amply. But in a coin other than you expected."

His goat eyes took on a look of abject pain. Fost, who knew the banker by sight and reputation but had never seen him up close, halfway expected to see a goat's bar-shaped pupils peering forth.

"I'm sorry Your Highness fails to appreciate my discretion. Mine is a fiduciary trust; the welfare of my accounts is in my hands." He held up brown claws dabbed with cornstarch powder to hide the age spots covering them. "When you have acquired more of the mellowing and maturity that aging brings, you will understand that my caution was motivated by sincere concern for your best interests. I not only look after my client's account, I attempt wholeheartedly to take the welfare of that client into account, too." He smiled at his small play on words.

Moriana looked as if she were about to spit on the deeply woven purple carpet. Dolefully, the banker ate another sweet. Fost shifted on the uncomfortable velvet upholstered stool a servitor had brought, and wished it had been Omsgib's table he'd rested his boots on. However, no sooner had they entered the elaborately graven portals of the House of Omsgib-Bir than they were ushered in to see the master himself, after first being courteously but firmly relieved of their weapons. Evidently, news of Moriana's victory in the Sky City, no matter how shortlived, had reached Omsgib's ears. Or maybe the goatlike gleam that came into his eyes whenever they fell on the swell of her breasts accounted for the solicitousness with which he'd greeted her.

"I don't see any need for further discussion," Moriana said stonily, marking the direction of the banker's gaze. "I am the Queen of the City in the Sky. I want the funds held in the City's accounts released to me. And I want them *now*. Any excuse for not releasing them I suggest you save for a court of arbitration."

He looked aggrieved and tossed three more candies into his mouth, one after the other.

"I do wish you'd not take that attitude, Highness."

"So you are going to try to weasel out!" She half-rose. Fost expected to see smoke rising from the roots of her hair, as had happened with Synalon when she was murderously angry.

Omsgib flung up his hands, as if to protect himself.

"No, no!" he bleated. "I mean—well, that is. . . ."

"Yes," Moriana finished for him. She permitted Fost to take her arm and draw her back into her chair.

"I believe . . ." started Omsgib, then his voice cracked. He ran a thick, pale worm of a tongue over bloodless lips. He sipped hurriedly from a silver goblet of wine at his elbow and cleared his throat. Seeing that he was in no real physical danger, his composure settled over him once again like a thick, greasy blanket. A small smile curled the corners of his mouth and his eyes regained their luster.

"I believe, Your Highness," the banker started again, "that on your last visit I pointed out that, from my standpoint as administrator of the Sky City's accounts, actual possession of the City accounted for more than legal niceties. A cruel fact, but a fact nonetheless, and as a responsible banker I must deal solely in facts.

"And the fact is, you are an exile, and therefore not properly Queen of the City in the Sky, any more now than before."

Her eyes glowed wrathfully beneath scowling brows. Her fingers tensed into fists, then uncurled again. The princess forced herself to take several deep breaths before speaking.

"That's as it may be. But there's no denying I'm the sole surviving heir of the royal family of the Sky City. On that basis you cannot deny me access to the funds."

He placed his palms together like a mendicant goat. His expression told that he was beginning to enjoy this exchange of verbal sword thrusts and thought he had the winning blade.

"I could not deny you access to the funds," he agreed sanctimoniously, "were that the case."

"Were what the case?" demanded Moriana, her face darkening with an inrush of angry blood.

"That you were the sole surviving heir."

She lunged to her feet with such speed that her chair fell over and its back cracked on the floor. Her hands tightened into hard fists and she leaned forward onto the desk. Omsgib cowered back, even though she was a full desk's width distant.

"What nonsense is this?" she cried.

Fost had to admire the way the banker recovered to face the raging princess.

"What I mean," Omsgib said, satisfaction in his oily voice, "is that you are the second party in two days to come forward claiming to be sole and rightful heir to the City."

"Who's the damned impostor?" Had her arms been long enough, Fost thought she would have reached across the desk to choke an answer from the banker.

"No impostor at all, or so I believe. She's a quite striking young lady, who goes to no pains to conceal her considerable personal beauty." He looked meaningfully at Moriana's businesslike garb of tunic and trousers and boots. "She's tall, like yourself, and as inclined to be overbearing. Her hair is as black as the soul of Darkness, if I may wax poetic. Her name . . ." He drummed thin fingers on the desktop while he studied the ceiling with one eye, the other closed. Moriana quivered with need to hear the name.

"Ah! I have it now," said Omsgib, donning a crudely counterfeited expression of recollection. "Her name is Synalon Etuul."

Squinting in the bright sunlight cascading in through the translucent skylight, Fost peered into faces he had only expected to see again in a nightmare.

"You're looking well, Long-*strider*," said Prince Rann Etuul, giving the peculiar Sky City inflection to Fost's Nevrym-given surname. "You should thank whoever broke your nose like that. It gives you an impressively rakish air."

"It was one of your damned lizard friends."

"Indeed?" Rann replied, one slim eyebrow arching. "*I* had no 'lizard friends.' If by chance you refer to one of the *Zr'gsz,* I might remind you it was your comrade Moriana who enlisted the Fallen Ones as friends." He smiled, showing a hint of fine, white tooth. "If that's the case, I sympathize. I narrowly escaped death from one of the reptile folk myself."

Fost looked down at the tabletop, cursing himself for letting fear-spawned anger speak for him. Even in the most secure room of the most prestigious negotiation and intermediary firm in Tolviroth Acerte, with the company's armed guards standing by in case one of the parties attacked the other, Rann jockeyed for advantage. And letting emotion run away with him, Fost knew, gave Rann considerable advantage.

"We both made our pacts with the Dark Ones, sister dear," said Synalon from where she lazily sprawled at Rann's side. "And they both proved worthless. Let's leave the past and see what the future provides, shall we?"

For the first time since the Safesure Intermediary Company guards had escorted her into the room, color came to Moriana's face.

"I made no pact with the Dark Ones!" she flared.

"You bargained with Their chosen," the darkhaired woman pointed out. "Surely, you didn't think that the Fallen Ones would do anything contrary to the interests of their masters?" It was Moriana's turn to avert her eyes and berate herself for giving advantage to a foe. She had thought exactly that, and she did not need the studied irony in Synalon's voice to tell her how foolish that thought had been.

Fost took a drink from the cup of wine at his elbow. One of the attendants, swaddled in white scale armor, looked to his sergeant, who nodded, and then stepped forth to refill the cup. The cup was of thin beaten silver, not for purpose of decoration but because a heavier one might be used as a bludgeon. Even one of ceramic might be broken to provide a sharp-edged, makeshift knife. Silver was too soft to hold an edge, and the flimsy cup would simply collapse if used to strike someone. The wine itself was scientifically diluted and its serving carefully overseen to produce a calming effect. Safesure took its responsibilities seriously, which was why Captain Arindin had recommended them so highly for this ticklish reunion. It was fortunate that the rival royal parties had encountered each other in Tolviroth Acerte, where secure neutral meeting ground could be had for a suitable price. Armed guards remained in the room with them; Wirixer mages were stationed outside, in case magic was called for. Fost tried to imagine dealing with Synalon and Rann in the common room of some country inn and found it too unsettling to ponder long.

Even in spite of the precautions, the safety of all concerned was beyond the company's ability to guarantee. Even though the Wirixer mages had been assembled, Fost knew all too well that if the sisters began tossing occult lethality about there was no way anyone in the world could stop it.

The silence in the room grew dry and scratchy with age. Fost cleared his throat.

"Excuse me for asking such a silly question," he said, quailing inwardly at the quick blue light of anger blazing in Synalon's eyes, "but why aren't you dead?"

She laughed. Her breasts shook vigorously to the full-throated merriment, threatening to break free of the inadequate restraint of her lacebird silk bodice.

"Ah, you poor, trusting fools. Moriana, you actually thought I'd step to my death in a fit of pique over a little setback?"

"As far as I could tell, you did," said Moriana with an evenness of tone that amazed Fost.

"Yes, beloved sibling, I did. And before even I stepped from the window, I sent a mental call out for my dear eagle Nightwind. I hardly had the chance to enjoy the feel of falling free when he was between my legs and carrying me safely away."

"And you, Rann?" piped up Erimenes, fidgeting at being excluded from the conversation. His and Ziore's jugs had posed a problem for the guards. Since there was nothing visible in either jar, and since the two most potent sorceresses were to be in the same room together anyway, it was decided a couple of genies made little difference. "How do you come to be sitting here, looking so hale and hardy? I thought Khirshagk's spear brought you down."

"It brought my eagle down, may he who cast that damned spear writhe in hellfire!"

Erimenes paled before the force of the prince's passion. The fury passed from Rann's tawny eyes and he relaxed.

"But Terror was the greatest of a great breed. The war eagles of the City are trained to preserve their rider's life at all costs. And though his every wingbeat added to his agony, Terror controlled our descent until he could set me safely on a hilltop. Then he died."

"My dear Rann, I do believe I detect sentiment in your voice." Some of Erimenes's cockiness had returned.

"No one cares what you believe, demon!" snapped Rann. His scars glowed like white-hot wires.

"If there's hellfire, Khirshagk's writhing in it," Fost cut in quickly. "He used that peculiar black smoking gem the Hissers took from the fumarole on Mt. Omizantrim and freed Istu with it. However the breaking of bonds Felarod created worked, it killed Khirshagk in the process."

"Lucky all in the City weren't killed," murmured Synalon. "I've tested the magic that bound Istu, and know its potency." She tapped her daintily pointed chin. "No, come to think of it, from my viewpoint it wasn't lucky at all, for if all within the City had been slain, I might have returned at once."

Moriana wasn't listening.

"There's hellfire," she said softly, staring unfocused at the center of the table. Silence crowded in again. Everyone knew why Synalon had tested the bonds pinioning Istu in the City's foundations, and it wasn't with a view toward strengthening them. Likewise, no one had to question how Moriana knew the reality of hellfire. She had seen it glowing through the slits that were the eyes of the Vicar of Istu, and it had touched her, left its mark on her.

"Perhaps if you'll explain how you came to be here," suggested Rann. Moriana scowled, not wishing to follow any path the prince pointed out. Hurriedly, Fost began talking, telling what had happened in the City after Synalon's apparent suicide. Soon, Moriana joined in the telling, and the two spirits as well.

As she listened, Synalon's fingers idly stroked at her exposed breastbone. When the tale came to the night of the Golden Dome, they slipped into the top of her gown, at which Rann cleared his throat and looked away. Fost imagined that the Safesure attendants were grateful just then that their helmets hid their expressions. They would certainly earn their fees this day.

When the bloody aftermath of Teom's orgy was told, Rann's eyes glowed and he massaged one fist, cracking the knuckles and nodding appreciation of Fost and Moriana's exploits. Then came the story of the Battle of the Black March, and he pounded his fist excitedly into his palm. He obviously wished he could have been there, commanding, fighting, taking in the ebb and flow of the battle. It was for such things the man lived—and it was in such things that Rann was a true genius.

Fost wondered whether Moriana, who had the narrative at this point, would tell of Zak'zar's apparition that had soured the victory celebration following the battle. She looked to him and stopped short.

"We had a visit from the Speaker of the People that night," he said, hearing her breath catch. "He showed us the fate that had befallen Kara-Est that day. How did you come to escape it?"

The rest was Moriana's to keep or give.

Synalon's fingers curled into fists.

"We would have fought the Hissers at Kara-Est," she growled, "but for the treachery of this worm beside me."

All stared at this, even the faceless attendants lining the whitewashed walls, for Rann's devotion to his princess was as legendary as his prowess in war and torture. The hair on Synalon's head began to untwine itself from its elaborate coiffure, and blue sparks crackled through it. Looking stricken, the guard sergeant started to draw his sword, knowing that it might be the last thing he ever did. But Moriana raised a slim hand.

"Stay," she said to the guard. "She does that when she's angry. It means nothing."

Synalon was known throughout the Realm for her behavior when angry. The sergeant did not look encouraged, but if Synalon uncorked anything horrible Moriana would catch the brunt of it, and it was Moriana who bid him not be concerned. He only hoped she wasn't going to commit suicide on *his* shift.

Rann had dropped his head until his sharp chin rested on the embroidered yoke of his dark brown tunic.

"I did what I thought best served the interests of my queen," he said quietly.

While Synalon sat looking disdainful and dripping the occasional fat blue spark to sizzle and die and leave small charred circles on the floor, Rann told how he had determined that resistance to the might of Istu was futile.

"I read the old accounts of the War of Powers," he said.

"The First War of Powers," Fost corrected dully.

Rann studied him for a moment.

"I suppose you're right in making the distinction. At any rate, I had some idea of the nature of the Black Lens, the form in which our scouts reported that Istu manifested himself. In that aspect the Demon can draw matter and energy irresistibly into himself, and only the mightiest of magics can forestall him."

"I would have fought!" shrieked Synalon. A blue nimbus flamed about her head.

"You would have died," answered Rann. Synalon whirled on him, raising her hand. Fost knew the gesture. Time slowed to a crawl before his eyes. The guardsmen sensed the intent but hesitated, not having expected the princess to turn on her own ally. Moriana made no motion, so it was up to Fost to act. He snatched up the goblet by his elbow and flung the contents onto the enraged princess.

A loud hiss and a cloud of steam filled the chamber. From outside came a dull thump. The Wirixer mages had detected the magics being mustered in the room; one had fainted upon realizing how potent they were. Synalon turned to Fost with eyes like lances of blue fire. For the courier, time seemed to flow like molasses. No matter how fast he reacted, it would be far too slow to stay his death. He remembered the searing caress of a salamander and wondered if a lightning bolt would feel the same.

Synalon tipped back her head and laughed.

"You're a brave fool, courier. You must still hear Hell Call ringing in your ears. Death was that close."

"I live," he said doggedly.

The laughter died.

"So you do. As does the renegade Rann. Perhaps you're not so much a fool, after all." .

"I could have told Your Highness as much," Rann said dryly.

"There's more to you than is immediately apparent, Longstrider, though it's not displeasing, either. It may please me one day to take you from my sister; I doubt she fully appreciates you." Before either party named could respond, the sorceress turned to Ziore. "And you, nun, I warn you. Don't try your emotion play on me a second time, unless you want to learn what true death is."

Again a long silence fell as all sat back and composed themselves, for the next round in this battle of wills.

"What precisely happened in Kara-Est, if it's not too much trouble to tell us?" demanded Erimenes, in a pet because the promised mayhem had failed to materialize.

The sergeant of the guard had dispatched one of the attendants to fetch a bowl of water and a towel to clean the wine from Synalon and the table. He entered without noticeable enthusiasm and began mopping up the sticky red mess. Synalon undulated beneath the caress of the cloth, making the man so nervous he dropped it three times. The last time one end fell down between Synalon's breasts. His hand shot reflexively in pursuit. Synalon raised an eyebrow at him, smiled. He threw up his hands, uttered a thin scream and fled the room.

"Now that the comic relief is over, we can get down to business," said Rann, rapping his knuckles on the table. "To answer your question, demon, I made preparations to evacuate Kara-Est, without advising Synalon. Then, the night before the City was to arrive overhead, I went to her to tell her the only logical thing we could do was get out." His eyes avoided his sovereign's.

"And she refused," said Moriana.

"Just so. As I had anticipated."

"So what happened?" Fost asked.

"I struck her with a Thailint drug dart. The chemical acts almost instantaneously. Not altogether so, unfortunately." He raised his right arm and drew up the tunic sleeve. The underside of his wiry arm showed angry red, as if recently scalded. "I'll bear the marks of her anger a long time."

"You deserved worse," Synalon said, but without heat.

"I did what I thought best," Rann repeated. "We had no hope of winning. And as far as I knew, Synalon was the strongest magician alive, and the only one with a faint hope of ever commanding the power to defeat Istu. But then and there, she had no hope at all."

"So what do you intend now?" asked Ziore.

"Isn't that obvious? We join forces against Istu and the Vridzish."

Moriana and Synalon jumped to their feet screaming denial; the Safesure attendants stood by the walls fairly quaking in their armor. They were well-tempered men and women, normally fearless, but this was like dancing with an unconstrained fire elemental. In the commotion, Fost's gaze met Rann's and perfect understanding flowed between them. The sensation made Fost's skin crawl, but he knew that he and the prince alike knew what must be done. Sharing a thought with the likes of Rann was not something Fost found comfortable.

For all their mutual hate, for all the many ways they were opposites, both royal sisters possessed intellects on the same order as their egos—enormous. And between them they knew almost all of the magic learned by humanity over the ages. Slowly, reluctantly, they calmed and resumed their places.

"He's right," Moriana said grudgingly. "Alone, neither of us has a chance against the Demon. Together . . ."

"Together, you've scarcely more of a chance," said Rann.

"Have you learned so much magic," Synalon said, looking at him narrowly, "that you can predict the future?"

"No. But I know history. Felarod and his Hundred— a hundred Athalar savants of the heyday of that city's skill in magic—couldn't contain the Demon of the Dark Ones. They had to invoke the World Spirit, and in that act almost died." He looked from one cousin to the other. "Recall that not even Felarod long survived his triumph."

"I don't fear dying to defeat the Demon!" shouted Moriana. She of all those assembled had the deepest hatred of the spawn of the Void.

Rann faced her coolly.

"What about dying uselessly? I don't know magic as

you do, but this I know. Even if you and Synalon act in perfect harmony, you have no more chance of overcoming Istu than I have of hiking to the Pink Moon."

"It sounds as if you're refuting your own argument," Fost said, arguing against himself as much as Rann. "If our joining forces won't bring Istu's fall, why should we take the risk? Either of us?"

"I'll tell you something, Longstrider," said Rann. "When we were antagonists I found myself wishing that we could work together, you and I. You continue to show yourself perceptive, and to prove the soundness of my judgment of you as a shrewd man, roughedged and not well schooled in subtlety, but able. I hope we can yet work together, Northblood."

Fost moistened his lips from his cup to hide what he assumed correctly to be an expression of unwonted pleasure. The prince was flattering him. And he seemed to mean it.

"But to your question. I still feel that the means of bringing down Istu can be found. Just because a weapon doesn't lie conveniently at hand doesn't mean it doesn't exist."

"Istu was overcome before." Instantly, Fost cursed himself for speaking. He was actually trying to elicit the prince's approval and had wound up mouthing the obvious.

Rann seemed not to notice.

"Just so. We can find the means." He smiled cheerlessly. "But there's the problem of staying alive until we do."

Moriana leaned forward across the table. She held her anger back with obvious effort, yet what her cousin said had merit.

"You've thought on the situation," she said with only the faintest hint of begrudging it to Rann. "Outline it for us, if you will."

Fost nodded to himself. Subconsciously at least, Moriana had accepted the necessity of joining with those who had been her deadliest foes. Now she spoke to Rann much as she must have when the two of them fought the Golden Barbarians together, years before.

"First," Rann started, "the strengths and weaknesses of our enemies. They have Istu, of course. But even the Demon of the Dark Ones has his limitations. According to the lore—and it's unanimous on this subject—Istu is in some way linked to the City itself. He's a creature of the Void, of the nothingness between suns. This world's as much a hostile environment to him as the bottom of the sea would be to us. The historical evidence indicates that he is most powerful when he is physically present in the City. Apparently, that was one reason Felarod bound him there; so strong are the forces binding him and the Sky City together that they might have drawn him forth from another prison, no matter what spells Felarod devised to hold him.

"The City itself provides severe limitations, at least to his movement. It is no longer constrained to follow the Quincunx. However, neither in the past nor in the days since Istu was freed has it ever been observed to go faster than the mile-an-hour pace it has maintained throughout the centuries. It *may* be able to go faster. It's safe to assume that speeding it up would tax even Istu's powers."

He steepled his fingers in front of his lips. Even Synalon listened now, with only a trace of contempt lingering on her face.

"Now, as to the People. Their population is limited, and even given that they put whole generations into hibernation to await this moment, they still must number vastly fewer than us. They do not work well at night. As Fost's friend Oracle discovered in old writings, the caste differences among the Hissers are more than social; it takes more gestation time and special nourishment for a mother to produce a noble *Zr'gsz*. Thus the lower caste ones are more numerous and are physically and mentally inferior to the higher orders. You can thank that fact for your present survival, Longstrider. The common Hissers at the March just didn't know how to deal with your one-man charge."

"I know," Fost said glumly.

"Thanks to the Watchers, the skystone mines are in disorder, and the Hissers' military might depends on their air power as heavily as did ours. Also, the Hissers have a severe disadvantage in terms of experience. Even among the Children of Expectation there can be few seasoned officers. They simply haven't fought any wars since Riomar shai-Gallri cast them from the Sky City, and really none since the War of Powers. So, though some of them like this Zak'zar may be shrewd, we still have a considerable edge in skill."

"You make it sound as if they were at the point of being whipped all the way back to Thendrun," Erimenes complained.

"Not at all, demon. Our forces, such as they are, are scattered throughout the lower half of the Realm. We have concentrations in Brev and Bilsinx, but let the Sky City appear over them and they fall just as Kara-Est did. Wirix is perhaps fallen; none has heard from them, either by messenger or magical communication, in over two weeks. We must assume the worst in this instance. The Dwarves of North Keep and the Nevrym foresters have made an open alliance with the *Zr'gsz;* and the Empire has rotted like a melon, from the inside out. Only at its peak long ago would the Imperial Army have counted for more than a moment's annoyance to the Hissers. It's victory at the Black March was almost totally illusory. No, friend Erimenes, even if the Fallen Ones lacked the aid of Istu we would still be like the drunk who fell in the cesspit. We'd be forced to stand on tiptoe to keep our noses out of the shit."

A nervous look passed among the listeners. Rann seldom used such earthy expression.

"What good does all this talk of military matters do?" demanded Synalon. "They have Istu; we have myself. And my sister, of course. What more needs to be discussed?"

"We are faced with two problems, cousin. The magical one posed by Istu, and whatever wizards the Hissers have. And the military threat of the Vridzish armies. We ignore either at our peril. I grant, if we undo Istu we win. But to do that we'll have to buy time. For that we'll need armies to keep their soldiers off our necks."

"Very well," said Moriana. "But our efforts need direction. Where do we seek the means of defeating Istu?"

"Athalau," Fost said, and was immediately sorry. Both sisters turned to stare at him. "That's our one and only lead. It was Athalar magic that broke Istu before. My knowledge of these things is limited, but nothing I've seen so much as hints at an answer elsewhere."

The others all began speaking at once, arguing, expostulating, objecting.

"Enough!" shouted Synalon after a few minutes. "The groundling's right. It turns my stomach to walk a path trod by Felarod, but the Dark Ones have proven no true friends. If nothing else we know where the means of defeating Istu once lay. Isn't that the best place to search now?"

Erimenes muttered something about Reductionism.

"Aren't you forgetting something?" Rann asked. All looked at him. "Felarod didn't defeat Istu alone. He needed a hundred Athalar savants. They weren't just trained but were specially bred to their talents. Where can we find their like today?"

And Fost put back his head and laughed the roaring wild laughter of the mad. Where, indeed?

CHAPTER SEVEN

Everyone looked at Fost. He teetered on the brink of hysteria, caught himself and drew back from it.

"I'm all right," he said. "I'm not crazy—not yet, anyway."

"Will you share this rare jest with us?" Synalon asked disdainfully.

"I know where the survivors of Felarod's Hundred went, and where to find their descendants. Yes, you do, too, you treacherous blue wisp, so don't try to look innocent."

Moriana looked from Fost to Erimenes, who was twiddling his thumbs and gazing at the skylight overhead.

"I know, too," she said quietly. "The Ethereals."

Erimenes made a face.

"You mean the folk who live by the Great Crater Lake north of the Ramparts?" asked Ziore.

"What's everyone talking about?" Synalon asked pettishly. "I'm sure I have no idea."

"Yes, you do, cousin dear," Rann said. "I paid a visit to the Ethereals while pursuing your sister and Longstrider after they escaped from the Sky City. A group of ascetics who live in the mists surrounding the lake. Totally divorced from reality." He spoke in a bantering tone, but with a small hint of respect.

"Do you think I pay attention to such trivial details?"

"Had you paid more mind to them, you might not be sitting here."

Synalon's lip curled in a snarl. The tang of ozone filled the room.

"But what do the Ethereals have to do with Felarod's

Hundred?" asked Ziore, easing some of the mounting tension with her question.

"The quality of education," Erimenes said, shaking his head sadly, "must have declined in the years following my death." He tugged thoughtfully at his chin. "But then, it's only to be expected. After me, Athalau's intellectual progress could only take a downward turn."

"It all happened ten thousand years ago, Erimenes," Fost pointed out. "It wasn't considered a necessary part of the curriculum where Ziore spent her life. Your teachings never addressed the War of Powers, as I recall." Erimenes turned his attention back to the skylight. The fact that Ziore had spent her physical life in a convent devoted to the abstemious tenets laid down by Erimenes the Ethical before his own death still produced friction between the genies.

"In answer to your question, Ziore," continued Fost, "I assume you do know the broad outlines of the legend, how Felarod needed the help of a hundred specially trained savants to summon the World Spirit and defeat Istu and the Hissers. You've probably also heard that ninety of the Hundred died from contact with such sheer power. And that the ten survivors were so horrified at the cosmic destruction they had helped wreak that they left Athalau, vowing to keep themselves isolated from humankind and magic."

"Yes," Ziore answered, frowning. "I heard versions of the story as a child, even in the convent."

"But did you hear where the survivors of the Hundred went after Felarod's victory?"

"No."

All eyes were on Fost now.

"They went to the Great Crater Lake," he said, "where their descendants now style themselves the Ethereals."

"Those cattle?" Synalon blurted, evidently remembering more of Rann's report than she'd admitted.

"Yes," Erimenes said, in leaden tones. "It's all true."

"And there's more to the tale," Fost said, grinning,

"to account for Erimenes's mournful expression. For years of their self-imposed exile, the Ethereals were without any kind of philosophical base. Schools of thought came and went, but each seemed tainted by the magic they had come to fear and despise.

"Then fourteen centuries ago, an itinerant sage of Athalau stumbled across their village. He brought with him tidings of a new philosophy sweeping through Athalau like a rising spring wind. It preached total denial of the physical world. Pleasures of the flesh, monetary concerns—and yes, magic. All these matters were shunned. It was a doctrine tailor-made for the Ethereals."

He gestured grandly.

"And the tailor who made it was none other than Erimenes, called in those days the Ethical."

"Hold me up to derision, if you will," Erimenes said, scowling. "Have you never made a mistake?"

"But do you think they'll help us, Fost?" asked Moriana.

"We can only ask."

"I'd best not be among those who negotiate with them," Rann observed wryly. He had tortured the villagers while seeking information and wouldn't be forgotten soon.

"But they've no concern with what goes on in the world," persisted Moriana.

"They'll see Istu's release as making it their concern," said Fost.

"It's been so long since damned Felarod's triumph," said Synalon. "What if they've lost what powers they had?"

"Don't damn Felarod too lightly, Highness," said Rann," since we find ourselves on his side now. I see no other course than to try the Ethereals and Athalau."

Synalon curtly ordered more wine, and the six of them, four mortal, two spectral, began laying plans.

The sun was low and its light the color of wine when the discussion was done. Rann nodded in satisfaction at the campaign they had outlined. Seeing this, the others sat back in their seats and relaxed a trifle. If Rann approved their planning, it meant that it was the best that could be done under the circumstances.

Whether the best was enough remained to be seen.

"Where are you staying, cousin?" Rann spoke, his eyes half-lidded.

"The Twisthorn Inn," Fost answered for Moriana, seeing her tense. He met her stare with steady eyes. "We have to trust them. I know the odds are that they'll betray us, but we'll have to chance that."

"I've had a bellyful of betrayal," Moriana said tautly.

"Perhaps if they gave their word?" suggested Ziore.

Erimenes emitted a strangled squawk. Ziore was his beloved, but it took all his self-control to swallow the scorn he had for her naivete.

"Would it be believed?" asked Rann.

"The word of the Queen of the City in the Sky is not to be doubted," said Synalon loftily.

"By what right now do you name yourself queen?" Moriana demanded, half rising and placing her hand on her empty scabbard.

Fost gripped her arm.

"She held the title longer than you did," he pointed out, "and you're both fugitives now.. When the Vridzish butcher you for their victory banquet, will you squabble over who'll be swallowed first?"

Fost felt the electric tension mounting. These were extraordinarily powerful sorceresses. The alliance, still fragile, threatened to come apart over this. He cleared his throat and raised his voice.

"By the Great Ultimate, I swear to take no action against anyone gathered here, save to defend myself or another of this party against treachery, until this War of Powers shall be settled." He paused, then, "For good or ill."

"Well spoken, if not concisely," Erimenes said. "You're sure your father wasn't a lawyer? Or a confidence man?"

"Swear," Fost said grimly, his eyes moving around the small circle. One by one they took the vow until Fost came to Synalon. Fost refused to break the gaze and, such was the intensity of his feeling, it was Synalon who turned away.

"If you insist," she said, making an irritable gesture with one hand, "I'll swear your silly little oath, as well."

"Then let's drink to it," Rann proposed. The toast was drunk. And Fost wondered what he was getting into.

In her official capacity before Synalon had driven her into exile, Moriana had dealt with many of the financial matters of the Sky City. Haggling for provisions and materiel proved second nature. And, after Rann had visited the House of Omsgib-Bir, money began to flow from the official coffers of the City. Fost was never sure what Rann had threatened, but the goatlike banker now fell over himself to supply ample amounts of money, presumably drawn against Sky City accounts. But such was Rann's effect on people that Fost didn't discount the possibility that Omsgib gave them money from his own pocket—out of fear.

While Moriana purchased supplies, Fost and Rann went to the waterfront district to find mercenaries seeking employment. Rann promptly sought out the biggest braggart of the lot, a big red-bearded man who wore his hair plaited into pigtails. Physically he was imposing enough, but it was obvious to Fost that the man knew even less of military arts than of discretion.

"You're the man I'm looking for," Rann told the giant.

"What's that, little man?" the giant bellowed. He obviously wanted to have some sport with the diminutive Rann. Fost waited to see the color of the fool's blood, but instead of a blade, Rann brought forth a well-filled purse and swung it slowly before the big man's bloodshot eyes.

"I hear you," the giant said, and followed Rann and a thoroughly bemused Fost to a booth in the shadows at the rear of the inn.

"What I'm about to tell you," Rann said conspiratorially, "must be kept in the strictest confidence. I am empowered by certain parties who cannot be named to raise a company of stalwart warriors to march to the relief of the Empire. As a man as well-informed as yourself is doubtless aware, the Empire is beset by inhuman foes camped along the River Marchant. We—those I represent—intend to mount an expedition to take the Hissers in the rear."

The big man nodded slowly and thoughtfully, though Fost doubted he understood a word in ten.

"And you want me to join this expedition."

Rann's eyebrows shot up in surprise.

"Why no, my good man! I want you to *lead* the expedition! You will, discreetly of course, raise a company and march north. Yours will be one of several secretly travelling to a rendezvous. However," he said quickly, as the man began to frown, "I don't doubt that with your obvious talents you'll find yourself in a position of authority. Perhaps even overall command." And to Fost's further astonishment, Rann simpered in a fashion that went well with the dandified accent he had adopted.

"How much?" the big man finally said, after his mind had slowly worked over the ramifications.

Rann swept his arm across the table, sowing circles that rang with deep, true tones. Coins of Tolvirot gold, not Imperial clay and tin, sprouted. The giant's eyes grew as big and round as the klenors winking seductively at him from amid the pools of spilled drink.

"Elhard Lanisol's your man," he said with ponderous sincerity.

The deal was quickly done. Half the princely sum scattered on the table went directly into the big man's pocket. The rest was to be used to begin recruiting.

Rann said he would return to meet Lanisol in a few days. Before Lanisol found out the name of his employer, Rann and Fost were pushing through the door and out into the street.

"You look as thick witted as our friend inside," laughed Rann.

Fost set his jaw. He wasn't going to ask for an explanation. Rann smiled and answered, as if he had.

"The Nevrymin and the Dwarves are openly ranked with the Vridzish," the prince explained. "It's safe to assume that other human allies of the Dark exist who keep their sympathies concealed. And I suspect there are such here in Tolviroth Acerte. And it is no assumption at all that they'll have heard about the small, scarred man and the expedition he's mounting to save the Empire."

"I don't follow you," Fost said reluctantly.

"The hypothetical minions of the Dark are going to learn that Moriana and Synalon have joined forces, and that they are spreading their coin liberally about Tolviroth Acerte. That much we cannot hide." He flicked a speck of soot from his shirt collar. "They'll wonder, of course, where we intend to go—and lo! the worthy Master Lanisol will tell them, as he's no doubt done to all in earshot by now."

"But you wouldn't tell him who you were. How will the spies know who's recruiting?"

Rann looked at him sidelong. Fost instantly regretted the question.

"How many men have you encountered matching my description, Longstrider? If it got back to someone with wit, this Zak'zar, say, that the renowned Prince Rann was accosting drunks under his own name to raise an army, what would that someone think? He'd feel the trap as sharply as if its jaws were closed about his ankle."

Fost still looked doubtful.

"Of course," Rann went on, "I'll have to hire a few legitimate mercenaries to march north to lend some credence to the tale. But mostly I seek out ones like Lanisol."

"Likely, he'll keep the money himself," said Fost, confused by the prince's devious mind.

"What of it? His ego won't let him keep quiet about the important secret mission that brought him such a weight of gold. That the story reaches the proper ears is all that matters." They rounded a corner and Rann lightly touched him on the sleeve. "Let's go in here, and see if the Blow On Inn is as ghastly as its name."

CHAPTER EIGHT

"So, friend Fost," asked Erimenes, expansive after a night spent cavorting with Ziore, "what do you think of our travelling companions? They're not such monsters, eh?"

Mostly occupied with trying not to think about the way his piebald riding dog's trot traumatized his kidneys, Fost didn't answer immediately. He let his gaze sweep the horizon, front to rear. The ground sank slowly behind into the green woods and metallic luster of the River Wirix, which could be glimpsed in its windings far away. To the right—north—the land became a sea of grass rippling on the frozen waves of hills. There in this season the grass grew taller than a man on dogback; from this it had gotten the name Highgrass Broad. In front rose a barrier that had grown day by day, dark when the sun hung in the west, but a dry yellow light when the sun still mounted the cloud-piled eastern sky. It was the rim of the central massif, a great slab of land that tilted upward from the foothills of the Thails to a line meandering south of Mount Omizantrim. Now the cliffs were near, sheer and forbidding, looking as if they'd been scooped out by a great trowel. They were over a thousand feet high, though numerous and perilous trails ascended the many faces. They planned on reaching the foot of one such trail, which Fost and Moriana both knew from their travels, by early afternoon, completing the climb to the top before night made the way too dangerous.

"Did you say something?" Fost asked, belatedly aware that the spirit had.

"That's what I like about you, Fost. Always on the alert."

"Ziore would never forgive me if I accidentally dropped your satchel halfway up the face of the rim."

"I've told you before, you have exceedingly dubious tastes in humor." Erimenes shook his head, tiny trails of vapor drifting from his forehead as he moved. "As I was saying, I believe you've learned that our new companions aren't the fiends you'd thought. Of course, I realized long ago that Rann and Synalon were not wholly lacking in merit. But then I had more intimate contact with them. . . ."

"Collaboration is the word, Erimenes."

The genie heaved a melodramatic sigh and drew himself up even straighter.

"For all your experience in the wide world, and for all my tutelage over this past year—think of it, Fost. We've spent almost a year in one another's company." Ignoring Fost's groan, he carried on brightly. "At any rate, though I've no doubt been a maturing influence on you, I find to my deepest regret that you are still callow, unable to appreciate the subtler motivations of your elders."

"*Your* motivations aren't subtle. They come down to only one thing. Hedonism."

"Fost, you must curb this tendency to stray from the subject." Erimenes wagged a finger at him. "Now, about Prince Rann and the exquisite Princess Synalon . . . ?"

Fost considered. Again his eyes made a quick circuit of his surroundings. The little party was strung in a winding line picking its way around clumps of scrub and outcroppings of rock. Moriana rode lead on her dog, heavy Highgrass war bow strung across the rounded pommel of her saddle. Next rode Fost, then Synalon and Rann at the rear on a shaggy red animal, his own, smaller Sky City bow likewise resting across his saddle-bow. This was caravan season, and bandit country.

"I don't know," he confessed. "I think Synalon's

insane, but all the same there's something I can't quite name about her . . . something magnificent, I think, though evil. And Rann . . ." He shook his head. "I've heard enough of his handiwork to keep me well-stocked in nightmares the rest of my life. But it's also said he's a genius. And I believe that, too. I can't forget that day in the City when I rescued Moriana and found myself singlehandedly facing both Istu and the whole damned army. I had no choice in that and ran like hell as soon as Moriana was freed. But down dropped Rann from the safety of his eagle to put himself between the monster and Synalon, though he knew his blade couldn't even scratch the thing. That's the bravest thing I've ever seen."

"It bothers you to find that your former foes aren't wholly the black villains you'd like to think them?"

Irritation darted through Fost. He smiled unevenly.

"You know, Erimenes, it's when you're at your most perceptive that you tend to be the most annoying." He let the reins lie across the dog's neck while he raised his broad-brimmed felt hat and smoothed lank black hair from his eyes. "It does gripe me, though, to concede any goodness in a creature like Rann."

"And Synalon, ah, but I perceive the lady herself comes to join our small soiree."

Fost looked around too sharply and almost lost his balance. Synalon had indeed nudged her mount into a gallop and drew up on the courier's left side.

"Greetings, milord Duke," she called gaily.

Fost felt himself blushing. He tried to stop and only caused a deeper reddening of his features.

"Are you unaccustomed to folk employing your proper title?" she asked, her voice as clear and sweet as a mountain spring, and seemingly as guileless.

"I—" The words stuck in his throat. He desperately needed a drink, though he'd last sipped from the canteen bouncing by his knee not ten minutes earlier. He cleared his throat and started over.

"Your Highness, I confess I don't really think of myself as a duke. Nor a knight, if it comes to that."

"But you had those titles granted you from the hand of the Emperor himself. What more could you want? For one of those tiresome Wise Ones to come down from Agift and personally hand you a ducal coronet?"

"No. In all truth, Highness, I never wished to be a knight, or a duke, either. I wanted only to be a free man, and to lead my life in peace."

He didn't need her laughter to tell him how silly his words sounded.

"Besides," he said quickly to cover his embarrassment, "Imperial titles don't mean much. The Emperor tosses them around the way dancing boys and girls strew sweets at every public function."

"So the honor was too common for you." She nodded sagely. "You are a proud man, Longstrider."

Damn the woman! She was watching him out of eyes the deep, strange blue of turquoise, laughing and yet not laughing.

"I will make you duke," she said softly. "But there is that which you must do."

He faced ahead in stony silence. Thirty yards in front of him rode Moriana, now looking neither left nor right, and by the set of her shoulders he realized she knew that Synalon spoke with him, and feared both to interfere and not to.

"I will not help you work treachery against Moriana," he said stiffly.

Her laughter bounced off the rock face and echoed downward.

"Ah, Sir Knight, you see fit to jest with me! But I assure you, sir, the ceremony of investiture would be much less traumatic than those of High Medurim you told us of—and considerably more *intimate*." Laughing still, she spurred her mount ahead to go alongside her sister.

Fost felt as if the heat in his ears would make his

hat burst into flame. Synalon could fling lightning bolts with words as well as magical gestures.

"Are you truly as ponderous of wit as that byplay made you appear?" Erimenes demanded indignantly.

"But she was . . . she was . . ."

"Of course she was," said Erimenes. "And is that such an unpleasant prospect? She is lovely, as lovely as your Moriana. Lovely in the manner of a cataract or a catamount, trickish and even lethal. But lovelier for all that."

"What would you know about it?" snarled Fost. Erimenes only smiled an offensively superior smile. Fost cursed himself for letting the spirit know just how deep his barb had sunk.

Not altogether willingly, he studied the dark-haired princess as she rode knee-to-knee with Moriana. They were in deep discussion now, seeming as casual as any two sisters out for a late summer ride. It was difficult to believe they had been—still were—the deadliest of enemies and bitterest of rivals. But not even Moriana could long maintain a bowstring tautness of wariness and suspicion indefinitely; with time had come relaxation and a certain fatalism. If Synalon betrayed her, no amount of worrying would stay her. As for Synalon, she had, once past her early tempest of objection, taken the arrangement with a calm that bordered on insouciance. Fost didn't know if this was more madness or confidence.

From behind she looked younger than her sister, though Moriana was younger by minutes. Not having addressed herself to war and physical exertion—of the martial sort—the black-haired sorceress was slimmer, almost girlish, though there was little girlish about the flare of her hips and the roundness of her buttocks so clearly visible through the thin cloth of her trousers.

Erimenes chuckled, and Fost shook his head as if that would clear it of such thoughts. He made himself concentrate on Synalon's garment, pretending that had been his intent all along. It was all of the sheerest silk, a blouse low-cut in front, trousers that fit like a second skin at the top. It was vastly impractical for travelling, but everyone knew better than to make an issue of it. Synalon was proud, strongminded.

Fost remembered the unfortunate scene with the dogseller back in the coastal village before they started their trek southward toward Athalau. The merchant had suggested to Synalon that she select something other than a stud dog, that if they encountered a bitch in heat he would bring them trouble. Fresh from High Medurim though Fost was, her answer had shocked him both with its content and its explicitness, and he was surprised to see Rann color and look away. It had taken even Erimenes several seconds to fully comprehend the possibilities she'd outlined.

But now Moriana was pointing ahead and Synalon wheeling her mount and riding back to him.

"Get to the ground," she shouted. "Find a hole and slip inside!" She flashed him a sunbright smile as she passed and then called her warning to Rann.

As he drew sword, he marveled at the way in which the woman infected even emergency with salacious innuendo. Up ahead he saw that Moriana had now nocked an arrow from the quiver at her back. Ziore was also pointing, her arm misty pink and hardly visible in the sunlight.

At first, he thought he saw a cloud, oblong and dark, floating into view above the hard yellow line of the Rim far off in the north. Then he saw the white, fleecy clouds rolling as if to meet it, and he knew what it was.

At a stately, ominous pace, the City in the Sky floated east.

Moriana sat erect in the saddle's stirrups, her dog prancing and sidestepping, tasting urgency in the air and the sweat smell of its rider. Her eyes were wild, wide and faraway. Her face had gone stark with a terrible rage and fear and grief and longing and a winter bleakness of soul. He looked behind and saw Synalon, too, rigidly upright and staring, and he knew then that they were truly sisters, twins.

Rann loped by, his bow slung across his shoulders in easy acknowledgement of the futility of battle.

"The Hissers are none too sharp of sight," he called, as happy as if he were on the hunt and were the hunter rather than the prey. "But they may be looking with more than earthly eyes. Time we went to ground."

Sheathing his sword, Fost did just that. He hoped Synalon and Moriana weren't too caught up in the tidal surge of their emotions to heed the prince's warning. He dismounted and got the burly creature to lie down in the lee of a large oilbush, dropped into loose soil beside it and began to burrow—and also to sneeze. The oilbush exuded a slippery, fragrant sap that aggravated Fost's allergies.

A thumping of paws, a scattering of small stones, and Rann was at his side, hauling his own dog down expertly and flopping belly-down at Fost's side. He grinned. To all appearances, he enjoyed this hugely.

Fost wasn't. His stomach tied itself in knots and his heart tried to beat its way to freedom. He felt blackness swim behind his eyes. Even if Istu had stood atop the highest tower of the Sky City, Fost could not have seen him from where he lay itching and sniffling next to a man who, until very recently, had been bending every effort to arrange a painful, messy death for him. But it was as if he could see the Demon of the Dark Ones, horned and great and invulnerable, and he was laughing, laughing. . . .

"Where's it going?" asked Erimenes. Eagerness almost masked the other tremor in his voice. Here was something Fost could find comfort in. Erimenes had at last found something to fear.

"Tolviroth Acerte, I'd judge." Rann shifted to a more comfortable position, cupped his hands around his eyes to cut the glare. "Damn! It's too far to make out anything. But still, I think we quit the City of Bankers just in time."

Fost felt a leaden weight condense in his stomach. He was a Realm-road courier and called no place home —and every place. But Tolviroth Acerte came close. And he had friends there. . . .

A swirling breeze tossed dirt into their faces. Rann blinked and spat, and Fost was glad to see him with even this small a human frailty.

"I don't like the timing," Rann murmured. "Unless the City lingered long conquering Wirix."

"What do you make of it, cousin?" came Synalon's call.

"Shh!" Erimenes hissed, turning skyblue in dread.

Rann laughed at the genie.

"If they can hear us at this distance, we're done for. Rest easy, jugged spirit." Fost noted that the prince didn't call Erimenes *demon*. It would have been incongruous with a real demon's presence so ominously close.

"No good," Rann answered with raised voice. "I fear High Medurim has seen the shadow of the City."

High Medurim. Fost saw crowded filthy childhood streets, wharves piled with bundles for distant ports, markets with bright colors and intriguing spices; he saw Oracle and Teom and yes, pale, hungering Temalla. His eyes turned wet and stung. He clutched handfuls of sand in futile anger. They spilled through his fingers and, he thought, so goes the world, so goes all I've known or loved.

He did not feel the time slip by and only noted it had passed when Rann touched him on the shoulder. He came back to himself to find the sun hidden by the cliffs and the City low in the darkening eastern sky, merging with the thunderheads of a distant storm.

CHAPTER NINE

Brev bustled as it had not in years. It was the least of the Quincunx cities. It owed what little prosperity it had to the geographic fact that it lay at one corner of the Quincunx and could serve as a center for trade. Before the binding of the City in the Sky to the Great Quincunx, Brev had been an anonymous spot on the map. Even in the ten millennia since that event, it had failed to distinguish itself. Thailot boasted skill in artificing and glassworking, particularly the grinding of lenses; Wirix had its sorcerors with their genetic manipulations; Kara-Est was Kara-Est, grandest seaport of the Realm and a high city of the world; Bilsinx, central of the five cities, was the strategic and economic center of the Sundered Realm.

Brev was a dispirited huddle of drab stone buildings with the Broken Lands to the west and the Steppe to the south—and occasionally the Sky City overhead. That was all.

Now envious Brev could hold her head up, for she was queen of the Quincunx. Kara-Est was destroyed, perhaps Wirix as well; the island city was taken and sacked, at the very least. Thailot huddled behind its hedge of mountains. The onion domes of Bilsinx watched over empty streets, her citizens following the Sky Citizens fleeing south to avoid the wrath of the City's new owners. For now, all roads led to Brev. The merchants rejoiced in the influx of bright gold, and her leaders spoke of the dawn of a new era.

The travellers had desired to keep word of their arrival quiet. It was too much to ask. They were greeted by shouts of acclaim, with speeches by members of the

126

ruling hereditary council, and rum punch and floral wreaths in the Triangle where the paths of the City converged. Fost and Moriana and the rest looked on with tired eyes, even the genies subdued and weary from the desperate pace they'd maintained since sighting the City.

Not even Rann had the heart to tell the crowds that their dawn would prove a false one.

The Palace was an appropriate setting for the grim meeting of the sisters and their loyal, if somewhat confused, subjects. It was drafty, cold and damp and dark, and lacking in adequate fireplaces. The halls had a few cracked windows that admitted breezes but little sunlight. What light there was inside came from lanterns with panes no one had cleaned in recent memory. Dusk rose out of the east when a steward ushered them into the council chamber. Blue and purple shadows lay like curtains across the windows. The rafters were all but invisible above, not so much from height as murk. Fost decided this was a perfect place to discuss the end of the world.

"Your Highnesses," greeted Colonel Ashentani, lately governor of Bilsinx. "It gives us all great pleasure to be reunited with you once again."

"We thank you," said Moriana, leaving them to wonder whether she meant both sisters or simply employed the royal we. "But let's have an end to ceremony. We've serious business to discuss."

The two were seated side-by-side at the head of the table. Rann sat to the left, nearest Synalon. Fost tucked Erimenes's jug under one arm and took his place at the foot of the table, hoping he would have no part in the proceedings so he could find a place to sleep.

Ashentani he recognized. Most of the others he didn't. Moriana did and Ziore picked the information from the surface of the princess's brain and relayed it to Fost. Mostly they were Sky City officers. For their part, Ziore told him, they were frightened by the events of the past few months, afraid of the Demon and the Fallen Ones, scared that they might make a slip that would put them out of favor with one or the other sister.

Toward one, however, Moriana felt cold hostility, which Ziore reported was returned in kind. Destirin Luhacs had succeeded Count Ultur V'Duuyek as commander of a Grassland mercenary regiment at Chanobit Creek. Moriana disliked the woman for the part her troops had played in smashing the army she and Darl Rhadaman had raised. Luhacs, a square-faced woman with eyes like blue ice, blamed Moriana for the death of the count, who had been her lover as well as her commander.

Further down the table sat Cerestan, the young lieutenant of the Sky Guard. He'd aged considerably since the first time Fost saw him. Since escaping the City and Istu's wrath, he had waged a quiet battle against the dangers besetting the refugees—hunger, thirst, exposure —as they fled first to Bilsinx and then to Brev. His eyes were sunk into pits and a hint of gray sprinkled his temples.

A servant came with mugs of steaming broth. Fost drained his in three swallows, almost revelling in the way it scalded his tongue. Though he barely tasted it, the warmth spread through his body and revitalized him. He felt closer to life than death for the first time in days.

"So that's our story," finished Synalon. "What of the Empire? Wirix?"

Colonel Ashentani squirmed uncomfortably in her chair.

"Well?" demanded Moriana. "We must know. Killing messengers bringing bad news is something I've never done." Moriana darted a quick look at her sister, who sat back in her chair and tented fingers in front of her slightly smiling lips.

"There are few facts," said Ashentani, "but they are grim enough. After Bilsinx fell and Brev collapsed, Wirix recalled its citizens from those cities. But there was a small colony of Wirixers in Samadum and it is from them we received news of Wirix's fall. The Fallen Ones launched an attack with small boats on the lake and their skyrafts above. When the City floated overhead, Istu appeared. He cast down lightnings, but the strength of the Institute was arrayed against him and the force of his bolts tempered. The Wirixer mages conjured an air elemental and set a waterspout against their invaders." Ashentani paused, noting she had the rapt attention of not only Moriana and Synalon but Rann, also. The small man sat with eyes half closed, evaluating her every word. She went on. "Istu bellowed in rage and disappeared."

"And then the Black Lens appeared in the Skywell," put in Rann.

"Yes," said Colonel Ashentani in a choked voice. "Istu absorbed the air sprite by drawing it into the blackness. Then the City crossed over Wirix."

"Tell me exactly what happened," said Rann, leaning forward now, his arms resting on the table, hands clenched.

"A black vortex descended from the Lens. It drove into the center of the city, digging to bedrock, coring Wirix like an apple. The government buildings were torn from their foundations but the Institute and most of the city proper were intact. The defenders, magicians and soldiers alike, were demoralized by the Demon's power. The purely physical storm that began when the vortex vanished destroyed what the Black Lens hadn't."

"And High Medurim?" Fost heard himself asking.

"Only rumors," answered the colonel. "Again the Demon used the Black Lens. The Hissers were dug in along the Marchant. The Lens blazed a black trail of death and devastation across the farmlands of the City States like a spear pointing straight at Medurim's heart."

"Enough poetry, damn you!" flared Fost. "What of the city?"

She shrugged, her face a mask showing the deprivation and horror she had lived with. Fost regretted his sharpness with her.

"The Imperial capital has fallen, whether captured like Wirix or eradicated like Kara-Est, I haven't been able to discover."

"Thank you, Colonel," Fost said softly. He turned his empty cup in his hands, staring into the depths as if to read some augury there. It was true. Medurim was no more, and likewise the friends he had known in both slums and palace.

After supper, Fost heard Cerestan's shrill voice asking the question he dreaded to hear.

"Why must we turn tail and run? Can't we *fight* the damned lizards?"

Fost feared that Synalon would renew her own objections to the plan and break the fragile coalition. Glancing up, he saw Rann twisting a linen napkin between his fingers with quiet vehemence and knew he wasn't the only one fearing for the alliance.

"Are you a master of magics?" snapped Synalon. The young officer recoiled at the fury flaming in her eyes. "Or do you presume to judge the decisions of your betters . . . and find them wanting?"

"No, Your Highness," he whispered, his face deathly white.

"Very well," said Synalon. "Now, caravans are bound from Tolviroth Acerte, some here, some for the Gate of the Mountains. A small cargo fleet should be standing off the Southern Waste near Athalau awaiting our word, if they met with no misfortune rounding Cape Storm. These carry supplies for our people. This is your task, Cerestan: remove the Sky Citizens and our allies to Athalau."

Gasps met the announcement. "But the barbarians of the Steppes—" "—impossible—" "But Athalau's buried in a living glacier—" "—impossible!"

"Impossible?" The hair began to rise on Synalon's head. She tossed back her spark-crackling hair and sneered. "If you find it impossible then I must depend on others not so easily daunted. You don't find this impossible, do you, Master Cerestan?" Her eyes fixed on the hapless young officer who had not joined in the chorus of protest at the announced exodus. "You've acquitted yourself ably. In honor of that, and in view of your increased responsibilities, I hereby appoint you Constable of the City in the Sky and charge you with seeing that the resettlement proceeds expeditiously."

As thunderstruck silence settled, Synalon turned to her sister and added, "With Moriana's approval, of course."

The anger that had been growing in Moriana's eyes faded.

"I approve," she said, clearly less than happy with her sister usurping power in this fashion. Moriana leaned forward and used the opportunity to regain her position of authority.

"As for the rest of you," Moriana said, sweeping the group with her gaze, "you know that Fost Longstrider and I penetrated the glacier which covers Athalau, as did Prince Rann." She looked at Rann who stared back with perfect calmness. "The way through this sentient glacier, who calls itself Guardian, has been opened before. We must convince it to trust us and open wide enough to accommodate all."

"It shall be done," said Colonel Ashentani, glaring at Cerestan.

"You all know the task ahead of us. Let's get to it, because we have no idea how much time the Fallen Ones will give us." All rose when Moriana did and silently left. She turned to Fost and stretched out a hand, saying, "I'm bone-tired. I'm going to bed." He took her hand and she squeezed his fingers as if they were her last grip on sanity.

A steward led them to their chambers. Glancing back, Fost saw the leaders clumped in excited knots, Rann sitting calmly with boots propped on the Count of

Brev's table and ignoring the commotion. Cerestan stood gazing after Moriana; Fost saw Synalon regarding the young officer with thoughtful intensity.

A tug on his hand drew him away and down the hall.

As it had every day of the week since leaving Brev, the wind blew icy in Fost's face. He shivered, gathered his cloak more closely about him and rode on. In a few more hours the sun would be high and beat on the travellers like hammers. But now, in the gray, early morn, the frigid breath of the Southern Waste scoured the barren land. He shifted his weight in the saddle, no more comfortable now for all the time he'd spent in it, and thought of Moriana.

It had been hard leaving her, but there hadn't been any other choice. They had to split, with one group going to the Great Crater Lake and the Ethereals, the other heading for the Gate of the Mountains and glacier containing Athalau. Alliance or no, oaths or no, it would have been sheer foolishness for Rann and Synalon to go one way and Fost and Moriana the other. Each princess had to be sure her interests were represented by both groups. To do so didn't guarantee safety, but to do otherwise was to invite betrayal.

Moriana had gone with Rann to Athalau and Fost guided Synalon to the Ethereals' village. Likewise, the genies had to split up. Erimenes, who had helped gain entrance to Athalau before, went with Moriana. Ziore rode with Synalon and Fost in hopes her ability to sway emotion would help convince the Ethereals to forsake their ancient isolation and join the battle against the Dark.

Orange and swollen, the sun peeked above a blanket of clouds stretched across the eastern horizon. Fost scanned the sky. Twice they had glimpsed skyrafts in the distance, and once they had scarcely managed to find shelter in a steep-walled arroyo when a twenty foot slab of stone passed soundlessly overhead. Rann's ruse must have failed; it was rare for the Vridzish to commit their aircraft this far south.

A few times they had glimpsed other riders. To Fost's surprise, the jet-haired princess made no objection to evading them. But as she pointed out, there was no honor—and damned little diversion—to be gained in battling brigands.

Beyond these incidents, little transpired. Several times Ziore detected the nearness of some hunting animal but was always able to deflect the creatures before they came near enough to attack. Unlike Moriana and Rann, neither Fost nor Synalon was a competent archer so they had taken plentiful provisions, and the necessity of hunting didn't slow them. Having reassured himself the sky was clear of foes, Fost's main concern was to keep an eye out for the fierce barbarians of the Steppe. Eventually some agreement would have to be reached with them to allow the passage of unprecedented numbers of northerners across their territory. It wouldn't help if Synalon reduced a score of them to cinders before Fost had a chance to open negotiations.

Synalon rode behind, wrapped in her cloak and her own thoughts.

"What are you thinking?" Ziore's voice asked from the satchel bumping at Fost's hip.

He started. He wasn't yet accustomed to the gentle feminine voice that now accompanied him or the equally gentle presence that went with it.

"I'm sorry," he mumbled, and quickly twisted off the lid of the nun's jar. "I forgot you were there. Erimenes would have made his presence known long before this."

A surprisingly girlish giggle emerged along with a streamer of pink smoke that swirled in a familiar fashion and became the form of Ziore.

"Erimenes can be trying sometimes. But still, he's awfully cute."

Fost couldn't think of anything to say to that and so rode in silence. The land here was almost flat, tan dotted with the green of occasional bushes as far as the eye could see. The very uniformity of the land was treacherous for it made the terrain seem flatter than it was. The Steppe boasted hills, ridges and deep gullies which could hide large bodies of foes until one was almost on top of them. The sameness of the land lulled one into thinking none could approach without being seen far off.

"I wish I knew what to make of our friend back there," he said.

"I, as well. Can we trust her? Moriana is afraid that she'll betray us."

"We don't have much choice. And she's got as much reason to hate the Dark Ones as Moriana. More, in fact."

"But she's not always rational." In spite of himself, Fost laughed at this. It was a marvel of understatement. "Perhaps her hatred of Moriana will overrule her bitterness toward the Lords of Infinite Night."

He took his black water flask from the satchel and drank. The taste of gruel was still in his mouth, and the tepid water the vessel provided did little to wash away the taste. He took a mouthful, swirled it around in his mouth, spat at a clump of amasinj bush. There was no need to conserve water; the flask magically replenished itself, as did the matching gruel bowl that rode in the satchel with Ziore.

"Have you had any luck at reading her?" he asked.

"She sensed it at once when I tried probing her at that first meeting, and since then I've been careful. Her emotions are so strong she can't altogether hide them. Her passions surge with the power of ocean waves, Fost. They practically swamp me."

Fost was grateful he didn't possess Ziore's sensitivity.

"I can't get past them to her thoughts. But some of the passions are clear. Pride. Ambition. Rage. Longing. So great they'd tear apart a lesser psyche."

"And Rann?" he asked. "Have you tried reading Rann?"

"He's got some manner of protection, or perhaps he is just good at shielding his thoughts."

"But no emotions? I imagine he's as cold as fresh caught cod."

Ziore's vaporous eyebrows rose and turned pinker.

"Not at all. He's almost as passionate as she. But I cannot define his passions as well as hers. Pride, great pride. Longing and rage, I think. And . . ." She paused as if afraid he'd ridicule her for saying the next. "And fear, I think."

His impulse was to laugh, and he held it down. A frown formed on his face as he rode. The nun was most likely wrong. She admitted that Rann's warped passions were harder for her to make out than his cousin's.

But what if she weren't wrong? What would it take to frighten a man like Rann?

Fost spent the rest of the day trying to push that thought from his mind.

The sun had passed its zenith when Synalon picked out the low dome of fog that squatted endlessly above the Great Crater Lake. When they made camp that evening, Fost judged they would reach the Ethereals' settlement early the next morning.

The three of them shared conversation over the small campfire. The first day Fost and Ziore had kept to themselves, wary of speaking to Synalon and frankly unsure of the reception they'd get if they tried. Slowly the ice had thawed and the two began to talk guardedly about the sorceress-queen. They still feared her, and Fost was a long way from liking her, but there was something about the empty immensity of the Steppes that made humans seek each other's company. Their differences all became trivial in the face of the lonely spaces and distant skies that dwarfed and mocked human fears and aspirations alike. Even Ziore, who was to all intents immortal, confessed to being made to feel ephemeral by the changeless waste.

Fost did most of the talking. To his surprise he had

found Synalon a good listener. She sat across the crackling fire, her cloak casually open as if to let the moonlight shine on breasts barely contained by her low, silken blouse. Her eyes were big and seemingly self-luminous, and always on him.

He spoke of his childhood in High Medurim, as he had to Moriana a year before when they journeyed to Athalau. Synalon encouraged him with questions, with attitudes of head and body implying receptive interest. She had a lively mind, he reflected, to have learned as much as she had of the difficult magical lore. His experiences as a slum child in Medurim must be as alien to the highborn sorceress as any work of demonomancy.

At times like this, with both moons high and waxing in the sky, Ziore was mostly silent, too. Fost almost lost awareness of his audience; he talked to the moon, himself, the restless wind, the insects that sang beneath the canopy of stars. He even found himself speaking of what he and Moriana had undergone together, after their flight from the very woman who sat watching him with such rapt intentness. He told of the journey south, the encounter with the Ethereals, the attack by Rann and his men at the foot of the Ramparts and what befell him and Moriana after they were separated. He told of Athalau, lost and splendid, and what he had found within. He told of how he had died and been revived and gone looking for the woman who had slain him. And he told of what he had gone through to find her. All this to the person who, for the past year, had personified evil in his thoughts. And she nodded in appreciation of the things he told her, even when what he spoke of was how he and the woman he loved had smashed the plans of this other.

It was lonely on the Steppe. The sound of his own voice was comforting.

After the need for speaking had burned itself out, he sat with his knees drawn up before him and his arms around them, staring into the slowly dying campfire. In a detached way, he was aware of Synalon scrutinizing him. Perhaps it was to the wind and stars he had spoken and not to her.

With a rustle of grass and fine cloth, she rose and stepped to his side. Her touch was both cool and hot upon his cheek.

"You're quite a man, Sir Longstrider."

He sat dead still. He had dreaded this moment—and yet he felt ambivalent. He had seen the looks she gave him as they rode from Tolviroth Acerte. If nothing else, he had piqued her interest by thwarting her consistently across a year; and she was beautiful, heart-stoppingly beautiful. The double moonlight fell as soft as a caress on her skin. He tensed, fearing her, fearing that within him which longed to respond to her.

But her fingers were soon withdrawn—too soon?—and she walked grand and serene back to her side of the fire. Trying not to betray the confusion he felt, he said a quick goodnight and stretched out on the ground, with his saddle beneath his head and Ziore at his side. He glanced from the silver and black of Synalon's form into the blank darkness of the Steppe where hunting beasts cried down the moons. In time he felt Ziore's touch upon his mind, soothing, lulling. He slept.

A timeless interval. Sleep departed. He was awake at once, sword in hand. A touch on his arm aroused him. His senses strained.

"Who is it?" he asked softly.

I, Fost. Ziore's feathery thoughts brushed across his mind. *Something's amiss.*

Aware of the strange stillness, he twisted about, studying the Steppes. The pink moon Astrith was gone and blue Raychan prepared to dip into the Golden Sea. Dark shapes huddled off across the flatness and movement flirted at the corners of his vision. He was wise to the wild and knew his brain created the motion. Whatever was going on, it wasn't happening in that direction.

Keeping his breath as regular as if he still slept, he

shifted and murmured to himself, preparing to roll onto
his other side. Ziore sent him no further thoughts. The
Athalar spirits never needed sleep, and he had been
content to fall asleep himself without caring whether
Synalon stayed awake or not. Ziore was a better sentry
than either of them, and could be trusted. It would have
been like Erimenes, before his apparent change of heart,
to let some toothy horror out of the Ramparts creep up
almost within distance to make its final savage leap
before rousing Fost.

He made another sleepy sound and rolled. At the
same time, he moved up one arm as if to pillow his
head. He used the motion to lessen the chance of firelight glinting off an eyeball and betraying his wakeful-
ness.

The fire had been tended since he'd dropped off to
sleep. It flickered low but not as low as he'd last seen.
Synalon sat beyond it so that the yellow tendrils of
light barely reached her. Her head was nodding, one
slim hand tracing elegant figures in the air in front of
her. With a shock, Fost realized she was not alone.

Her companion sat farther from the fire than she.
With the black mountains at its back, Fost couldn't
limn it by the stars it blocked. But by the faint glimmer
from above he saw—or thought he saw—a Dwarf.

That's odd, he thought to Ziore. The creature had
a Dwarf's outsized head and stumpy limbs yet it appeared taller than Synalon.

I'm frightened. He felt a contact on his arm and
twitched, barely stifling a yelp of surprise. *I need to
touch something—somebody.*

He knew of Ziore's illusory touch from Moriana;
Oracle had known the same trick though he'd never
used it to hold hands as the genie was doing.

It's all right, he thought back. *But what* is *that thing?*
Synalon glanced his way. He quickly shut his eyes.

*I don't know. But it scares me. It broadcasts no emo-
tions that I can detect. Fost, I . . . I fear to probe it.*

He squeezed her hand.

Then don't. I don't think it'd be wise to fool with that thing, whatever it is.

Are we betrayed?

He felt his muscles winding tighter. The question lay like a lump of lead in his mind.

We can't assume anything. Wait and see.

He opened his eyes. Synalon sat alone. Her chin was sunk to her breastbone. Asleep or not, she showed no sign of movement.

Fost rolled over again. Even with Ziore's help, he was a long time finding sleep. And when he did, it was filled with dreams of Dwarves and twisted faces and roses as black as death.

CHAPTER TEN

Tendrils of fog reached for Fost's face, making him think he rode through cotton. He could scarcely see the alert, upright ears of his dog a few feet in front of his face. The padding of his dog's footfalls came as though from far away. Behind, Synalon's dog existed only as rhythmic sounds even more remote.

Now and again the whiteness parted briefly, eddying around a clump of rock or a sickly looking shrub. But for these occasional sights, and the jogging of his mount's steps, Fost would have thought he was standing still, lost in the mist.

For the tenth time in the last five minutes he fought down the urge to ask Ziore if she was sure she knew where they were going. Erimenes had reluctantly led him and Moriana to the Ethereals' village, the only alternative being freezing to death in a blizzard. He had sensed the nearness of humans and steered his companions toward them. Ziore had the same senses and used them. But with Fost's visual world constricted to a sphere the radius of his arm, it was hard for him to believe that Ziore knew her way.

Abruptly the mist parted. Before him rose a random clump of huts rudely made from chunks of slag cast up when a meteorite had struck the Steppe during the contest between Felarod and the World Spirit on one side and Istu on the other. A few pale folk, as wispy as the mists through which he rode, drifted without purpose among the buildings. The smell of drying seaweed and an open latrine assailed his nostrils.

"See," Ziore said smugly. "I told you I steered us truly."

He felt an impact behind his right leg. His dog jumped, doubling back with a snarl. He swatted it briskly on the head before it snapped at Synalon's mount which had blundered into it. He cursed under his breath. This collision was his fault. He'd been so surprised at seeing the Ethereals' village that he hadn't given the agreed upon two tugs on the rope tied between Synalon's saddle and his own. He looked back to see the princess rearranging her garments and got the impression she had drawn her black silk tunic open wide to let the damp mist play across her breasts and belly. He saw color on her cheeks. She smiled; he quickly looked away.

"We're here," he said unnecessarily, feeling the need to be saying something to cover the awkwardness he felt.

Synalon gestured imperiously to him to lead the way. They wound their way around sad, slumping huts to the large round building in the center of the settlement. Fost recognized this as the temple where the Ethereals gathered to meditate. As the two reined in before the irregular door, a man emerged, stooping to pass beneath the sagging lintel. Fost recognized him as well.

"Greetings, strangers," the Ethereal said in a high, sweet voice. "I know not what brings you, but you are welcome to rest. And who knows? You may come to share the wisdom of our ways and give up the distress and discord of the material world, which is the world of illusion."

"It's plain to see we received the more difficult task," Synalon remarked sardonically.

"Greetings yourself," said Fost, swinging off his dog. "*I'm* no stranger. The woman with me is. Meet Her Royal Highness, Synalon Etuul, Princess of the City in the Sky, currently in exile. Your Highness, this is Itenyim, of the Ethereals. He's in exile, too. From reality."

"That's not very diplomatic," Ziore chided softly.

Fost shrugged it off. He hadn't realized how bitter he was toward the Ethereals.

"We employ no titles here," said the Ethereal, ignoring Fost's jibe. "But you are welcome."

Synalon stayed on her dog, regarding the Ethereal. She had taken him for a woman at first, because of the slim, frail form and the effeminate features. But the bone structure of the face and the protuberant Adam's apple were clearly masculine, as was the body clad in a simple, dirty green robe that hung to the knees.

"I see the temple wall's finally caved in," remarked Fost, gesturing to a gap in the melted rock wall. "They put me to work there when Moriana and I stayed here before. I wasn't at it long enough to do much good, it appears. Where's Selamyl?"

A shadow crossed the flawless features.

"Selamyl met with misfortune after you and the woman departed."

"A misfortune named Rann?" The Ethereal didn't answer. Not looking at Synalon, Fost said, "Well, round up your people as best you can. We need to talk to them at once."

"They are about their dances and duties and meditations."

"Those dances and duties and meditations are about to be permanently interrupted," said Fost briskly. "Tell them that unless they listen to the princess and me they are going to have visitors who make Rann look as saintly as Erimenes himself."

Itenyim's face, already alabaster, turned a shade lighter. He turned and walked off, almost hurrying. A strap was broken on his sandal, giving him a limp.

"Saintly?" asked Synalon, arching a brow.

"They think he is," said Fost. "I told you they were divorced from reality."

"Return to Athalau?" The Ethereal woman's face was a marble mask of incomprehension. "That's impossible."

"It had better not be impossible," Fost said, "or you and I and the princess and every other human being in the Realm are going to be dead before this winter's snow is melted."

"Life is illusion," answered the woman.

Fost bared his teeth. He had the urge to grab her and shake loose her complacency. But that wouldn't only be wrong, it'd be futile. If these people had resisted Rann's special brand of persuasiveness as long as they had, mere shaking wouldn't do any good.

"Are the Dark Ones an illusion?" he asked, voice ragged with exasperation. "They're what we face."

A ripple passed through the small crowd assembled in the temple. At least, mention of the Dark Ones got some response.

"What have these matters to do with us?" asked another.

Fost glanced at Synalon, at ease beside him on a three-legged stool that gave every indication of collapsing beneath her. Her lips were curled, and it wasn't just at the odor of stale clothing and indifferently washed bodies that permeated the low-roofed building. Even the air current blowing between the door and the hole in the wall failed to freshen the atmosphere.

"Do you know what's happened?" he asked.

It was a foolish question. He didn't need the sheeplike faces turned to his, some already showing unmistakable traces of boredom, to tell him so.

"We do not trouble ourselves with the gross affairs of the world beyond our village," said Itenyim loftily.

"The world outside your village is about to trouble *you*, however," Fost said, "and what it will do to you is more than a little gross. The Fallen Ones are back in control of the Sky City, my friends, and Istu rides it like a raft."

His listeners shrank away.

"The Demon is loose?" another woman asked. Fost nodded.

The Ethereals turned to one another and spoke in

subdued, quavering tones. Their ancestors had turned their backs on their own past, but fear of the *Zr'gsz* and of the Demon of the Dark Ones lay deep in human bones.

"Istu knows who you are," Fost said, which was quite possible. "He hates you for what your forebears helped do to him."

"But have we not made amends?" Itenyim gasped. "Our fathers and mothers forsook Athalau and came to this spot in the wilderness out of remorse for what they had wrought. Is this not enough?"

The air exploded from Synalon's lungs in a surprised snort. Fost scarcely believed what he heard. The Ethereals were hoping Istu would forgive them for their ancestors helping to cast him down!

"Nothing you could do would be enough," said Synalon. "The Demon of the Dark Ones knows as little of forgiveness as he knows of mercy. What he *does* know would shrivel your souls if you heard." The effect her words produced on the Ethereals hardly seemed great. By normal standards they were still impassive.

"What is it you want of us?" asked a more or less male voice from the rear of the temple.

Fost felt like cheering. They'd gotten through to at least one of the Ethereals.

"What we're asking is grave, I won't deny. We need some of you—as many as we can get—to come with us to Athalau. There we must find the Nexus and use it to get in touch with the World Spirit, as Felarod and your ancestors did ten thousand years ago."

"But it was for shame at what they'd helped Felarod do that our ancestors came here," someone cried.

"They helped save the world," Fost shouted back.

"The material world." Itenyim practically sneered. "Had the world been destroyed, think of the generations that would have been spared from suffering its illusions."

Be calm, Fost, Ziore urged him from her jug. Given the Ethereals' historic dislike for Athalar magic, she had agreed it was best she not show herself to them.

"Suffering?" Fost spat the word. "For all that the world is illusion, Master Itenyim, you acknowledge suffering as real. And I tell you the suffering the Hissers and their ally have inflicted, and will continue to inflict unless stopped, is a thousand times greater than anything humanity has suffered from the illusions of the material world."

"But the sufferings of the body are nothing," the first woman intoned, as if reciting a litany. "Serenity of the spirit is all."

"Faugh!" Synalon shook her hair back angrily and glared at the several score Ethereals crowded into the temple.

"I've always thought myself selfish, but it seems these dung eaters have some things to teach me. Do you think, you vapid bitch, that the sufferings Istu inflicts are of the flesh alone?" She laughed savagely. "Perhaps I should give your soul a touch of hellfire, a small taste of what Istu can do. That might teach you a measure of compassion, unless it turns you mad—or kills you outright." She fixed the Ethereal woman with her eyes. A tiny whimper escaped the woman's throat. She began to writhe as if held in place by invisible bonds. The muscles on her neck stood out in stark relief, but she could not look away from the suns that were Synalon's eyes.

Fost roughly grabbed Synalon's arm. Instantly, she turned the full force of her hell gaze on him. He reeled as agony exploded at the center of his being. It was as if all the loss, despair, and agony of a thousand lifetimes were made into a stake impaling his soul. He spent an eternity shrieking into mocking emptiness.

Then the horror was gone, leaving his mind staggering and weak. He felt Synalon's feverishly hot hand grip his.

"I couldn't stop the spell in time to spare you."

Dazed as he was, Fost still knew that this woman, who could slay with a single glance of her cobalt eyes, was apologizing to him. He nodded weakly, unable to speak. Dimly, he heard the sobbing of the Ethereal woman.

None of the Ethereals moved to help her. All eyes were on Synalon, who stared back at them with fierce contempt.

What do we do now? Fost asked Ziore. *It looks like the diplomatic approach isn't working.*

I don't know, she responded despairingly. *I'm trying to sway them. But I can't change even one's emotion!*

"I'm sorry for what my companion did," Fost said, expecting a deathbolt at every syllable. "But the world is under a death sentence. It will be carried out unless you help us."

"We've spent ten millennia trying to expiate the guilt of our forebears," said an Ethereal in the front row. "Now you're asking that we shoulder that burden anew."

Fost sagged. He could find no words to answer.

"Guilt, Cuivris?" a voice asked from the open doorway. "I will show you guilt."

Every head turned. Fost blinked and stared as Selamyl, the Ethereal who had tried by guile and argument to restrain him and Moriana from leaving before, made his way painfully into the hall.

"I thought you said he was dead," Fost said to Itenyim.

"I said nothing of the sort."

Nor had he, Fost recalled. It had only been said that Selamyl was one of Rann's victims.

He had obviously been a victim. Once he had stood even taller than Fost. Now he was hunched in on himself and shrunken so that the bones of his cheeks poked out through parchment skin. His grace had been almost painful to watch for one less fluid; now he hobbled in a broken walk, supporting himself with a cane fashioned from the haft of some tool.

"I live, friend Fost. And you truly are my friend. I owe you much."

"It was his fault you were injured!" Itenyim said heatedly.

"If fault lies anywhere, it lies with he who struck the blow. You would like to believe the fault was mine, though, wouldn't you, Itenyim? That I brought this on myself when I tried to stop you from telling Rann where our guests had gone?" Itenyim dropped his eyes. "No, I was not slain. But I came close enough to death to make me think. Since then I have spent much time away from the others, contemplating what you and the golden-haired princess told me. It is we who live an illusion."

Itenyim looked at Fost, his eyes swimming with tears.

"He's mad. His wound deranged him. Don't believe what he says."

Selamyl laughed. The others drew back, leaving him in a circle of loneliness.

"The outsider knows truth when he hears it," he said. "And speaking of truth, didn't I hear you say something of guilt when I came to the door, Cuivris? Well, here's a truth. Whether we like it or not, we are wardens of the Nexus and its secrets. If we do not act, those secrets and the Powers they command, will fall into the hands of the servants of the Dark. Is this why we came here ten thousand years ago? So that we could help undo all the sacrifice and devastation the War of Powers brought to pass?

"Istu is freed. A new War of Powers is at hand. If we do not act, it is lost. And the responsibility is ours. *Ours!*"

The Ethereals looked from Itenyim to Selamyl, who loomed above them like the idol of a pagan god. Slowly and subtly, they edged from Itenyim and drew closer to the crippled man.

"Do we murder the world?" Selamyl asked. For the first time in ten thousand years, the voice of an Ethereal rang as harsh as the blow of a hammer onto an anvil.

"Do we let our dread of working evil cause a greater evil still? Or do we turn our faces from illusion, leave behind our toys and scents and contemplation of the emptiness behind our eyes to do this thing which must be done, that only we in all the world can accomplish?"

One by one the Ethereals rose to their feet and came to stand by Selamyl. Soon, only Itenyim remained seated.

A small sound woke Fost. Habit brought him up with blade in hand, even though the strange, deadly creatures of the Ramparts—the legacy of the first War of Powers —never ventured into the Ethereals' village.

Synalon stood in the doorway holding a small lamp. She wore a nightdress of pale flannel that covered her from neck to ankles and hid the curvings of her body. Fost wondered how she'd managed to pack the bulky garment. He swallowed. Somehow, the effect made him hunger for her more than nakedness would have.

"May I come in?" she asked. Taking his silence for assent, she glided in and put the lamp on a jut of black slag in the wall. She pressed her palms together on the flat of his sword. "You were so masterful today."

Gingerly, he freed the blade from her grip and slid the weapon back into its sheath.

"I?" he said. "Being masterful with these people is futile."

"You swayed Selamyl." She sat with her hip touching him. Her flesh burned like a brand through thick flannel and thin blanket. "No, my lord. You give yourself too little credit."

She reached out to stroke his cheek. He turned away.

"I can't take credit for what another's done. And I'm no lord."

"Ah, I forgot. The Emperor's ennobling you wasn't sufficient for your pride." She leaned close. "I will make you a noble. Then none can question your right to a title—not even yourself."

"I guess I can't gracefully refuse, can I?"

"No. You cannot." Her mouth descended to his. Her lips were cool, the contact light. Her tongue swept lightly in a circuit of his mouth. He shivered. His hands wanted to grab her, but he held them rigid at his sides. He couldn't bring himself to cooperate.

"You are reluctant?" she asked, raising her head and smiling down at him. "Do I displease you?"

"No," he croaked. "Never."

The smile widened. Her nails traced tingling lines down his cheek, his jaw, throat, chest. Her eyes did not leave his. He felt his muscles tightening, felt his groin tingle in pleasurable anticipation.

Moriana! he thought.

Synalon was not without sensitivity. She caught his thought, his emotion.

"Do nothing for now, milord. Nothing."

The blanket passed his hips. She worked her magic caress down until his organ stood stiff and bucking and his buttocks left the pallet in a spasm of pleasure.

"You don't find me displeasing at all." Her eyes released his. Her hair fell in a black cascade over his belly, cool and fragrant, dancing with highlights of golden flame. Her lips closed like a noose of fire and ice. He gasped at the first suction, gripped her shoulders with increasing desire. Shudders wracked his body, increased in intensity. He tried to speak but his tongue turned thick and his jaw trembled.

The wet friction was excruciating as she moved up and down. Fost's every sense heightened, expanded. He felt the flannel, the firmness of her flesh, the heavy breasts swinging rhythmically so that finger-hard nipples brushed his thighs through the fabric. He grew drunk on the smell of her hair and the oil lamp and the moss used to seal the walls, on the scent of the night and the musk of her excitement. Up and down she moved, her tongue never resting.

Then came the explosion from within.

His fingers clamped on her shoulders with bruising force. Her mouth was avid and hungry and infinitely delightful.

She raised her head. She licked her lips and brushed back her hair.

"Now the edge is off, milord. The ceremony can truly begin."

She sat up straddling him and pulled the gown off over her head. Her pale, blue-veined, carnelian-tipped breasts rode up with it, then dropped to swing free. She pulled her hair from the garment's folds, shook it back, looked down on Fost as if from a great height.

Though he was spent, the sight of her beauty electrified him. He felt himself stiffening again, an obelisk lifted in honor of the triangle of black fur below her smooth stomach.

She raised herself on her knees and shuffled upward along him. He grunted as pleasure stabbed into him when she brushed the tip of his manhood. Then she was poised above his face, mysterious and gilded in lamplight. She lowered herself. He had a last thought of Ziore in her satchel beside the bed before his lips touched coarse, dewy hair. His tongue emerged and swept through the tangle to slick, succulent flesh. Synalon shivered delicately, cupped her breasts with her hands, then thrust her pelvis forward so that his tongue probed deep inside her.

Small, insistent animal sounds rolled from her throat. His tongue swirled within her, savoring both taste and texture. She was maddening and beautiful and he was drunk on her. His tongue withdrew, sought, found; it pressed in.

Her cries filled up the small chamber. Her fingers knotted painfully in his hair but he was lost in his pleasurable task. His tongue flirted, teased, bored in.

She screamed.

Walls of pliant flesh clamped on his head. All he heard was the hollow drumbeat of her pulse, racing, outpacing his. He felt her perfect body tremble, felt her leaving, raised his hands and seized her. At last she tore herself away, her body shining with sweat.

"It is as I thought," she said, her voice husky. "You are truly fit for a Queen of the Sky City."

His mind slipped out of gear and coursed back to the night before and the Dwarflike shape by the campfire. What was it? What had it offered? Some connection between that and Synalon's current passion was almost made, then slipped away from him.

She flowed down like water, her breasts falling heavy upon his firmly muscled chest, her mouth seeking his. Fost's fingers trembled on her buttocks as she lowered her hips and took him in. And then the ancient, insistent motion possessed them both. He forgot all but the heat and pressure and pleasure.

CHAPTER ELEVEN

"If you're going to kill me," said Moriana, "this is a good place to do it." Her words were almost lost in the wind moaning through the Gate of the Mountains.

Impassively, Rann studied her across the fire. His yellow eyes cast back the light like a cat's. At the third point of a triangle around the small fire wavered Erimenes's blue, misty pillar. The genie looked from one to another.

Moriana prodded the fire with a stick. Blue flames crackled toward the slit of cloudy sky visible high above.

"You say nothing, Prince."

"I didn't realize comment was called for, Princess," replied Rann.

"I see no need to fence with words. I don't trust you." She angrily threw the stick away.

The prince sat within his cloak. Moriana stared at him across the flames as if she could penetrate that narrow skull and lay bare the thoughts within. But Rann was protected against her probing. He remained unreachable, unreadable.

Their journey from Brev had passed in festering silence. Fost and Synalon had been enemies but had no cherished tradition of enmity. But there was bad blood between Erimenes and Moriana and between the spirit and the scarfaced prince.

It had not been a pleasant trip.

But the journey neared its end. Less than a day south lay the fringes of the glacier. Moriana must face the challenge of convincing Guardian to open a way into Athalau, not just for her and Rann, but for the vast

mob of soldiers and civilians making its way south
from the devastated Realm. And beyond that was the
problem of defending the city and the people against
the wrath of Istu.

Tension twisted within her, a slowly fraying cord
near to breaking. She sought release in anger and the
dangerous pastime of baiting her cousin.

"You want me to believe you're on our side. Why
should I believe that?"

Erimenes's eyes widened in anticipation. Moriana
lashed at Rann with bitter words, practically taunting
him. Rann was not known to suffer such jibes in silence.

"What you believe means little to me," Rann said
after a time, "except if it affects our chances for success.
But I perceive you mean to have this out now, whether
or not this is the right time for such disputes. Listen
well, cousin. I would see the Fallen Ones cast out of
our City in the Sky, and the Demon of the Dark Ones
imprisoned once more—or better, destroyed."

"Why should you care?" She remembered the ruined
face of old Kralfi who carried the marks of Rann's
handiwork to the grave.

"You may not be pleased to be reminded of this, but
I'm as human as you are." He raised a finger to quell
her objection. "Oh, I've done things you find repellent.
I don't apologize for them. I merely wish to point out
that my deeds notwithstanding, I am a man, not a
Zr'gsz. If the Hissers bring down the blade, it falls on
my neck, as well. So I am 'on' your side, like it or not."

"Why not join with the Dark Ones? You've done so
before."

"*I've* never done so. Synalon served the Dark Ones
for a time. I served her." He tipped back his hands and
thrust his forefingers against the bridge of his nose. "I
might ask why you do not choose to throw in *your* lot
with the Fallen Ones—as you've done before."

"Because they betrayed me!"

"And didn't the Dark Ones betray Synalon? Think

a moment, cousin dear. Her hatred for you springs from mere rivalry. The Dark Ones misled her. You've threatened her ambitions; they've wounded her pride. Which hatred do you think will prove more implacable?"

"Don't listen to him," said Erimenes. "He's too glib. He means you no good, him or that damned Synalon."

"And how much good have you done the princess, demon?" snapped Rann. "I remember when you were all aquiver to see Moriana tortured."

"I, uh, that is . . ." Erimenes looked at the rocky ground and fell silent.

"You disclaim all loyalty to the Dark?" Moriana flung the words at Rann like a gauntlet. "Why do you choose to serve Synalon, who would be the handmaiden of the Lords of Infinite Night?"

"Would *you* have had me?" he asked, almost too quietly to hear above the wind's lament. "You who turned her face in revulsion when the bird riders brought me back from the Thails? You always spurned me when we were both young because I couldn't learn magic while you seemed to absorb it through your fingertips. What the savages did to me only confirmed what you'd secretly thought: I was less than a man."

"That's not true!" she screamed. "I offered sympathy. You wouldn't have it!"

"Not so, cousin. Pity, perhaps. Pity without understanding. You never attempted to understand me. I who loved you hopelessly, from the time we were both children." She turned red, her cheeks burning. He laughed. "Yes, my attentions made you uncomfortable when we were both young. I always imagined it was a relief to you, what the Thailint did to me."

"No, never that!" She squeezed shut her eyes.

"Synalon understood. We understood each other perfectly. She was neither gentle nor kind, but she understood."

Moriana sobbed brokenly, huddled in on herself, shaking. Erimenes looked from her to the prince.

"A sad tale. Is this your justification for the evil you've wrought? Do I understand that you must torture innocent victims to death because you're not appreciated?"

"You understand nothing, demon!" Rann shouted at him. He turned away in a swirl of his dark cloak and stared up the pass.

There were voices in the dark, and they were laughing, laughing.

Frantic in its fear and pain, the soul raced around the Skywell. It darted inward as if to cast itself through the Well. Istu reached, tweaked with a taloned thumb and forefinger. Its hues blazed up in yellow pain. It collapsed quivering on the pavement.

Istu chuckled.

"See here," he said to the one standing silently, watching the Demon at his play. He prodded the prostrate soul with one black fingertip. "The colors of a soul, stripped of obscuring flesh, reveal its nature. Here on the outside is the yellow of pretense. This green layer beneath is lust. Below that the pink of sloth, the turquoise of indecision, and so on." The taloned finger sank into the midsection of the soul, which still twitched uncontrollably. "And at the core, we find a pure white light. Interesting. And odd, considering who this was in life. So many of the souls we took at that place were hollow at the core."

The night was chill with the promise of early autumn and lay heavy upon the People. Nothing stirred on the streets radiating from the Well of Winds. The Demon, his captive soul, and Zak'zar, Speaker of the People, seemed alone in the City.

"Is it necessary to torment that soul so?" Zak'zar asked. "You'll reap more in the weeks to come."

Istu prodded the soul again. It thrashed spastically, then lay still when the finger was withdrawn.

"Why should you care?"

"I knew this one in life."

Istu squatted on his haunches in unthinking imitation of the black basalt statue of him across the Well.

"You seem fascinated by the pale, pink ones. Would you have me leave a few alive for you as pets?"

"I was chosen of all the generations of the People to become Speaker when the Instrumentality at last fulfilled his function and freed you to bring us vengeance and victory. I was chosen because I could deal with the pale ones and understand their ways." He spread his hands in front of him, palms down. "With understanding comes a certain sympathy. It troubles me that our victory means the eradication of the enemy ones."

"You are soft," Istu sneered.

"I merely appreciate that those soft-skinned folk have virtues of their own. The interest of the People is mine to safeguard; I deplore that we and the Soft Ones cannot coexist. We could learn from them."

"Is this why you insisted we accept the ludicrous entreaties of the Dwarves and those traitors from the Nevrym Forest, to ally ourselves with them? As if their pathetic efforts contributed anything of worth." The great horned head shook, obliterating stars. "And why couldn't I complete the destruction of those last three cities, as I did with Kara-Est? I was born to extinguish suns, mortal. I dislike staying my hand."

"We still have to complete the reduction of this continent," said Zak'zar softly. "And the world beyond that. Our victory is far from assured."

Istu swelled with rage, but Zak'zar carried on.

"I requested that you spare the cities we took because many things have transpired in the world since you and my kind were forced from it. We may find knowledge that will ease our way to triumph. Or we may learn of a deadly threat in time to avert it.

"As for accepting the Dwarves and Nevrymin as allies, why not? If they do our work for us, we will be victorious all the quicker. I fear that time presses."

"Why should that be? I am Istu, spawn of the Dark Ones. Doubt your own strength, if you will. Doubt not mine. The Pale Ones cannot stop me."

"And yet some of them are bound for Athalau," said Zak'zar, "and it was in Athalau that you found your downfall last time."

A bellow of rage rebounded from the starred dome of the sky. Istu grew to a black pillar of wrath, raising mountain-smashing fists high as he glared down at the small, small figure of Zak'zar.

"No one slights the power of Istu!"

"Pardon if I gave offense, Lord Istu. I only pointed out the truth. My abilities in this was another factor in the Dark Ones selecting me as Speaker." At this reminder of Zak'zar's mandate from Powers greater even than his, the Demon subsided a little. "I would remind you, great Istu, that the Dark Ones themselves agreed to the wisdom of my proposal to expedite the conquest of the Realm by making alliances with those foolish enough to think our victory might profit them. And likewise, They share my concern over efforts to reach Athalau. As you well know, They even take steps of Their own to counter the menace posed by the Nexus and the World Spirit."

"I wonder at that," the Demon said sullenly. "The Dark Ones have already broken Their faith with that woman once. Do They think They can dupe her again?"

"In my study of the Pale Ones," said Zak'zar, crossing his arms and nodding in concentration, "I've found that humans are cursed with a thing called *hope*."

"When I was bound in the depths of the City, sometimes my thoughts turned to the prospect that once again I would know my world-destroying freedom. In a word, I hoped." Istu shook his horned head. "Well do you name it a curse."

"After all," said Zak'zar, "why do Fairspeaker and Mauna aid us so eagerly? Their minds should tell them the best they can win is a stay of execution. But hope tells them otherwise, and it's hope they listen to."

Istu's eyes flared bright yellow in the blackness of his face.

"Verily does the black-haired witch hope in vain," he thundered. "I have not forgotten how she lured me forth to pain and humiliation. I shall cherish her soul within mine. And this I will give her: often, very often I will give her clothing of flesh to wear so that she may know my vengeance again. And the same for her fair-haired sister. I had but a taste of her and will have more."

"I thought you kept all your captive souls in the spirit jars in the warehouse."

"Most. Those are the subjects of my passing interest, like the ones I collected in High Medurim, like this miserable baggage here." He nudged the soul with his foot. It huddled in on itself and shook. "But there are those I would add to my permanent collection. Those two are among them."

"Even so." Zak'zar bowed. "I would ask a boon."

"Ask," said Istu, waving a magnanimous claw. "You are the Chosen of my progenitors."

"Release this soul and the one you keep next to it. I care little for the souls of the soft-skinned strangers, but these I knew. They deserve better."

"I will not," said Istu, hunching his shoulders. "They were the only ones of their kind. They are special items. I won't part with them. Not until they begin to bore me."

"As you will." Zak'zar bowed again and glided away. Istu glowered after him. When the Speaker was gone, Istu gave the cringing soul another petulant kick, picked it up by the scruff and rammed it into its red clay jar. He placed the jug carefully in its spot among the others and went off to find his own repose.

In the morning, he returned to gloat once more over his collection. What he saw made him shake his enormous head in disbelief. Anger flared nova-bright within him.

Two jars that rested side by side containing the souls

of Emperor Teom and his sister-wife Temalla had been smashed. The souls were flown to oblivion, unreclaimable. In his fury, Istu danced on the other jars, stamping them into powder beneath clawed feet. Invisible in the sunlight, the freed souls swirled about his columnar legs and were gone.

When the last jar was crushed and its spirit departed, the fit left Istu. He contemplated what he had done. He had a shrewd notion of the culprit responsible. He might have gone then and sought out the knave. Certainly, Istu could punish him in such a way that would make up for the diversion lost in the forms of bottled souls.

Instead, Istu began to laugh. At the sound of his laughter, birds fell dead for miles around.

"It is a grave thing you ask of me." Each word came slow and heavy like the fall of mountains. "I must think on it a while."

"Marvelous!" cried Erimenes. "What's 'a while,' you immense fugitive from an icehouse? Until the sun goes out? Or merely next year?"

"Tsk tsk," said the glacier named Guardian. The boom of its voice hammered the sheer walls of the Gate of the Mountains bringing a fall of boulders thudding into the pass a few hundred yards behind the travellers. "Were you not of the blessed kindred of Athalau, good Anemones, I should almost think you precipitous."

Erimenes emitted a squeal of rage and began tearing at the fringe of blue hair surrounding the base of his long, narrow head. The sentient glacier's inability—or refusal—to pronounce his name properly enraged him more than the living ice mountain's geologic deliberations.

Gloom filled the pass deepened by the mist spilling down from Guardian that formed a grayish layer thirty feet off the canyon floor. Light and warmth seldom penetrated here yet the cliff base was dotted with clumps of small blue flowers that seemed little daunted by the darkness and chill.

The Rampart Mountains had a heart of cold stone; the rocks of the canyon were those Guardian had swept up into himself on his slow advance from the Southern Waste. They had been ground smooth within the glacier's body and eventually tumbled from the face as it rolled ever onward. In time, Guardian would swallow them anew to begin the cycle anew unless climatic conditions did not permit him to continue his involuntary progress along the narrow canyon.

On one of those polished rocks sat Rann, apparently at ease. Watching him as she paced in front of the glacier, Moriana wondered at his outward calm. He didn't take frustration and delay philosophically; none of the Etuul blood ever had. Under normal conditions he should have been pacing even more vigorously than she. Instead he sat quiet and self-possessed.

Moriana wondered what had gotten into her cousin. His demeanor made her doubt he intended treachery. But still, he was *too* calm.

"Come and rest yourself, cousin," he said, smiling. "The glacier will take its own time answering. No amount of stalking to and fro will hurry it."

She paused, glaring at him more from reflex than anything else. She finally shrugged and seated herself on a rock not too near Rann's.

"I cannot rightfully deny entry to you, Princess, nor to you Irimunas, for you are rightfully Athalar." The words boomed out, making Moriana jump in surprise. Rann regarded her with calm indulgence. "But to let so many folk in as you propose? I do not know."

As before when talking to Guardian, Moriana found herself straining as if this would hurry the words. But that trick of colossal energies released when the World Spirit was summoned by Felarod that had given the glacier life had not otherwise altered its nature. Guardian thought and spoke glacier-fashion. If anything, this speech was a breakneck babble by its standards.

"I have been tricked before," rumbled Guardian. "A

human named Rann told me he followed to aid you, when in fact he meant you harm and that pleasant, near-sighted fellow with you—Fost, by name."

"Why can't he remember *my* name?" grumbled Erimenes.

"Yes, it was a mistake to let Rann into Athalau. His friends burned a hole through my back with a horrid fire sprite." The ice face shuddered. A sheet of ice split from the glacier with a resounding crack and fell, showering Moriana and Rann with sharp fragments. "It was worse than the ice worms who gnaw at me from within."

Rann yawned, stretched, stood.

"Prince Rann is a very bad man," he said. "You should not judge the rest of us by what he did."

Another pause. Rann stood with arms crossed while Moriana paced.

"You are right, human," came back the answer in time, when the sun had begun to bulge from the top of the eastern cliff and burn away the mist. "But still, so many. Would that not endanger Athalau?"

"As I understand it," Rann said, placing hands on hips, "your task was to preserve the city from agents of the Dark Ones. The princess has told you the *Zr'gsz* have freed Istu and once more ravage the continent. Presently, they will turn their attentions this way."

"All the more reason to guard my city with zeal."

"*My* city, indeed," grumbled Erimenes.

"Not even one as vast and mighty as you can hope to resist Istu, Guardian," said Rann. "But you hold within you the means of defeating him. You hold the Nexus by which Felarod drew up the wrath of the World Spirit. We must reach the Nexus. The World Spirit is the only power great enough to help us."

The glacier sat in silence, save for the creakings and groanings from deep within as the sun heated the miles-wide expanse of its body. Eventually Rann sat back down. Moriana joined him. The cool cloud had ceased to stream down Guardian's face. It was fast becoming warm. Moriana dozed.

"Very well."

She jumped at the words. Rann still sat on his rock, as collected as ever. He put aside his scimitar which he had been burnishing to a mirror sheen and stood, awaiting the glacier's verdict.

"My responsibility is clear. I must open a path large enough to permit many people to enter Athalau, that they might use the Nexus to bring down the Demon once more."

Moriana sighed in relief.

"Now, my friends, you must move back. This will not be easy for me and could endanger you if you're too close."

Moriana and Rann retreated and heard Guardian say, "So many people. Surely they can put an end to those cursed ice worms."

Out of sight around the winding of the Gate, Moriana found a chunk of dark quartz that had tumbled from above and sat. Her need for action thwarted by the nature of Guardian, she now found herself drawn irresistibly toward sleep. She heard Erimenes and Rann conversing in low, neutral tones, and let consciousness slip away.

An earsplitting crack awakened her. Others followed in rapid succession, louder and louder, mounting toward a crescendo of noise that dwarfed even the roar of Omizantrim in full eruption. She stared up the canyon, saw clouds of mist and glittering ice crystals billow forth like smoke.

She saw movement from the corner of her eye. Before she could react, Rann was upon her, wrapping steel-cable arms around her and forcing her back against the cliff.

Treachery! she thought, unable to fight her cousin off.

Erimenes's satchel swung from Rann's arm, and she wondered if the genie had entered into intrigue with the prince.

Then twenty tons of stone hurtled down, noiseless against the awful tumult, and buried the rock on which she had been sitting.

In time, hearing returned. In the ringing stillness Rann and Moriana picked themselves up from the tangle in which they'd lain at the foot of the cliff. They picked their way through the rubble strewn along the floor of the pass.

"Great Ultimate," Moriana whispered as they rounded the bend. Rann's fingers tightened on her arm.

It was as if a great maw had yawned wide in the glacier's face. Thirty feet tall, three times that in width, a passageway had been opened into the glacier's guts. Was it Moriana's imagination or could she truly see, far within, a glimmer of that subtle, lovely radiance given off by Athalau?

Erimenes was weeping.

"To think that my city might live again," he sobbed.

"You won't forget the ice worms, will you?" echoed Guardian's voice from the great, dark archway.

CHAPTER TWELVE

The Steppe was carpeted with wildflowers, the white blooms covering the land like early snowfall but rippling like the surface of a lake changing to the whims of the wind. Sitting atop a knoll whose bare skeleton of rock protruded like a lizard's spine, Fost surveyed the straggling line of men and women wading knee-deep through the flowers and tried to sort his feelings.

One hundred thirty-eight Ethereals had followed the crippled Selamyl from their village to take the arduous path to Athalau, leaving behind a handful of the aged and the reluctant. Ten of the travellers had died already. Fost wondered how many more would follow.

There were dark things in the Ramparts, not natural life but one of the grimmer legacies of the first War of Powers. A score of times they had come forth to beset the travellers, occasionally in the daytime and often at night. In the darkness all Fost had been able to make out of the attackers were glowing eyes and gaping maws filled with teeth that glinted wetly in the moonlight. Sometimes the attackers were many and small, but savage. Other times it would be a great, lone beast like the creatures that had come on them during the day. Those had been similar, huge armored things with spiked tails and burning demon eyes. Fost was almost grateful that most of the attacks occurred at night.

Synalon had plied her battle magic, accounting for most of the creatures when they came. She and Fost had complete charge of the caravan's safety. The Ethereals had no concept of self-defense, nor any will to do so. They would stand looking vacant, even wistful, as a swarm of creatures like stinking scaled rats tore them to shreds. It was tribute to Synalon's sorcery more than Fost's bladecraft that so few had fallen.

"Yet they keep on," he marvelled aloud. He had feared the Ethereals would lose heart and turn back as soon as misfortune fell. But they took the dangers and the deaths the same way they took the trudging hardship of the trek itself, with a stolid lack of concern. Fost began to see, as Rann had before him, that beneath their veneer of fecklessness and fragility these Ethereals had a strength of their own.

"We've made good time," said Synalon from behind him. "Three hundred miles in two weeks, afoot. We shall soon be at the Gate of the Mountains."

Fost nodded, looking back down at the long file of Ethereals. Many straggled to one side or the other of the winding trail foraging for berries and edible roots. It was something the Ethereals were good at, and supplies had not yet become a problem.

Nor did the straggling bother Fost. As long as none drifted out of sight, it mattered little whether the Ethereals marched in line or not. With only two of them to guard so large a flock, it was luck alone that had kept the varied wolves from taking more.

"Why so downcast?" Synalon chided him. She flung out her arms and drew in a deep breath, causing her breasts to lift dramatically in the thin shirt. The nipples stood out in bold relief against the taut fabric, and he saw their ruddy color. "It's a lovely day. The sun is high and hot and feels good on the skin, and the wind from the Ramparts still bears the chill of the Waste at its back to take the sting from the heat. And the flowers raise their heads all about, and their perfume fills the air. Aren't these pleasing to you, my Fost?"

"I never thought I'd hear such sentiments from you."

The music of her laugh filled the air.

"You've spent too much time with my dour sister. She's always striving after tomorrow. I am content to live with today, taking the sensations it gives me and enjoying them as best I can." She looked at Ziore. "Don't go all sour on me, little nun. I do lay plans against the future—aye, and hopes as well. But there are days when I immerse myself in the moment and revel in the million flavors of life."

"Then why did you ally yourself with the Dark Ones?" Fost asked before good sense could stop the words. "They are the foes of life."

A shadow passed over her finely sculpted face like a cloud crossing the sun.

"I thought they could give me power, and that power would open gates to new sensations. What must it be like to stride among the stars as Istu did? To know at once the chill and heat of the Void, to shout into airlessness and race the light of suns?" She sighed deeply. "But you shall now hear something I seldom say. I was wrong. The Dark knows no bitterer foe than I now."

Does it? Fost wondered, remembering the dying firelight and the great black Dwarf beyond. But the perverse imp of defiance that made him blurt his question about Synalon's earlier pact with the Elder Lords had retreated, and he said nothing. Synalon loved him with a fiercely hot passion, physically at least, and he both feared and hoped that love extended to other dimensions. But she remained the mad, mercurial creature who had ruled the Sky City with a whim of steel and flame, and it wasn't safe to presume too far upon her good feelings.

"Your philosophy is similar to what Erimenes now believes," Ziore commented.

"Ah, but I'm wiser than your Athalar sage, little sister," Synalon cried, "For I have long since learned that lesson and did not have to wait until I was dead." Her hand shot out with a speed that reminded Fost of the *Zr'gsz* blood in her veins. She caught him by the wrist. She drew his scarred hand to her lips and kissed it gently. "And now, my dear Fost, you shall learn why my way is wisest, to wring each moment dry of sensation without thought to the next."

"What?"

"Look to the northern horizon, dear one."

He did. His heart dropped into the bottom of his belly.

Like a fleet of ships upon the waves, they rode the air in a bobbing black line across the sky. Still too distant to be clearly seen, shimmering slightly in the waves of heat rising from the Steppe, the skyrafts grew even as Fost watched. Form and detail sharpened. His sword slid into his hand with a fluid motion.

Synalon sent her mount stiff-legged down the face of the knoll, sliding and staggering amid a slippage of small, loose stones. Fost followed, hoping his dog wouldn't break a leg.

Synalon called for the Ethereals to close up into a group.

"No!" Fost shouted, and quailed as she turned a furious look on him. "Have them scatter and hide the best they can. The Hissers are missile troops when they ride their rafts. If the Ethereals clump together, *Zr'gsz* darts will go through them like a sickle through ripe wheat."

Her dog reached the foot of the ridge and galloped toward where Selamyl still dragged himself inexorably forward with his cane. Fost's beast pounded after.

She let him do the talking. He hurriedly outlined the danger to the Ethereals' leader, and what must be done. Selamyl smiled benignly.

"Holding perfectly still is a thing my folk are good at," he said. He turned and began speaking, gesturing into the scrub around them.

One by one the Ethereals disappeared. Fost's eyes widened at the completeness with which they vanished.

The Ethereals lacked wilderness craft but they could divorce their minds utterly from their bodies and drift among their dreams, immune to physical discomfort. Their bodies bent into unlikely shapes to take advantage of the sparse cover—and then they froze. In a matter of minutes, Fost saw only Selamyl. Then he, too, disappeared.

"Impressive," said Synalon. "But remember the *Zr'gsz* are airborne. They'll hunt the Ethereals from a different perspective."

"But Oracle told me their eyesight is poor. Their eyes are attuned to movement rather than detail. If the Ethereals stay immobile, we have a chance."

"I think I can help," Ziore said urgently. "This close to Athalau my powers are greater, like Erimenes's. I cannot turn the Hissers away, but I can slow small numbers of them."

Anything that helped counteract the blindingly swift reflexes of the Vridzish would be of immeasurable aid.

Synalon's eyes glowed beneath half-lowered lids. Her lips moved as she spoke to herself. Ziore shuddered and drew away from the sorceress. Fost felt a thrill as though his nerve ends were lightly brushed by powers beyond his ken.

The rafts drew near, a score, two dozen. Fost's eyes unfocused. He blinked, realizing that there was a blurring of the line of dark stone rafts. A Hisser, highborn from his size and green cuirass, pointed and shouted a sibilant command. The formation split to avoid the disturbance, some going around, others up and over.

The air darkened, swirled, coalesced. A winged shape hung in air, a tiger's head swiveling at the end of a long snake's neck. At least six legs dangled from the bloated body. Fost couldn't be sure because the thing swam in and out of focus.

As the leading raft passed overhead, the thing half rolled, drumming the air with its wings. A claw shot up, up to and *through* the underside of the raft. The pilot hunched over the globe at the rear suddenly gave a ringing shriek. The claw drew down pulling the Hisser's smoking guts with it through the skystone.

"Great Ultimate," Fost whispered.

"I think you've seen this magic before. Back in the tower of Kest-i-Mond."

He recalled the striped ape monster, blinded by a deathbolt that failed to save the enchanter who cast it, and the nightmare chase it had given him through the corridors of the sorceror's keep. Fost's blade had passed harmlessly through it, and it flowed through solid walls and doorways as though they were air. Only by luring it into an open fumarole Kest-i-Mond had built his castle over had Fost avoided death. Synalon's magic now was identical with what he'd faced—and barely triumphed over.

Slung stones and javelins sleeted down at the winged creature. They passed through it like smoke. Clawed limbs lashed out again and again. The monster delighted in eviscerating *Zr'gsz* and tearing out hearts to fling them in the faces of its foes.

"They'll never get past that horror," said Fost. Relief almost overwhelmed his dread of the monster.

Synalon frowned. A spot of darkness appeared in the air beside the winged beast, grew. The tiger-headed thing saw it, struck at it with a claw. The beast's arm disappeared. The black hole caught the arm and drew the monster in. It uttered a wail that raked down Fost's spine. Then it was gone. The hole winked out of existence.

Synalon's hair crackled with sparks.

"Damn! They've a mage with them who draws on Istu's power."

As she spoke, a beam of black light lanced down at her. She gestured contemptuously. It bent abruptly to dig a smoking rent in the ground.

"Even with the Demon's help he has no touch for offensive magic," Synalon sneered. "But I fear he can negate any spells I attack with."

"Is Istu near?" asked Fost, peering all around.

"No, but his power can augment that of any he favors. I myself sought to tap the power of his sleeping mind—as you may recall."

He had a fleeting urge to strike her. He remembered too well. She had planned to sacrifice Moriana to the sleeping Demon as a bribe for his assistance. Fost had barely rescued the golden-haired princess.

Synalon's hands moved, weaving a new spell. A crack opened in the earth below the sky fleet. A billion black hornets billowed forth to surround the rafts. Stoic as they were, the Hissers began to scream and fling themselves over the edges of their vessels to escape the maddening stings.

Fost couldn't see the enemy sorceror. But he must have acted because the swarm became a cloud of tiny sparks burning unbearably bright, falling to the Steppe in an incandescent rain.

The rafts were almost overhead. Arrows began to pelt the landscape, javelins and stones striking with thumps like hail. Synalon's lips drew back taut.

"They know what we're doing. They're trying to slay the Ethereals."

"They're shooting blind," Fost said. Evidently the Vridzish had spotted the Ethereals at a distance and knew they were near, but couldn't pinpoint them. With their eerie self-control, many of the Ethereals died without a sound, without stirring.

The rafts came close enough to speed missiles at the mounted pair. Fost steeled himself. He had no shield and his mail vest would provide little protection against hard-driven arrows.

Synalon waved her hand. The barrage of missiles dropped, arrows and javelins aflame, the stones molten lumps.

"Had they enough archers they could swamp me," she said. "But they don't."

The skyrafts veered off, milling aimlessly in the sky. Fost awaited a new spell from Synalon. None came.

"I do what their mage does," she explained. "I conserve strength."

The rafts spread out, formed a circle around the two and touched down. The craft each held six to eight Vridzish. Six to eight too many for Fost's liking.

The Hissers rushed forth, the nobles splendid in their cloaks and armor, the paler scaled lowborn warriors clad in loincloths and carrying obsidian spears and axes. Some of the latter carried shortswords of plain steel looted from a human armory. Oracle had predicted this would happen. Obsidian held a keener edge than steel but it was brittle. As Vridzish weapons were broken or lost, they had to be replaced. Picking up fallen human weapons proved easier than chipping new ones from glass.

It was small comfort. Two of the shortsword-armed Hissers stopped and hauled an Ethereal woman to her feet. Her face never lost its dreamy look as they plunged their swords repeatedly into her body.

Synalon pointed three times with her finger. Three lines of blue lightning stabbed forth. The two slayers and an officer nearby charred and fell. Synalon laughed delightedly at her handiwork.

"The whoreson can't guard against that!"

The Vridzish commander shouted and waved his sword. The Hissers advanced on Fost and Synalon at a trot. Both dismounted, preparing for battle.

Lightning flared in such rapid succession that Fost was momentarily deafened and blinded. But if the *Zr'gsz* mage couldn't fend off her deadly short range lightning, neither had Synalon speed or strength to cinder all their enemies before they reached the embattled pair.

Instinct made him lash out even before his vision

cleared. Fost felt his blade slash through something brittle; then came the unmistakable sensation of steel cleaving flesh. A Hisser gasped and fell, the broken halves of a mace dropping to the Steppe.

A score of the reptiles surrounded the pair. Fost's dog snarled and leaped, taking a deep gash down one side but bearing two of them to the ground. A trio of low-born Hissers closed on Fost. His eyes searched rapidly and found a small stone lying near his foot. He kicked it between two of the Vridzish.

They were stupid. Their eyes followed the rock and then not even their inhuman speed saved them from Fost's whining blade. He swung left, right, left again and black blood gushed over him.

A noble loomed up ahead swinging an obsidian-edged sword. Fost hurled himself backward. The black stone blade moaned past. Fost felt nothing but as he backpedalled he saw that his tunic was parted in a line running across his chest and blood welled through a sleeve.

Synalon glided forward, her rapier twitching before her like a giant insect's antenna. She attacked the officer, and he retreated a step. Steel rang on stone, and then the tip of the slender sword whipped around a parry to score a heavily muscled forearm.

The *Zr'gsz* whistled in rage and struck, battling Synalon's blade out of the way. She danced back. He smiled then, teeth bright in his dark face, and advanced.

As quickly as he had advanced, he stopped. His eyes rolled up in his head showing greenish white balls. He stiffened. Every muscle swelled into relief on his powerful body, and he began vibrating in the grip of an awful spasm. A keening sounded only to be drowned in a froth of blood. He fell, kicking grooves in the soil. He finally lay still.

"My sword skill's too paltry to put all my faith in it," Synalon said from behind Fost. "Come on then, bastards. My venom's good for many more!"

And they did come on, barely giving Fost time to clamber to his feet. He and Synalon fought back to back as the Vridzish rushed. It seemed that each new attack must be the last; Fost didn't know how he parried the blinding strokes of mace and axe and sword. The *Zr'gsz* crowded in on all sides, jostling each other, making it difficult to attack. Fost buried his sword over and over until he was black with their blood. Synalon's poisonous sting littered the ground with convulsing victims. But there were too many Hissers, and beyond the circle of hard, dark faces Fost saw several score others still hunting down the Ethereals.

His face and arms stung from myriad shallow cuts. He dared not even glance over his shoulder at Synalon, but from her constant low-voiced cursing he guessed she was in no better shape.

He refused to have it end like this. The thought of dying filled him with rage.

"O, Ust!" he bellowed. "Give me the strength to slay these sons of darkness!" Madness came on him, and he waded in among the Vridzish.

He scattered a dozen of the lower caste warriors. Another officer faced him. His speed outmatched Fost's berserker fury. Each stroke of his mace drove Fost's blade perilously near the man's own flesh. Sweat blinded Fost.

Then the noble's head departed its shoulders atop a column of blood.

"Again I greet you, O Chosen of Ust," said Jennas, hetwoman of the bear clan, as she flicked black blood from the six-foot blade of her greatsword. "This is getting to be a habit," she added in a quieter voice.

The timely arrival of the Ust-alayakits threw the *Zr'gsz* into confusion. Jennas wheeled her bear Chubchuk away and launched herself against their common foe. The long hair and body fat of the bears provided excellent armor; the beasts absorbed savage blows without harm. Fost saw the plumed *Zr'gsz* captain fell a male bear rider only to have another rider roll down on him like an avalanche. The rider was a grossly fat woman with a steel cap strapped atop wiry red curls. The Hisser threw up his shining green blade. A giant axe swept down with all the force of that huge body. The green sword snapped. The axehead hurled on. Through gorgeous plume, through green helmet, through skull and body until it sank into the cold ground of the Steppe. The *Zr'gsz* was sheared in two, the halves quivering over dead legs for a second before falling in separate directions.

The Hissers ran for their rafts. The fat woman laughed and threw her giant axe into the air. It cartwheeled up until it was outlined against the swollen disk of the setting sun. Then it returned, a huge hand snared it and the battle was done.

Flames danced high against the nighttime sky. Drunken and boisterous, the bear riders staggered in a victory dance around the bonfire.

Fost sat with Jennas and the monstrous redheaded woman, Vancha Broad-Ax. Her great axe, Little Sister, was laid carefully on the ground by her huge rump where she patted it from time to time and crooned appreciatively to it. The Bear folk still talked about the way she'd struck down the *Zr'gsz* noble that afternoon. Fost had never seen anything like it, and to judge from the talk of the Ust-alayakits, neither had they.

"I had the proper motivation," Vancha boomed in a voice as big as she was. "Ust has kept little Jennas apprised of what goes on in the world north of our Steppe, by means of visions." She laid a companionly slab of arm across "little Jennas's" shoulders, who was every bit as tall as Fost and just as powerful. The hetwoman smiled, but her amber eyes were troubled.

"It's good to see you again, Fost," the hetwoman said as Vancha poured herself a fresh mug of rakshak, the liquid fire that these nomads drank. "It is as Ust foretold." She looked away quickly.

Fost felt a tingling and glanced over his shoulder. Synalon sat away from the fire on a saddle taken from the corpse of Fost's dog. Her arms were folded beneath her breasts, and she regarded the courier with sullen, smouldering eyes. He bit his lip and turned away.

When the Vridzish had fled, Synalon had seized him and hugged him tight. Her lips had sought his; the slaying had aroused passions in her that wouldn't be put off. Yet he had shrugged her off to share a tearful embrace with Jennas. Only when he had literally felt Synalon's gaze laid across his back like a whip had he turned from Jennas to see the anger and hurt glowing in Synalon's eyes.

Though Synalon drank nothing, she had grown more sullen since the sun fell from the sky. When a young bravo had swaggered up and tried to put his arm around her, she had given him a glare charged with more than anger. He cried out in a high-pitched voice and fled, stumbling and falling into the fire and being badly singed before his fellows dragged him out. The bear riders were of a rough humor and thought this a capital joke. Fost read darker implications in it.

"So you're herding these two-legged sheep to Athalau," Vancha said, her immense paw settling on his arm. She nodded toward the Ethereals, who sat like so many pallid statues. Silently Fost counted the unmoving figures. They didn't number one hundred. There was only one way of learning if they would be enough for the dangerous task ahead of them.

"Well, we're glad to strike a blow against the foul lizards. We'll gladly escort you to the Gate of the Mountains, won't we, Jennas?"

"What say?" Jennas asked, shaking herself. "Oh, yes, we must do anything we can to help. Ust wills it."

Vancha's pig eyes, as green and hard as emeralds, narrowed into slits amid fat.

"Something's eating you, girl." The eyes flicked to Fost. "I think I know what it is, too."

"Thank you, Vancha, but you do not know."

Fost studied the hetwoman. He had thought her handsome at first, but in the months they had spent together chasing Moriana all over the Sundered Realm, he had come to know the beauty in her strongly sculpted features, her high, proud cheekbones and close-cropped shock of reddish hair. And in ways he loved her, though he told himself Moriana took preeminence.

He hated himself for hurting her, but she knew from the start that he loved Moriana and would go to her if possible. It hadn't stopped them from becoming lovers.

It would be harder for Jennas to understand why they couldn't resume their relationship. He set down his mug, stretched, managed a good imitation of a yawn that turned into the real thing.

"It has been one hell of a day," he said. "I'm going to bed."

Vancha rose and gave him a fond, spine-crushing squeeze. Across the campfire Ziore told dirty jokes to the younger warriors. She knew a surprising number for a nun. The trip to Medurim had given her more than any of the warriors.

He nodded to Jennas, not able to meet her eyes. He turned and walked off into the darkness, away from them, away from Synalon, too. It had all become too much for him. He wanted only to be alone.

He heard the crunch of a step behind him. His spine turned icy with premonition.

"Fost." It was Jennas, soft-voiced, diffident. "There's something I must tell you." She took him by the shoulders.

Her hands were slapped away.

"Get away from him!" screamed Synalon. "I'll share him with my sister, but he's not going to be soiled by any filthy barbarian bitch!"

Jennas turned to face the sorceress. Her face was calm in the orange firelight. Around the fire voices were raised, asking what was amiss. Torches were lifted and the bear riders came at a run, sensing something deadly wrong.

"You thought to sneak off with him and seduce him," hissed Synalon. "Perhaps you got away with this before. But he's too good for the likes of you!"

"He can make his own choices," Jennas said in a level voice.

"He'll not choose you!" Synalon lunged forward. Fost caught the flash of steel and gasped.

The bear riders growled and closed in.

"No! Get back!" cried Jennas as she sidestepped, dodging the gleaming arc of Synalon's dagger. "It's between me and her! Leave us be!"

Reluctantly, the bear riders stopped where they stood.

"That's enough," Jennas told Synalon. "I've no quarrel with you."

"I challenge you!" spat Synalon. Her face was an icy mask of fury. "I'll not even use magic. But still I'll have your heart, you slut!"

She lunged forward, her right arm a blur. Jennas jumped back, not quite fast enough. The slim dagger opened a long gash in her arm. Her face hardened. A heavy-bladed knife appeared in her right hand. She crouched, holding the weapon low for a disembowelling stroke, while Synalon circled her like a stalking panther.

"Fost, Fost, what's going on?" cried Ziore. "Can't you stop them?"

He started forward.

"No!" Jennas cried without turning. "You can do nothing. This was meant to be."

Synalon moved in. Jennas's blade met hers with a skirring sound. Grimacing, the princess struck again and again. She could not penetrate the steel ring of Jennas's defenses. With a catlike scream of rage, Synalon launched herself at Jennas. Though the bear rider was heavier, Synalon bore her to the ground. But only for a moment. Jennas's brawny arm caught Synalon by one pale shoulder and flung her away.

In an instant Jennas was astride the prostrate princess, eyes wide, dagger poised for the deathstroke. Then the killing light went out of her eyes. She lowered her arm.

Synalon thrust upward. The needle-slim blade bit through mail and leather, punctured skin, slipped between ribs to pierce the woman's heart. Jennas jerked, reeled backward and fell heavily. The sorceress jumped to her feet waving the bloody dagger.

"Kill her! Kill the witch!" somebody cried as the bear riders rushed to their chieftain's aid.

"No!" Jennas's voice was strong but ragged with pain. "It—ah!—it was a fair fight. She challenged and I accepted."

"She struck when you stayed your hand," growled a bear rider.

"The fight was fair." Jennas's body shook. She clamped her jaw against the pain. Blood welled around her teeth. "You must not harm her. She must yet play her part or all . . . oh . . . all is lost."

She looked around wildly.

"Vancha! Promise me. You will aid the outlanders as we promised. Do it for our people, or they shall . . . pass."

The redhead thrust herself forward, shouldering aside the warriors as if they were children.

"I will," she said through the tears streaming down her cheeks.

Jennas's back arched. When the spasm passed, she said weakly, "Fost."

"I'm here." He knelt by her side and took her head, cradling it in his lap. His own face shone with tears.

"I know," she said in an almost normal voice. "Do not blame yourself. This was all . . . foretold." She seized his arm in an iron grip. "Keep well, Longstrider.

For the sake of your people and mine . . . and your golden-haired princess. And, ah . . . remember Jennas, who loved you."

Her head lolled back on lifeless muscles.

The Ust-alayakits surged toward Synalon, raising blades and torches. A huge figure stepped between them and her. An axe head glittered against the stars, came howling down to split a stone in a shower of sparks.

"No!" roared Vancha Broad-Ax. "You'll obey our hetwoman's command or I swear I'll butcher the lot of you!" Her face dissolved in tears, her huge body shaking. But the fat-ringed hands that gripped the black haft were as steady as rock. All knew that what Vancha Broad-Ax promised, she performed. The Ust-alayakits drew back.

Heedless, Fost let Jennas fall and lunged for Synalon, ripping his sword from his scabbard.

"You murdering bitch!" he shouted, cocking his arm to run her through.

"Will it be you to break the oath, then?" she asked, a smile playing at the corners of her mouth.

"What do you mean?"

"The oath we swore in Tolviroth Acerte. Was it just words to you?"

"But you've broken it, you murderous . . . *thing*. You killed Jennas."

"Oh? Perhaps my memory fails me," she said, tilting her head as if listening to a distant voice. "When we swore that oath together, I do not recall Jennas being there."

The strength went out of Fost. His sword tip drooped to the ground. His knees gave way beneath him.

He sensed a nearness, looked up to see Vancha against the stars.

"What Jennas commanded shall be done, outlander," she said. "We shall aid you in reaching the Gate of the Mountains, and you and your witch-woman will come to no harm. But I beg you, stay out of my sight from this moment on. I would not betray my hetwoman's last wish!"

With a sob, she turned and fled. One by one, the Ust-alayakits turned and walked away until he was alone with Synalon and Ziore and a grief as boundless as the uncaring skies above.

CHAPTER THIRTEEN

Fost stared in amazement. When the bird rider patrol had spotted them at the head of the pass and winged low enough to shout down that the way into Athalau lay open, Fost assumed that Guardian had opened a narrow passage as he had done previously. Or Moriana had found an iceworm tunnel and convinced the glacier to let the humans use it. Instead, a great arched tunnel yawned ahead. Synalon's dog trotted around the bend and stopped beside the bear Fost rode.

"My sister's done well."

Fost only grunted. He could still scarcely bear to speak to Synalon. Though last night, only a night after Jennas's murder, when she had come to him—that had required no talking.

Wings cracking like sails in a stiff wind, a flight of bird riders passed low overhead and disappeared through the entrance. Fost heard the scraping of a cane, and Selamyl came into view. He stopped. His face lit with awe and wonder, and then he dragged himself on.

Vancha Broad-Ax appeared at the head of the file of Ethereals. Seeing the entry opened in the living ice, she stopped and stared for a long moment. She turned then to Fost, looked through him, wheeled her huge mount and went back the way she had come. Shouts echoing down the canyon told Fost the bear riders were going home. Jennas's last command had been fulfilled.

Another shout brought Fost's head around. His heart jumped in spite of grief and bone-deep weariness, and he kicked the bear into a lumbering run toward the tunnel and the woman and the blue figure just stepping from it.

In all his fevered adolescent fantasies, Fost had never even remotely imagined that he might pass a night in fabled Athalau, lying abed on silken sheets with a beautiful princess. Of course, if he had dreamed of the horrors and travails that went along with the fulfillment of that never-entertained fantasy, he probably would have slit his wrists.

The six of them had exchanged terse greetings over dinner in a dormitory in the center of Athalau, next to the Palace of Esoteric Wisdom. On convincing Guardian to open the pathway, Rann had sent back a message via Moriana for a squadron of bird riders to come ahead and provide defensive strength. Their meat that evening was an antelope the flyers had shot in the foothills, quartered and flown in.

After dinner, Fost and Moriana bid good night to Synalon and Rann. Fost had dreaded this moment but Synalon did not explode with temper, did nothing but smile and nod in a specially meaningful way before going off with her eunuch cousin. Moriana watched them go.

"They're up to something," she said quietly. "I mistrust them."

They ensconced Ziore and Erimenes in a room on the bottom floor of the dormitory where the sounds of their reunion wouldn't keep the others awake all night. Then Fost and Moriana climbed the stairs to their chamber on the second floor for a more intimate welcoming of their own.

Half-drowsing afterward, Fost lay on his side, running his fingers through Moriana's hair. It was fine and soft—like Synalon's. He shook himself. He didn't want to take that pathway.

"What's the matter?" Moriana asked sleepily.

"I was just wondering about this room. The bed

smells fresh and these sheets certainly don't seem two hundred years old."

"We had Rann's bird riders fly in the bedding this afternoon," she said. "As for the sheets, they're of Athalar make and meant to last."

"It's just as well," he said, glancing down at the rumpled bedding.

She smiled lazily.

"Let's test them again," she said, reaching for him.

Finishing, they drowsed for a time, woke, made love again. Privately Fost marvelled at his own response. Synalon had been wringing him dry every night since the first time in the Ethereal's village. But he wanted to lose himself in the taste and scent and feel of Moriana, the textures and tempos of her body, and it was as if he hadn't been with a woman in weeks.

When they were done, he rose and poured them both wine from a crystal decanter.

"It's hard to believe this hasn't gone to vinegar," he said, carrying the cups to the bed.

"The Athalar magics were versatile." She sipped the wine. "I hope their knowledge can be recovered."

They had made a good start that day, and a vital one. As they had walked the long road leading from the Gate of the Mountains down into the softly glowing city, Fost had remarked that he hoped they would be able to find the Nexus in time. It'd be brutal irony to make it all the way here and then not find that which they sought.

"I don't know where it lies," Erimenes said. "But I think it will be no problem. The Ethereals have Athalau in their blood. Being present in the city works on me, makes my powers grow. They will know where they are to go, mark my words."

And it was true. Selamyl had no sooner set foot on the rim of the depression in which the city lay than he stopped and went as rigid as a hunting dog catching

a scent. Fost thought it simple wonder at first. There
was reason enough for that. One didn't have to be of
Athalar descent to marvel at the beauty of the place,
its soaring spires and well-ordered colonnades, a sym-
phony of form and shape and color. A smooth, seam-
less substance paved the road that sloped gently before
them into the heart of the city. Over all shone the
sourceless, shifting, polychromatic and restful light of
Athalau.

Here and there blocks or stalactites of ice had fallen
and damaged buildings. Fost, Moriana and Rann, who
had all been there before, kept hands on sword hilts
and a watchful eye for iceworms. These creatures, some
big enough to swallow a man whole, infested the glacier
to Guardian's annoyance, and had over the years fil-
tered down to lair in the city.

But neither the unconscious vandalism of falling
ice nor the invasion of the deadly worms detracted from
Athalau's beauty. Yet it was not the beauty that gripped
Selamyl or the others as they came up behind him to
stand transfixed.

"I . . . I remember," Selamyl said in a distant voice.
"This was meant to be." As the quiet syllables echoed
through the vast dome of ice, he set off at a vigorous
walk down the road, neglecting now to use his cane.

No one had seen an Ethereal hurry before, let alone
a crippled one, but one by one the rest came out of their
trance and followed, some trotting to catch up. As if
he had walked these boulevards every day of his life,
Selamyl led them to a wide plaza at the center of the
city, which was dominated by the most striking building
in Athalau, a tower carved from a single giant ruby
whose top was lost in the ice above. He turned down
the street flanking the plaza and walked quickly to a
building whose front was mostly blocked by a great
chunk of ice fallen from above, crushing the marble
portico.

He looked in dismay at the obstruction, and then

down at the sinister rusty stains on the pavement under his feet.

"What has happened here? We must get in."

Rann stepped forward, a curious half-smile on his hips. He scuffed at one stain with the toe of his boot.

"Blood," he explained. "Mine."

Fost and Moriana looked at each other. They knew this place, and what had happened to it. It was the Palace of Esoteric Wisdom, once holding the Amulet of Living Flame and the treacherous Destiny Stone. The ice had not fallen by random chance. Erimenes had called it down to crush Rann and his bird riders, who had tracked Fost and the others here to seize the Amulet for Synalon.

But the way into the Palace was not entirely blocked. Fost scrambled up with Rann close behind. Together they helped Selamyl over the rubble. He led them through the nave without a glance at the altar which had held the two talismans. To a stairway, down; deep below, beyond a door Erimenes swore had not been opened since before his time, to where the Nexus lay.

It didn't look like much. It was only a pattern traced on the floor in some dull metal, a square mandala with various nodes, widening in the metallic track in a distribution that said chance but whispered some hidden design. It stretched thirty feet on a side with ten feet of floor surrounding it, a domed ceiling rising twenty feet overhead. Fost looked at Moriana, who shrugged. He could tell by the disappointment in her eyes that she felt nothing of power here.

But Selamyl walked in with eyes aglow to the center of the Nexus and fell to his knees in rapture. And one by one, the Ethereals followed him in, trancelike in their movements, and each moved to a spot on the design and dropped in turn to a kneeling posture, as if by prearrangement.

Now Fost sat on the edge of the bed gazing down at the princess.

"Tell me what happened after you left Brev," she asked, and he did so. She caught her breath when he mentioned waking in the middle of the night to see Synalon in conversation with the black Dwarf, though he admitted it might have been some trick of the light. Moriana said nothing to this, but her expression was eloquently skeptical.

She squeezed his hand during the account of the battle with the skyrafts. When he came to what happened next he broke down and sobbed and, holding him, Moriana cried, too. She had been jealous of Jennas once, but had come to honor and even love the brave, wise woman who had done so much to aid Fost.

"I don't know why Synalon did it," Fost said over and over, shaking his head. "It was insane. She had no way of knowing the bear riders wouldn't tear her apart."

"She is insane," agreed Moriana. "Rann has spoken of difficulties he had with her, trying to build a strategy on the shifting sands of her whim." She sat up, gathering the sheets around her, drew up her knees and rested her chin on them, frowning. "But perhaps it was no mere freak of her temper that made her act so. Perhaps it was planned, to impede our bringing the Ethereals here."

Fost looked away. A cold lump settled in the pit of his stomach.

"There was more to it than that," he said reluctantly. And he told her the story of his seduction by Synalon.

When he finished he heard nothing but her measured breathing at his back. He thought he'd hurt her too badly for forgiveness and waited to be ordered from the room.

What came weren't harsh words but a gentle touch on his shoulder.

"Fost, dear Fost." She raised herself, leaning against him. "I should have warned you. I saw she admired you." She took his chin and swung his face to hers. "I know my sister's ways. She is beautiful and knows how to wield her beauty like a paintbrush or a sword. I think I would not have things otherwise. The man who could resist her attentions once would be more than human." Her mouth twisted. "Or less than a man, like Rann." She kissed him.

A while later he said, "But what of us? Do you think she'll make trouble because it's you I want?"

"Didn't she say something about sharing you with me? I think she accepts our relationship—for now." He felt her draw away. "Do you want that, too? To parcel yourself out to both her and me?"

He took her in his arms and let his body answer.

The city came to life again for the first time in almost two hundred years. The caravans Moriana had dispatched from Tolviroth Acerte weeks before arrived bringing sorely needed supplies. The merchant fleet lay at anchor in Dawngold Bay thirty miles east of Athalau, and Guardian obligingly opened a new passageway to permit the supplies to be portaged overland and into the city. He did so eagerly because it was always a source of deep sadness for the glacier that he had watched over the death of the city. Now he could take part in Athalau's rebirth. Sometimes he chuckled to himself, the sounds of his pleasure booming through the tunnels and streets.

No one felt mirth at the word the fleet brought with them. The party Moriana sent out to meet the ships was astonished to find twice as many ships riding anchor in the mouth of the Gulf of Veluz. The extra vessels were refugees fleeing the wrath of Istu, which had descended on Tolviroth Acerte not long after Moriana and the rest departed. The survivors were shocked and scarcely coherent but reported that the city had been captured, not utterly obliterated as Kara-Est had been. It was small comfort.

Under the surprisingly steady guidance of the youthful Cerestan, refugees began to stream into Athalau

from Brev. And not only from Brev and Bilsinx but
from as far north as the Black March. Word had spread
that mankind would make its last stand in the icebound
citadel of the south. Perhaps, as Rann speculated, Zak'-
zar had spread the rumors himself in hope of straining
Athalau's tenuous supply lines to breaking. There were
other cities that had yet to suffer the attentions of the
Sky City: Port Zorn in the east, Duth and Kolinth and
those of the other City States that had not lain in the
City's path from the Black March to Medurim, Thailot
and Deepwater and the Sjeddland cities west of the
Thails. But it was also true that Athalau offered the
best hope for humanity's survival—the only hope.

If it was the Vridzish's wish to weaken the defenders
of Athalau with hunger, that tactic was in vain. The
supplies Moriana had ordered to the lost city were
plentiful and great stores of travellers' fare lay in the
vaults beneath Athalau. This was magically preserved
dried food meant to sustain life over long journeys. It
was scarcely palatable, but it did what it was intended
to do. Moreover, game teemed in the Ramparts this
season; hunting was good, if risky. Eventually the food
stocks would run low, but Rann doubted the Fallen
Ones would feel they had the leisure to wait. Every day
the humans explored Athalau increased their chances of
being able to successfully summon the World Spirit. It
soon became apparent that the *Zr'gsz* would not wait.
Bird riders reported that the Sky City passed first Bilsinx
and then Brev, and Istu smashed each city flat. But they
were abandoned by then. He reaped few souls for his
collection.

The *Zr'gsz* reacted violently when the survivors of
the fight with the Palace of Esoteric Wisdom reported
back, launching savage attacks against the long columns
of refugees and airlifting in an army of foot soldiers
from the north, risking the increasingly rare skyrafts in
the face of the fierce storms that blew in from the Joreal
Ocean in this season.

And there was another danger they faced.

Prince Rann was in the field again, at the head of the reunited forces of the Sky City. No longer were the lizard men and their stone rafts a frightening novelty as they had been when Moriana led the aerial fleet against the City in the Sky; no longer were the Sky Citizens fighting halfheartedly to defend the throne of a queen many thought an usurper and worse. The soldiers of the City and their allies fought with all the skill and courage for which they were renowned—and with a cornered animal savagery, too. When Rann's eagles spread their wings above the rafts of the People, the slaughter they worked was fearful.

Despite all anyone could do, the slaughter the Vridzish worked on the refugees was frightful, too. It was impossible to protect the mile-long columns of trudging, desperate folk. But Cerestan did well, luring an army three times the size of his into an envelopment and massacring it to a man, with a force of Bilsinxt and Sky City cavalry. After that, the attacks on the refugees slacked off.

Encouraging as the humans' successes in the field were, they were insubstantial. It was a bitter war; if the humans lost, they were doomed, but all they could win was a respite, the chance to follow one breath with another until the City and the Demon arrived.

Moriana desperately prepared herself for the coming duel with Istu. The Ethereals had moved into the Palace of Esoteric Wisdom as if it had been built for them and began a strict regimen of meditation and study. Moriana studied, too, in the vast and varied Athalau libraries. Her knowledge grew, but not her confidence.

There was no way to test the Nexus or try calling upon the World Spirit until the actual time came to face Istu. The summoning of the World Spirit had been too much for Felarod and nine-tenths of his Hundred; already Moriana had fewer Ethereals to work with. She dared not risk them prematurely.

She bore the burden well. Sometimes she awakened Fost at night with weeping, but when he held her in his arms all she could speak of was her fear that the best wasn't good enough, that the evil she had loosed upon the world would consume it and humankind.

When she returned to fitful drowsing, Fost brooded over the near certainty that even victory would cost him Moriana. He never let her know of his concern. But sometimes when she slept, he shed tears, too.

During the hectic days he occupied himself with a task as necessary as Rann's. He began the eradication of the iceworms, first in the city and then in the glacier. Guardian was a good and true ally and the humans owed him much.

"Is this a fitting occupation for an itinerant hero?" Erimenes demanded one day as Fost trudged from an iceworm tunnel at the head of a weary, battered squad. "You should be off soldiering, covering yourself with glory like Rann and Cerestan."

"I'd sooner be covered in shit," Fost growled. "I'll never make a soldier. I admit, sometimes I take joy in fighting and bringing an enemy down, though I'm none too sure that's worthy. Man to man's a challenge. Mass to mass is butchery and chance."

The genies mostly spent time together, and even Fost admitted—to himself—that he was touched by the joy Erimenes took in sharing the rebirth of his city with Ziore. However, the philosopher did go into sulks for several days when Rann flatly refused to permit him to accompany a raiding party.

Synalon kept her distance, studying in libraries as Moriana did, or in her chambers in the dormitory next to the Palace with the door closed. Moriana muttered dark suspicions of what her sister did, but had no time to act on them.

Until one night a month after they arrived in Athalau. . . .

Fost tramped down the arched corridor of the dormitory feeling as if his boots were cast of lead and his joints made of jelly. It had been a grim, brutal day hunting the worms. Two men of his ten hadn't returned. Fost was glad Erimenes had been at a museum sneering to Ziore about how art had deteriorated since his day instead of being with Fost. Erimenes had by and large lost the habit of cheering when his own side took casualties, but Fost wouldn't have liked to tempt him. There were many deep holes within the glacier where a spirit jar could be cast down.

The floor rumbled to a cheer beneath his feet. Prince Rann was being toasted in the refectory. He had another victory to his credit. The *Zr'gsz* had sent a hundred rafts probing into the Gate of the Mountains itself. Anticipating such a move, Rann had long since laid plans with the nomads of the Steppes, who reluctantly cooperated. Only the Ust-alayakit tribe stayed aloof.

When the Hisser rafts were well into the narrow ravine, a storm of boulders, arrows and javelins came crashing down on them from above. As the surviving rafts climbed clear to meet their attackers, Rann and the Sky Guard swept out of the sun like a firestorm from Omizantrim. The humans took a handful of casualties, none among the bird riders. Not one of the rafts escaped.

Fost had to admit the strange, compact man with the devastated face had earned the cheers. Especially since he seemed to work miracles against the *Zr'gsz*. He was a monster, of that there was no doubt. Fost had seen his handiwork. And yet, and yet . . . without the scarred prince the humans would have already lost.

On top of such a day, this was too much to think about so Fost went into the suite he shared with Moriana and fell asleep.

It seemed he had just drifted into blackness when a scream roused him. He jumped to his feet, yanked his sword from the scabbard and ran into a footstool. Cursing and clutching his shin, Fost found a cloak, wrapped it around himself and went hopping into the hall.

Down the corridor stood Rann. The naked arc of a scimitar gleamed blue in the prince's hand. Fost's blood chilled. Then he realized Rann also sought the source of the cry.

"Upstairs," he said. He turned and dashed for the stairway. He heard Rann following.

He came out on the third floor. Moriana stood in an open door from which a strange blue light spilled. It was the door to Synalon's room. Moriana looked in with horror that metamorphosed slowly to anger as Fost watched.

He ran to her as she raised a trembling finger and pointed it like a weapon at her sister.

"You—" Fury choked her. "You *traitor!*"

He came to the door and looked in. Synalon sat on the bed wearing some confection like azure mist that clearly showed the lush outlines of her body even in the dimness. Witchlights danced in clay saucers on the floor.

Across from the black-haired princess sat a gigantic black Dwarf.

CHAPTER FOURTEEN

The Messenger of the Dark Ones rose. He smiled, his teeth startlingly white against the midnight of his face.

"I see our discussion is at an end, daughter," he said to Synalon. "To you others, farewell. I regret not having the chance to speak with you before since I shall not see you again—alive." He faded and vanished, leaving only his taunting laughter hanging in the air.

Moriana's eyes blazed.

"You—"

"No," Fost shouted, moving as fast as he ever had. He thrust past Moriana and stood, arms outspread, between the furious princess and her sister. "Hear her out."

"Get out of my way."

Fost saw Rann standing just behind Moriana in the door. The scars on his face glowed whitely. Fost knew with certainty that this was betrayal and that the prince was about to drive his curved blade into Moriana's oblivious back.

Then Rann pushed past, taking his place at Fost's side, raising a hand to Synalon who rose from her bed with death in her eye.

"This is fair, I think. Neither of you casts a death-bolt without slaying the both of us. Now, Highnesses, will you talk?"

Fost felt his neck hairs rise. The air crackled with potent magics barely held in restraint. He waited to die and wondered what the Hell Call would be like.

It didn't happen. Moriana was first to drop her threatening hand, but Synalon followed reluctantly.

"I see nothing to talk about." She gazed past Fost without warmth.

"What were you doing, Synalon? Do you deny that creature is a sending of the Dark Ones?"

"I do not." Haughtily, she tossed back her head. "It was the Messenger of the Lords of Elder Dark himself. I have spoken with him before."

"What did you discuss?" Rann asked in a casual tone, as if mentioning how nice the weather had been that day.

"We discussed my sabotaging your plans to raise the World Spirit against Istu."

Moriana's hand shot forth. Fost grabbed it.

"Wait, dammit!" He swiveled his head and said in desperation, "Explain and explain quickly or we're all dead."

Synalon started to bristle.

"I'd be pleased to hear an explanation, as well," Rann drawled.

She shook back her hair and straightened her shoulders, as if preparing herself for a wearisome task.

"Very well. Shortly after we left Brev the Messenger appeared to me, after Fost had gone to sleep. He proposed that I rejoin the Dark Ones. He said I had proven wanting before but that if I acted rapidly and well I could earn back my lost grace—and more."

Moriana dropped her arm. She shook her head in dejection.

"How could you? How could even you?"

"I could not!" Synalon laughed. "What kind of fool do you take me for, sister mine? Think me a traitor if you will. But I would be a stupid groundling if I trusted anything the Dark Ones said to me."

"Then why did you tell him you'd go along?" Fost demanded.

"I thought better of you, Longstrider. Is it not obvious? The Dark Ones fear what we do here. They are not certain Istu can prevail so they sought to ensure their success from within. It takes great energy for the

Lords to intervene on this plane, even through the agency of their Messenger. So I let them think I was mooncalf enough to heed them, and they wasted their efforts on me. I may have saved us, sister. Small thanks I'll get."

"I don't believe it," Moriana stated flatly.

"But what of you?" Synalon flung at her. "Can we trust *you?* You've treated with the servitors of the Dark before—*daughter of Thendrun!*"

Moriana sagged. She caught the doorframe to support herself. Fost longed to go to her and hold her but sensed it wasn't safe to move.

"He told you," Moriana said in a weak voice.

"Yes." Synalon raised her head triumphantly. "Is it so strange that we are drawn to Darkness, dear sister, with the heritage we share?"

"I . . . I couldn't bring myself to tell you," whispered Moriana. She turned away. "Best we die here and let others carry on the fight. We are tainted, touched by the Void and the Night. We do not deserve to return to the City in the Sky."

"Are you so weak?" Synalon screamed at her. "Go then. Open your veins and spill your blood upon the floor, if you despise it so! I care not what I do or do not deserve, nor whether I am sprung from *Zr'gsz* or even if one was my father! I will wreak my revenge upon those who betrayed and used me, and all who stand with them." She strode forward, pushing Fost and Rann aside as easily as if they were children and seized Moriana's shoulders, spinning her roughly around. "Perhaps *you* do not deserve to stand in the streets of our City again, sister. Then don't! But *I* shall! The City is all I've ever loved. I shall possess it again—and only death can stop me!"

In the stunned silence following her outburst they all heard the frantic footsteps in the corridor beyond. Synalon shoved her sister from her as a small boy in the tabard of a Bilsinxt drummer looked nervously around the door.

"Your Highnesses," he said in a shrill voice. "Th-they sent me from below to fetch you. The Sky City has just entered the Gate of the Mountains!"

Their footsteps rang loudly in Fost's ears as he and the others crowded into the chamber where the Nexus lay. Light appeared from everywhere; no torches were needed in Athalau. The Ethereals had been stirring on their pallets in the nave of the Palace of Esoteric Wisdom when Moriana and the rest raced by. Now they filed into the chamber as they had on that first day.

This time they did not take up kneeling positions on the dull steel pattern. Instead they lined themselves along the walls.

"The time is come, mistress?" Selamyl asked Moriana.

She hesitated, then said, "The time is come."

Selamyl strode forward and took his position in the middle of the line and faced the far wall. Soundlessly the others glided forward and knelt, each upon one of the nodes that seemed strewn at random throughout the mandala. With a sinking feeling, Fost saw how few there truly were. Many of the nodes were unoccupied and the silvery patch in the center looked like a gap left by a missing tooth.

He didn't see how they could ever succeed.

"What would Felarod do, were he here now?" Moriana asked aloud.

"You must find your own way," said Selamyl. His eyes were closed, his voice seemed to come from all around. "Flow with the universe. The World Spirit will guide you."

"Can you—can you reach the Spirit?" she asked.

"Yes."

"Then do so."

Silence. Fost felt it gnawing inside him like an animal demanding release, felt the tension begin to build and set his limbs trembling. He wanted to scream at the inactivity.

Moriana shifted to stand beside him, and her hand sought his. He willed his hand not to quaver and knew he failed. He looked around. Synalon stood nearby with lifted chin, feigning disinterest. Rann stood with folded arms, his head thrust forward, his yellow eyes wide beneath thin brows.

A greenish glow bathed Rann's face. Fost stared at him for a second, then turned back to the center of the room.

The metallic tracery on the floor had come to life. The green glow flowed from it suffusing the room. The kneeling Ethereals had become translucent. Each slender body shone like a lamp but without heat.

He became aware of a faint pulsation of the light. Shouts rebounded down the stairway from above, and it seemed there was an outcry in the streets.

"Behold the Nexus," came Selamyl's voice. "It is Athalau itself. This is the center."

"And the World Spirit?" Moriana could barely force out the words.

"It comes."

A chill wind tore at Zak'zar's face and felt as if it would strip away the skin. His cloak cracked behind him like a whip. It was agony to be abroad in this cold night with the icy breath of the Waste upon him. The others of the People lay abed wrapped against the chill. But his place was upon the rampart of the floating City.

Istu stood beside him, set apart from the night only by the absolute blackness of his being unmarred by stars. His yellow eyes watched the rugged terrain below unfold. The City followed his will, its course matching the winding of the black slash that wandered through the mountains.

He stiffened, raised his head as if testing the wind for some scent, some sound.

"What is it?" Zak'zar asked, shouting to be heard above the keening wind.

Istu raised a taloned hand to still him. Then he crumpled his hands into fists and shook them in the face of the south.

"My curse upon you! I lay my curse on Athalau and all within!"

"What's happening?"

Istu's eyes swept down. Zak'zar thought the Demon would slay him in his unreasoning fury. But the mad glare subsided. Istu spoke.

"In Athalau. I feel it, I hear it, it wounds my ears! The Pale Ones have summoned the World Spirit."

Zak'zar felt strength ebbing.

"Have we lost, then?"

"No!" Great shards of rock detached themselves from the walls below and slid into the Gate of the Mountains as the Demon's voice beat down upon them. "Never! They lack Felarod, and knowledge, and I am strong! Never again shall I be bound. *Never!*"

Zak'zar gripped the stone guardwall and stared ahead. In the distance he saw a pool of paleness lying against the blackness of the mountains. A glacier. Within it lay his fate.

The wind tore at his eyes.

Hours passed like days, like years.

"Vast is the World Spirit," Selamyl said when Moriana asked him if the summoning was done, if the Spirit had risen to smite its starborn foe. "It is slow to anger but its wrath is great."

Fost sat with his back against the wall of the Nexus chamber. He drifted in and out of sleep. When his body realized that no amount of adrenaline was going to make things happen any quicker, it surrendered to the exertions of the day before. But still an urgency nagged at him causing him to half-rise from sleep and dream images.

At some point a servant brought the spirit jars. Fost roused enough to listen briefly to Erimenes describing how the whole city now pulsed with the same green light that came from the Nexus. Fost thought the pattern's glow brighter than before, but thinking took too great an effort and he slept again.

He came awake abruptly, sensing something vital was about to happen.

The first thing he saw was the City in the Sky. He shook his head, shut his eyes and opened them again. Still it hung in the midst of his vision, above sharp peaks turned molten gold by the rising sun.

"Disconcerting, isn't it?" Erimenes chuckled dryly at his elbow. "My humble contribution."

"You *caused* that?" Somehow, a vision of what was happening miles away had been conjured forth, inside the room.

"Well . . . no. But it was I who remembered the old stories and told the princess how to call it up."

Moriana stood where she had before, staring at the picture which occupied one whole wall of the chamber.

"And the Spirit?" he asked. "Has it come yet?"

"No," said Ziore from his other side. Her face was stark with worry. "And soon it will be too late. Poor Moriana."

"It is come."

The chamber reverberated to the words. The voice was Selamyl's and yet was not. It was deeper, transformed, as vital and surging as the boom of surf on sand.

Moriana raised her eyes to the scene of the Sky City. It jumped forward. Fost gasped. Then he realized that it was the picture that moved with such speed, not the City itself. He saw the black, horned shape on the parapet and felt a cold greater than that of the Waste seize his bones.

"I call upon the World Spirit to destroy the Demon Istu!" Her words rang out like trumpets.

Fost caught his breath.

Nothing happened.

"World Spirit! Strike! Raise up your power against the dark destroyer as you did ten thousand years ago!"

Fost felt it now. The energy enfolded him, restoring strength to his limbs, clearing his weary, scratchy eyes. Each breath was wine. But still nothing happened, no energies leapt forward to oppose the black Demon.

"World Spirit!" screamed Moriana. *"What's wrong?"*

"Will," said that voice which had once belonged to Selamyl. "It needs a will to guide it."

"But what of you, you Ethereals?"

A pause. Fost thought of the awesome deliberation of Guardian. The world was much bigger than the glacier. Would the Spirit be commensurately slower?

"We . . ." For the first time that transcendent voice faltered. "We lack the will. We have forgotten how to strike out in anger and lack the time to learn."

Synalon rose, stretched catlike and sensuous.

"One thing I've plenty of is will. Sister, shall I?"

Moriana stared into the green fire of the Nexus. This was what she'd feared, that she must enter rapport with the World Spirit and risk the dissolution of that small spark that was her soul, her inner being, her self. The time had come for her to match the dedication already shown by the Ethereals.

"No," Moriana said and stepped forward.

Fost leaped to his feet, lunged forward and caught her wrist, crying, "You can't!"

"I must." Her voice was calm.

"You'll die!"

"And what of that?" She reached out and stroked his cheek with the backs of her fingers. They rasped on stubble. "I must do this. Only then can I expiate the wrong I created when I helped the Fallen Ones capture the City."

She dropped her hand.

"I love you," she said. "Live long and take what happiness you find." And she stepped into the middle of the Nexus.

Green fire enveloped her. Fost cried out again and started to follow. A steel claw caught his arm. He struggled, then turned back in fury. Ziore held his wrist. There was nothing wispy or insubstantial about her now.

"Do you think she wants you to throw your life away?" the genie asked.

"But . . ."

"You cannot help her now. You can only distract her."

He stepped back. And the power came up through the floor and shook him and his mind reeled toward blackness.

At the molten core of the planet burned anger.

But it was rage without form, without direction. That vast organism which was the World possessed a thousand senses and each one cried out that something was deathly wrong. A pathogen had invaded its system, a black presence, both alien and destructive. It knew that something must be done but it didn't know what or how.

A feeling tickled the edge of its being, tiny but insistent. Slowly the feeling penetrated it. Slowly it responded.

It sensed other presences, miniscule, separate from and at the same time part of it. It flowed toward them. Somehow it knew that here was the means to channel its anger, to bring its mighty wrath to bear on the wrongness.

It touched the lesser entities and became one with them. It stopped. Had it been aware, it would have known confusion. There was nothing, no direction, no guidance, nothing to purge the irritant.

Then a new presence touched it. Will burned within, a hot, white light. Like a plant questing toward the sun, the World Spirit moved to merge itself with this thing of Will.

* * *

At the core of Moriana's being burned anger.

Her City was held captive by an enemy who had betrayed her to possess it. She felt it hanging almost overhead now, and her being ached with the longing for it. But more even than the *Zr'gsz,* she hated their Demon ally. He had defiled her, laid surrogate hands of stone on her and ravished her body while his hell-glowing eyes raped her soul. For that her rage would tear the skies asunder, to visit vengeance upon Istu.

Your enemy is near! she thought. *Now reach!*

The mountain called the Throat of the Dark Ones exploded.

It blasted itself skyward, a mountain launched as a missile into the dawn, riding a column of incandescent gas and ash and the dust of pulverized rock. The *Zr'gsz* skystone mines disappeared, and those who worked them and those who fought to slow the work. So violent was the blast that huge hunks of the shattered mountain entered orbit around the world to spiral down slowly until the tenuous arms of the atmosphere tangled them and drew them to flaming end.

Such was Moriana's wrath united with the wrath of the World.

Though the wavefront of the blast and the titan sound that rode upon it would not reach the Ramparts for over an hour, Istu felt Mount Omizantrim die. He clawed at the heavens and bellowed his rage. His ancient enemy was come. The fight would be to the death this time.

He turned and strode to the center of the City. His bowed legs straddled the Well of Winds. He spread forth the blackness of his arms. He reached outward, began to flow downward, his form subsiding and swelling to fill the Well. The Black Lens appeared where he had been, glistening, pregnant with power.

* * *

A thirty-foot wall of water washed over the island of Wirix and scoured it clean, driven by the blast that slew Omizantrim.

But the Wrath had only begun.

With the senses she now shared with another, Moriana knew that her first stroke had missed. She struck again—

—and a range of mountains thrust themselves above the sea on the far side of the world, dark and humped and water-glistening like the back of an aquatic monster.

And again—

—and storm clouds gathered above the Ramparts, a thousand times faster than the normal gathering of clouds. They piled higher, black on black, shot through with lightning. In the streets of the Sky City the Fallen Ones cried out in fear and wonder.

And again—

—and part of the Northern Continent split off and sank into the sea with a crack and a roar and a rushing of water.

Fury raged in silence upon the wall of the Nexus chamber. Fost's back was to the wall and his eyes were wide. He had control of his limbs again, but the power still surged like a drug in his veins.

"Moriana! What's happening?" cried Ziore.

"I . . . I cannot control it." Her voice penetrated the bones of those in the chamber, transmuted as Selamyl's had been.

The room shook then. Synalon lurched into Rann; Fost fell, cracking his knees painfully on the stone. Imaged on the wall, the western Ramparts tumbled like eightpins to the throes of an earthquake. The Ethereals and Moriana sat statue-still, unmoved by the spasm beneath the earth.

The gathering clouds had grown to a black anvil

thunderhead, a mountain above mountains. The watchers saw a sheet of lightning flash from the thunderhead and shear off a slice of the City's starboard rim in a coruscating spray of molten stone. Synalon shrieked as if it were her own flesh being sundered.

Maddened, the Demon retaliated. A black funnel grew from the underside of the Lens and stabbed down. It bit into the ice over Athalau and began tearing chunks from the glacier's body. A moan rolled through Athalau, pitched almost below hearing, so that it rang deep in the bones of the humans within.

"The Demon's killing Guardian," shouted Fost. "Can't you do something?"

"Yes," said Moriana. That much she could do. She folded power around herself, around Guardian, wrapping the glacier in a cocoon of forces that held him steady against the pull of the vortex.

Istu squealed with rage as his funnel ceased to bite. He lashed downward repeatedly. But he could no longer gouge the ice that armored Athalau.

"What now?" asked Zak'zar from the edge of the Skywell.

"Wait," said Istu, "and you shall see."

Moriana kept trying to wield the power of the World Spirit, to smite Istu with all the force at her command. The watchers in the chamber beneath the Palace saw earthquake and waterspout and eruption devastate the land. The World Spirit flailed about like a blind beast only landing blows near its foe by accident.

"Moriana, you've got to stop," screamed Ziore as they watched Paramount, Lord of Trees, hurled down to smash a hundred lesser trees beneath it. "You'll destroy the Realm without harming Istu!"

"What can I do? I cannot aim the power. If only I had some way to focus on the City, on Istu!"

Synalon shook back her long black hair and turned from the Nexus.

"I knew I'd find a part to play in this farce," she said. "Rann, summon me a bird tender. I wish my eagle made ready at once."

He gaped at her.

"Because *I* will be the focus my sister needs."

"Highness! Why?"

CHAPTER FIFTEEN

"Madness," declared Rann.

"Not so, cousin. Moriana and I are twins. There is a link between us, though we've spent our lives denying it." She looked back at her sister, who sat like some green idol in the center of the Nexus. "And my hatred is great. Give me your power, sister. I shall wield it with a fine rage."

Moriana did not move. Perhaps she could not; perhaps she was frozen forever in that position with her legs folded under her, her hands resting on her thighs. So complete was her lack of response that Fost feared she had died or utterly lost her identity in the immensity of the World Spirit.

Then, "Yes," filled the chamber.

Rann raised a hand to halt Synalon as she went to the door.

"You'll need an escort, cousin. Someone to make sure you have time to achieve rapport with Moriana."

"You propose I take an army? Where do we get the time for that?"

"A small escort will have a chance to approach the City unseen." He hitched up his sword belt. "With your permission, Highness."

"I'm coming, too," blurted Fost.

A shadow crossed Synalon's face.

"No!" said Moriana firmly, though her expression didn't change.

"Let me congratulate you on your courage, Fost!" cried Erimenes. "This is the ultimate adventure of a lifetime."

He whirled to face the genie.

"It's not courage. I'm doing this because I'm afraid, dammit. I've thought I'd carried on with this mad venture for love or loneliness or from sheer curiosity. But there's another reason. I'm afraid to live in a world that gods and devils use as their playground. We're just pawns to them, all of us. I can't take that, do you understand?"

"Go then," said Moriana with resignation. Still she remained immobile, apparently lifeless.

Rann clasped forearms with Fost and left the chamber at a run. Fost paused, then picked up Ziore's jug and carried it into the Nexus, jumping across the burning lines and avoiding the nodes. His head swam to tidal surges of power, but he made it, depositing the jug at Moriana's side. He stooped and kissed her forehead; it was icy. Then he turned and ran for the door, slowing only to scoop up Erimenes's jar.

"Farewell, my love!" sang Erimenes. "I'm off to the wars!"

"Dear Erimenes," sighed Ziore, wavering at Moriana's side. She waved, sparks flying from her fingertips as they crossed a node.

"Goodbye," said Moriana.

Fost felt emotion choke him. The word echoed in his brain with grim finality.

"Their counterattack has failed," said Zak'zar.

Istu's laugh rumbled from the Well.

"They've realized that without a mind the scope of Felarod's they cannot wield their power with any precision. They were doing themselves more damage than I inflicted."

"Surely, they haven't given up."

"Your faith in the Pale Ones is touching, Speaker. But it matters not. They've shown they cannot harm me. While I . . ." He chuckled like a poisoned spring. "Watch, and you shall see."

* * *

From the surface of the orange-red sun a wisp of star-stuff was pared like skin from a fruit. An invisible force bent it into a flaming hoop, a strand, and drew it across space toward a green world waiting eighty million miles away. . . .

The roar of eagles' wings filled the corridor Guardian had opened to the east. Four war birds flew in a line, their wingtips brushing the frigid walls. Fost hunched close to the neck of his mount and tried to decide whether he preferred the claustrophobic feeling the shining walls rushing by gave him or the dread of falling from the bird.

"Thank you for bringing me along, Fost," said Erimenes at his side. "I always knew you were a considerate soul.

"Don't thank me yet, Erimenes. You yourself said Istu could destroy you."

"And so he can. But he can destroy me as easily if I'm cowering in the belly of this garrulous glacier. I'd rather be where the battle rages and the blood flows."

"I'm glad you enjoy the prospect," said Fost grimly. He shifted the buckler strapped to his left arm so its bronze-bound rim wouldn't gouge his hip. "As for me, I'm ready to swallow the bravado speech I made back in the Palace, syllable by syllable."

"Nonsense, Fost. You, too, feel the thrill of approaching battle. And this isn't just any fight, you know. Your feats this day will live in ballads forever, as long as there are men to sing them."

"There may not be, after today."

They broke into the light. Fost squinted and let his eagle have its head. It was huge, almost as large as the midnight-black Nightwind Synalon rode, brown with white head and a white bib on its chest, and it knew what to do far better than Fost.

Rann's eagle, as gray as a cloudy sky, moved into the lead. The fourth bird was pure white. Its rider raised a gloved hand in salute to Fost as they took station on opposite sides of Nightwind. Fost waved back. Cerestan was a fool for coming along, but Fost was in no position to be critical.

Rann banked. Fost felt his bird tilt to follow the leftward turn, surging upward toward the City hanging above them, black against muttering storm clouds. He tried not to panic, tried not to think about losing his seat and tumbling end over end to the hard rocks below. He was strapped into the saddle and had both hands clinging to the harness. He looked up, up. . . .

The sun reached down and drove its fist into the middle of the glacier.

As the solar prominence Istu had torn from the face of the sun bathed the glacier in flame, great clouds of steam billowed upward with a serpent's hiss magnified a millionfold. A groaning scream rang through Athalau, shaking loose great spires of ice, toppling ancient buildings. Men, women and children fled through the streets, covering their ears as they ran.

Zak'zar reeled back from the rimwall, shielding his eyes against the hellish brilliance. The Sky City began to rock with the force of the superheated steam boiling from below.

When the Speaker's eyes worked again, he beheld Istu standing braced on the rimwall, laughing and laughing as he raised his arms to bring down more sunfire.

Hot water washed down the nave of the Palace of Esoteric Wisdom and cascaded over the steps. The Ethereals did not stir as the tide came surging around them. They were one with the World Spirit and beyond feeling; some had turned dark, no longer touched with the green glow. These would never again feel physical agony.

"Princess." The word was ground from a giant mill of agony. "Princess, I . . . I melt! I cannot shield you much longer." The words came scarcely less quickly than a human would have spoken, so great was Guardian's pain.

"Moriana, do something!" cried Ziore.

"I can stop the waters from flooding the city," Moriana said, and this was done, the near-scalding tide receding until only an inch of cooling water swirled on the floor. "But I cannot stop the burning.

"If Synalon doesn't reach the City soon, we all shall die with Guardian."

"Great merciful heavens," cried Erimenes. "What's going on?"

"They don't seem merciful to me. And I don't know," snapped Fost, more intent on remaining on top of his eagle than on examining their plight.

There had come a blinding streak of light. It had been obscured at once by an explosion of steam. Only because the bird riders had flown to the eastern edge of Guardian were they saved from being scalded to death. Fost managed to blink back the green line of afterimage that split his sight, and he occasionally saw flashes of the fire streaming down from above through rents in the cloud as though a curtain were being drawn aside to give him a view of Hell.

He glimpsed motion to his right and looked that way. The gray eagle flapped alongside. Rann held up a gauntleted fist, then drove it upward and forward. The gray climbed away.

"What's that mean?" Erimenes asked.

"It means we go on."

The steam-laden winds buffeted them like the fetid breath of Hell. The clouds proved a blessing; they were shielded from observation from above. But Fost wondered if they veered into that fall of sunfire.

* * *

Guardian struggled to retain life.

"Princess, the pain. I . . . I am almost pierced through."

"I'm sorry. I can do nothing until my sister reaches the Sky City." Moriana had the awful thought, *if she does. If the sunflame didn't take her. Her and Fost.* The thoughts were strong enough to stand out against the inchoate background of the World Spirit.

"I must die soon. I cannot be helped. But . . . save Athalau. I have done . . . done my best . . . to . . . guard . . . her."

"I shall, good and faithful Guardian." The words, "If I can," went unspoken.

Rann shot an arrow through the face that appeared, peering over a rimwall that loomed ghostly in the fog. Fost's eagle burst from the mist wing to wing with Nightwind. The giant black bird slashed a Hisser's head from his shoulders with a vicious stroke of his beak and shrieked triumph as he settled his claws once more on the gray-green stone of his home.

Rann's bird dropped toward a group of Vridzish racing to the wall. Rann shot another, cast aside his bow and leaped from the saddle as his bird came down like fury among the foe. Then Fost's own bird thumped to a landing. Fost forgot about the prince as he struggled to free himself from the safety strap before the half-dozen charging *Zr'gsz* reached him.

He had a powerful ally in the bird. Screaming in rage, it struck out with beak and talon, disembowelling and dismembering. But the wild movements threw Fost around in the saddle so furiously he couldn't free himself.

Then the bird stood alone amid black-bloodied corpses. Fost tore free the strap and jumped to the ground. His sword sang from its sheath. He felt power and control merge harmoniously within and knew he would fight well this day.

"Sister, I am ready!" he heard Synalon cry at his back. Cerestan engaged a knot of Hissers off to the left. More came at Fost, and he sprang to meet them with a roar of hatred.

His first blow tore apart one's face. His second took a clawed arm off at the shoulder. His third sent greasy ropes of intestines spilling about a Hisser's knees.

A whistling scream sounded and he saw his war bird reel back, blood fountaining from the stump of its neck. A huge *Zr'gsz* noble had taken the head off with a single stroke of an obsidian-edged sword. Fost ducked under the cut meant to remove his head; his sword slashed at the dark, bulging neck. He ripped his sword free and turned to face the lizard men streaming toward him with weapons in their claws.

"There's no way out for me now," he cried. "So come ahead and we'll do this right!"

The Vridzish advanced.

The agonized groans of the glacier cut off as though severed by a knife.

"He's dead," Ziore said, and began sobbing.

Though she felt the glacier's passing, Moriana never heard the nun. Her whole being strained to hold together under the terrific pressure of rapport with the World Spirit. It was like being twisted and pulled and compressed all at the same time, a million vectors tearing at her soul. She probed for her sister's mind and prayed she could hang on until contact was made.

As Erimenes predicted, Fost earned himself a place in the ballads that day. The spirit cheered hysterically from the jug while the tall man slew and slew like a figure out of legend. He used every trick of swordplay he knew, both fair and foul, and threw in alley fighting from boyhood days in Medurim. He hacked and stabbed and slashed, then smashed faces with his buckler. When an axe-blow split the shield, he hurled it in someone's

face, picked up an abandoned shortsword and fought
on tirelessly.

But Fost saw through the haze of blood and sweat
in his eyes that Rann was the true hero. Fost fought
with preternatural strength and fury, but Rann . . .
Rann fought as no man ever had, nor would again.
With scimitar in his left hand and his knife in the
right, Rann walked among the Hissers like death in-
carnate. He disdained to parry, but no blade touched
him. His weapons were in constant, blurring motion,
the dagger picking at eyes and throats and exposed
bellies; the scimitar slashed left and right and curved
around the guard of an unsuspecting enemy to bring
bloody death.

The tide of Hissers slackened. Fost staggered back
against the wall. To his surprise he saw Cerestan still
fought on. Synalon stood with arms upraised, straining
to make contact with Moriana. Fost wondered how
much longer any of them would be alive.

A figure strode down the narrow street, a green cloak
flapping from its shoulders, a sword in hand. It stopped
before the prince.

"You are Prince Rann," said the newcomer. His skin
was almost black, and he towered above the diminutive
prince.

"And you are Zak'zar." The scimitar whipped forward. With blinding speed, the sword snapped to guard.
But the prince's stroke was never meant to connect.
Instead, black blood from the scimitar's last victim
spattered Zak'zar's eyes. He blinked and fell back a
step. Rann lunged.

Zak'zar's reflexes were still those of a *Zr'gsz*. His
blade flashed. Rann's dagger whipped up—not fast
enough. Fost saw the green blade cave in the right side
of Rann's face, saw the tawny eye split in blood.

Synalon screamed.

"Get away from her, Fost!" Erimenes's shout sent
him running to the right, heedless of whether he was

attacked or not. He stepped on a javelin dropped by a skewered Hisser, went down, rolled and came up staring toward the wall.

Synalon!

He couldn't look at her directly. Energy pulsed from her, fierce and white and hot. The bird rider's garb she had worn burned away in an instant leaving her naked and splendid and terrible. Forces ebbed and flowed around her like the aurora, ghosts of color barely hinting at the potent energy fields of which they were the only visible part.

He got to his feet, looked back in time to see Rann spinning and ducking under the sweep of Zak'zar's sword. Rann whirled in a complete circle, getting inside the *Zr'gsz's* guard. His scimitar struck under the armpit, bit through metal and Fost thought he heard the grating crunch when it hit the spine. Zak'zar dropped his sword with a clang. His hands spasmodically opened and closed twice, he vomited green-black blood, and died.

Rann stood over his foe's body for several heartbeats, then collapsed across the inert form.

More Hissers appeared. Several ran at Synalon. She gestured, and they turned to pillars of ash, slumping and beginning to flow, becoming incandescent piles of heated sand.

"You must flee," Synalon said in a voice as vast as the sky. "No one will pursue."

She started walking forward. Cerestan lurched after, limping on one leg, determined not to leave the side of his queen. She sensed him, half-turned.

"No."

It was too late. He entered the deadly embrace of the energies surrounding her and, with a last startled cry, turned to ash himself.

"Go, Fost!" Erimenes shouted. "Great Ultimate, you've done it! You're free! There're two eagles left. Take one and go!"

Fost turned and ran—straight for Rann.

"What are you doing, fool?" shrieked the genie. "Leave him. You fool, save your own skin!"

Fost stooped and grabbed Rann's wrist. He checked for a pulse.

"He's dead, Fost. By the Five Holy Ones, flee *now!*"

He felt the faint flutter of a pulse and rose, swinging the prince across his shoulders. He marvelled at how light he was, then noticed the sunfire had died out and the steam was beginning to dissipate.

"He wouldn't have done the same for you. You fool, you incredible fool!"

Synalon approached. She saw him and smiled. A ripple of sensation passed through him, desire and revulsion and hate and admiration all at once. She was no longer merely human. She came straight on. He dodged to the side of the street, teetering to balance Rann on his back. Synalon swept past. He felt the tingle of the energies. She was growing taller, and at the far end of the street Istu waded through buildings to meet her.

Fost turned to the rimwall and ran like hell.

It was birth and orgasm and death. Moriana's soul expanded in all directions, contracted to a point, and a blazing line surged between her and Synalon. Energy sluiced through her, filling Synalon, possessing and being possessed by her. For a moment the two points came together, merged. Synalon screamed. But Moriana was already fading, and it did not jolt her to look into her sister and see herself.

They broke apart. Moriana was a spark, and she was dimming. Her task was done. Synalon had been right; her malice was the perfect focus for the vengeful energies of the World Spirit. Now Moriana could relax, quit fighting to maintain identity, be absorbed into the World Spirit and know peace. She plummeted down. . . .

And was caught by a gentle, unyielding grip.

I have you now, my child, came Ziore's thought. *I won't let go.*

Moriana began to swim back upward through the layers of the World Spirit's mind, back toward herself.

Istu lashed at Synalon with his talons. She skipped aside and the swipe brought down a spindly tower. She felt the power in her hand. She struck. Istu felt fire in his bowels and screamed. Her laughter eclipsed his cry of anguish.

The eagle dropped in a dizzying spiral groundward. Somehow, Fost hung on. He heard a tumult at his back as if the sky was breaking open. He dared not look back, nor did he know how the war eagle Nightwind fared, with a half-dead Prince Rann strapped to its back.

An immense round pit yawned beneath. He realized that the flare had burned through Guardian and into Athalau; he saw where the tops of lofty spires were melted and vitrified from the awful heat. He shut his eyes, squeezing out tears.

"Goodbye, Guardian," he said. There seemed little else to say.

"He's dead?" asked Erimenes. Fost only nodded. "Oh, no, no, no!" The spirit chanted a liturgy of negation, and Fost was amazed at the real pain his voice.

The ground wheeled wildly below. The white war bird that had been Cerestan's braked with her wings and landed roughly in the scorched plaza near a silent, dry fountain. She staggered and collapsed under Fost's weight. The courier rolled free. The bird raised her head and sucked in great, ragged gulps of air.

Fost struggled to his feet and started toward the Palace of Esoteric Wisdom at a lurching run. His thoughts were of Moriana.

"Wait," said Erimenes. "Look. Above."

The Sky City careened across a sky gone mad. Black clouds whirled crazily and the storm beat at the City with fists of wind and rain and lightning. Rocks exploded from the Ramparts to smash among the buildings of the floating City. The earth shifted violently beneath Fost's feet and flung him to the ground.

The tremor went on and on. Fost spread his arms and clung to the pavement. Erimenes shouted something that was swallowed in the din of crashing buildings.

The shaking subsided. Fost looked up again.

Some trick of the forces allowed Fost to see only Istu and Synalon facing each other on the parapet. They battled with forces he neither saw nor comprehended.

Though she must have grown several times her natural size, Synalon was still dwarfed by Istu's midnight bulk. She flickered like a flame, dodging the Demon's increasingly clumsy charges. The World Spirit's energies flowed through her to tear at the minion of the Dark Ones.

Suddenly, she darted in, closing with the Demon. He threw back his head and bellowed. To Fost it seemed the slim white arms reached *inside* the blackness of Istu's body.

A gasp burst from the watchers below. Synalon planted her feet and raised the gigantic form of the Demon of the Dark Ones above her head as if he were a child. For a moment, she held him there. He writhed and kicked with clawed feet, roaring with a shrill and frightened voice. She laughed, the sound vibrating in all their skulls.

Then she cast the Demon over the edge.

Over and over Istu tumbled. He changed shape as he fell, became a bird, a block, a blob, a fluttering leaf, crumbling, becoming dust, becoming . . .

Nothing.

Fost felt a tightness in his throat and a stinging in his eyes. Istu had been the very soul of evil, but Istu had been old, had immeasurably endured—and died alone. In this way alone could he claim kinship with the mortals he had oppressed. Like them he died, toy of uncaring gods.

Synalon stood poised on the brink, arms outflung in triumph, infinitely desirable and infinitely frightening. Her hair streamed out like a banner as she rode the Sky City like a raft, wild across the seething sky, faster than ever it had gone before.

And then the City in the Sky struck a mountain peak. It exploded into a million fragments, and Synalon Etuul was joined forever with the City she loved.

EPILOGUE

Erimenes wept for the damage done to Athalau. Limping across the plaza, trying not to put too much weight on a sprained ankle, Fost thought that the devastation didn't look too bad. The city had been staunchly built and most of the buildings had survived.

He stood for a time gazing at the front of the Palace of Esoteric Wisdom without fully realizing where he was. He had lost a lot of blood from wounds he never remembered receiving. He swayed a little and tried to summon the courage to descend into the basement of the Palace and confront what awaited him in the chamber of the Nexus.

Then someone emerged from the Palace onto the portico. She came unsteadily, supported by a young man and a woman in the Sky Guard uniforms.

But she came.

When she saw Fost, Moriana broke away from her helpers and ran down the steps. They met halfway across the street, threw arms around each other, sank weeping as their knees gave way.

They kissed. At length Fost pulled back. He could only look at her, unbelieving.

When he trusted himself to speak, he asked softly, "The Ethereals?"

Her eyes fell. A tear traced a trail down one cheek. He shut his own eyes and lowered his forehead to touch hers. The sweat on her hair stung a cut; he didn't pull away.

"And the ones who went with you?"

"Cerestan got too close to Synalon after the power began flowing through her. Rann fought Zak'zar and killed him. He was badly hurt, though. I carried him to the rimwall and strapped him to Nightwind's back."

"Where is he now?"

"I lost sight of him when I got on Cerestan's eagle." He bared his teeth and shook his head. "I hate to say it but I hope he got away. You should have seen him fight, Moriana. I've never seen anything like it."

She paused, then said, "I hope he made it, too." He barely heard her words they came so softly.

He glanced around to see Erimenes staring at the Palace and fingering his chin. The genie's face was drawn with worry.

"Your Highness," Erimenes said, his voice quaking with emotion. "I don't mean to interrupt, but . . . that is . . ." And while he groped for words to express his fears and hopes, a voice hailed them from the cracked steps of the Palace.

"Highness! You forgot your satchel!"

The trooper brought the battered leather satchel down and laid it reverently next to Erimenes's. He and Ziore dove into each other's arms. Their forms blended into a wavering purple column.

"She was the one who saved me," Moriana said. "When I was slipping away, losing myself in the World Spirit, she stopped me, helped me find my way back."

"She's got my gratitude," Fost said, hugging Moriana to him. "What was it like?"

A tremor passed through her.

"Do we have to talk about it now?"

"Never, if you prefer."

"I may."

He raised his head, asking, "What're they pointing at down there?"

She looked up at a group who stood at the foot of the Ruby Tower which had miraculously survived the battle.

"I don't—wait! The sun! It's . . . it's in the west now. It should be well north this time of year."

"Then . . ."

"It's true!" cried Erimenes. "The world's tipped back on its axis. Athalau is free from the ice forever!" He wept again, tears of joy, and the others joined him.

Moriana's tears turned sorrowful again, and she clung to Fost.

"Oh, Fost, think of what we've lost! All the people who died. And Guardian. And my City!" She pressed her face into his shoulder. "And my sister. I only knew her for an instant. One instant out of all our lives." Her tears poured bitter and free on his mailed shoulder.

"But think of what we've won," he told her. "Our lives. The lives of every human who still survives in the Realm—in the whole world. And," he said, his face hardening, "a respite from the gods. And you've *got* a city, Athalau."

He took her face in his hands and lifted it to his. He paused an instant, uncomfortable, then said, "And we've got each other."

She grinned and kissed him on the nose.

"That didn't hurt," she said, and he knew she read his thoughts.

Then he took her by the arm and they rose. Toward them came the folk of their city, of the reborn Athalau, and all were singing.

PLAYBOY'S BEST SCIENCE FICTION AND FANTASY

Richard C. Meredith

_____16552	AT THE NARROW PASSAGE	$1.95
_____16564	NO BROTHER, NO FRIEND	$1.95
_____16572	VESTIGES OF TIME	$1.95

John Morressy

_____16900	GRAYMANTLE	$2.50
_____16689	IRONBRAND	$2.25

Frederik Pohl, Martin H. Greenberg
& Joseph D. Olander

_____16917	GALAXY: VOLUME ONE	$2.50
_____16926	GALAXY: VOLUME TWO	$2.50

William Rotsler

_____16633	THE FAR FRONTIER	$1.95

George Takei & Robert Asprin

_____16581	MIRROR FRIEND, MIRROR FOE	$1.95

Robert E. Vardeman & Victor Milán

_____16754	THE CITY IN THE GLACIER	$2.25
_____21085	THE DESTINY STONE	$2.50
_____16986	THE FALLEN ONES	$2.50
_____16999	IN THE SHADOW OF OMIZANTRIM	$2.50
_____16732	THE SUNDERED REALM	$2.25

William Jon Watkins

_____16608	WHAT ROUGH BEAST	$1.95

Joan Winston

_____16573	THE MAKING OF THE TREK CONVENTIONS	$2.25

1181-5